Born in the backroom of a fictional bookshop in a provincial town in Northern France in order to provide a safe haven for all works created under its auspices, P&P developed their own unique graphic style before launching their first graphic novel, La Vie En Rose in 2022.

This was followed a year later by A Boat Called Wish and The Komplete Klaxon

Also by P & P

La Vie En Rose (2022)
A Boat Called Wish (2023)
The Komplete Klaxon (2023)

*This book is dedicated
with love and thanks to all our actors.*

©2025
Sue Coxon and Mark Stewart-Jones

ISBN: 9798290247007

pandppublishing@gmail.com

THE BALLAD OF SERGEI YATOPIWEL*

(*pronounced *sair*-gay yar-*toppy*-vell.)

P.&P.

THE·GREAT·GLOBE·ITSELF,
YE·ALL·WHICH·IT·INHERIT·SHALL·DISSOLVE.
AND·LIKE·THIS·INSUBSTANTIAL·PAGEANT·FADED,
LEAVE·NOT·A·RACK·BEHIND.

William Shakespeare, The Tempest

<u>For Will</u>
Hal Lavache

<u>For Hal</u>
Will Lavache

Hal? ... Hal?

Are you sure that we are awake? It seems to me that yet we sleep, we dream...

Hal? Where are you?

I'm right here, Baby.

But WHERE are we?

ACT ONE

ACT ONE   SCENE ONE

THAT'S SERGEI YATOPIWEL!
CREEEEAK!

AND IT'S ACTUALLY PRONOUNCED SAIR-GAY YA-TOPPY-VELL!
BUT YOU DON'T NEED TO WORRY ABOUT THAT!
YOU JUST NEED TO FUCK OFF!

ACT ONE   SCENE TWO

10

16

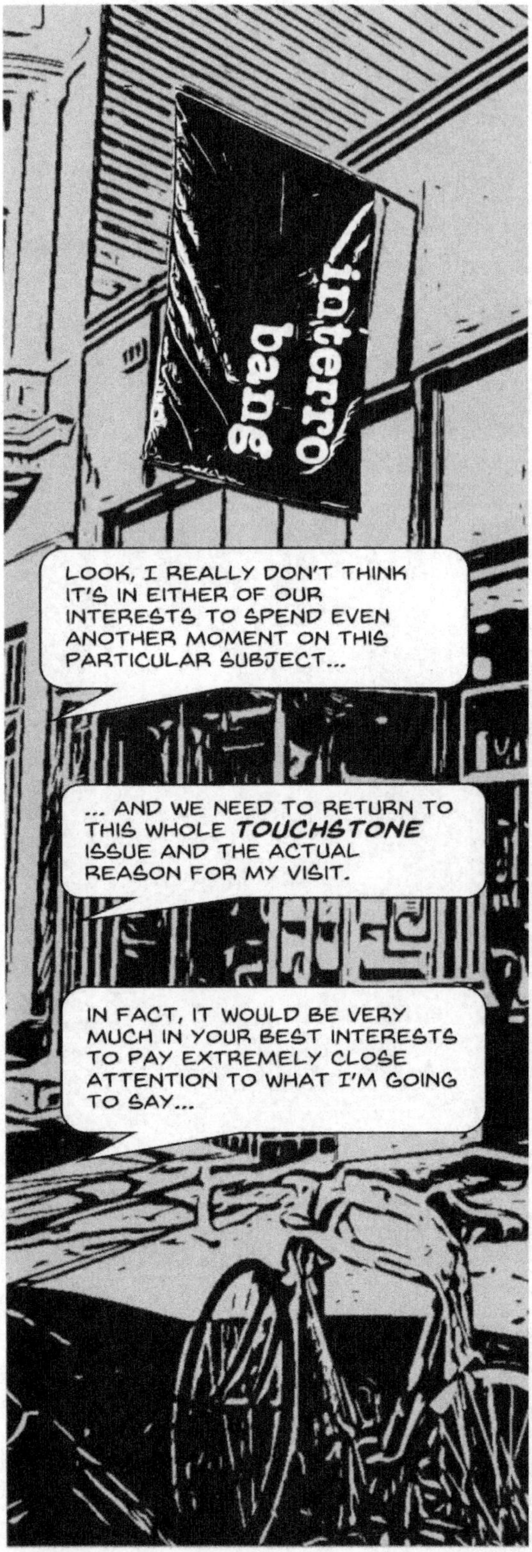

ACT ONE   SCENE THREE

18

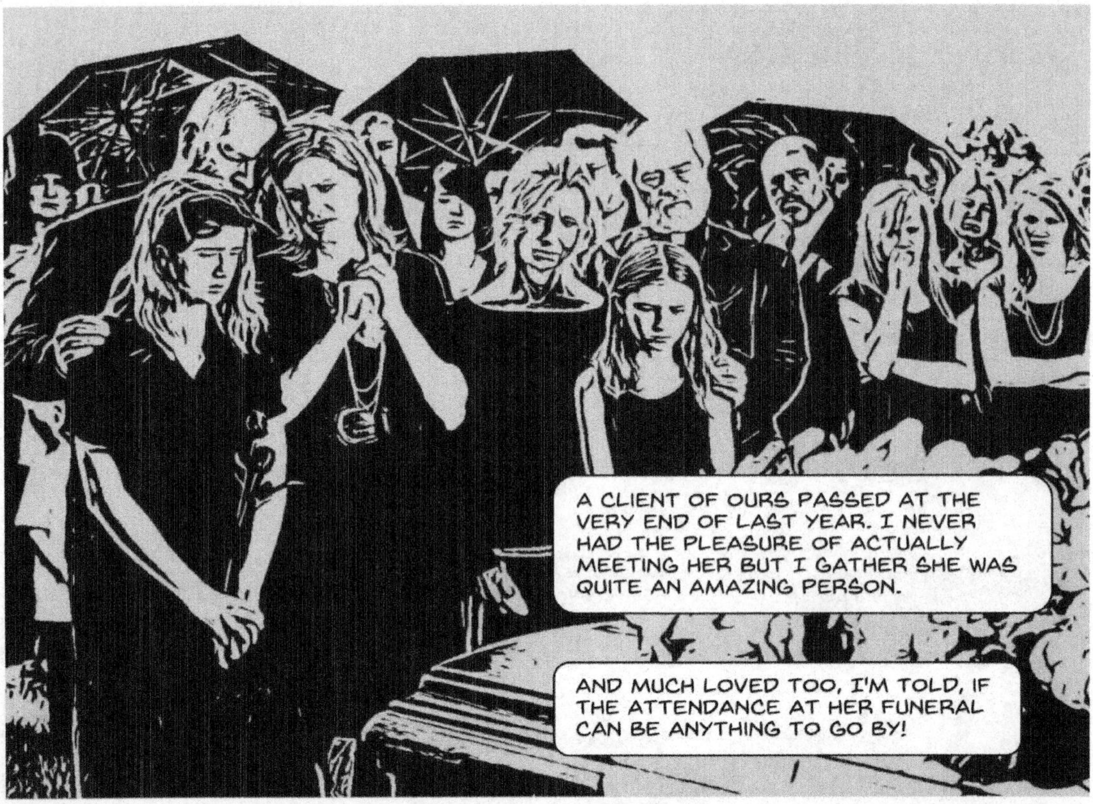

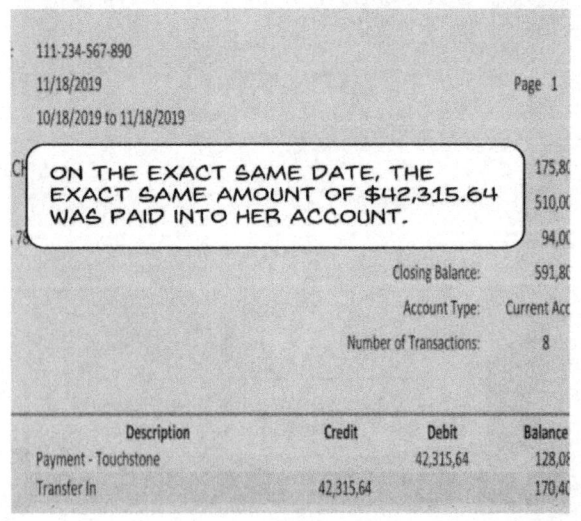
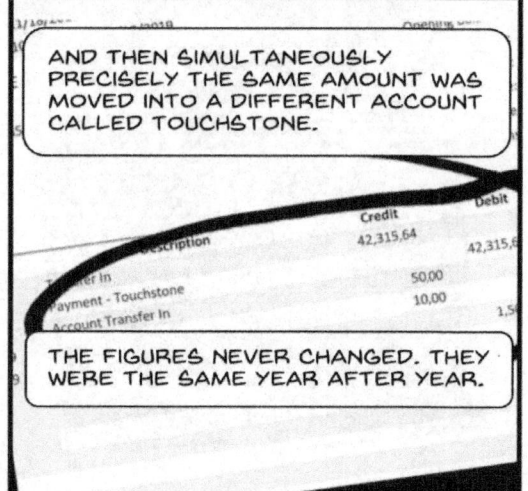

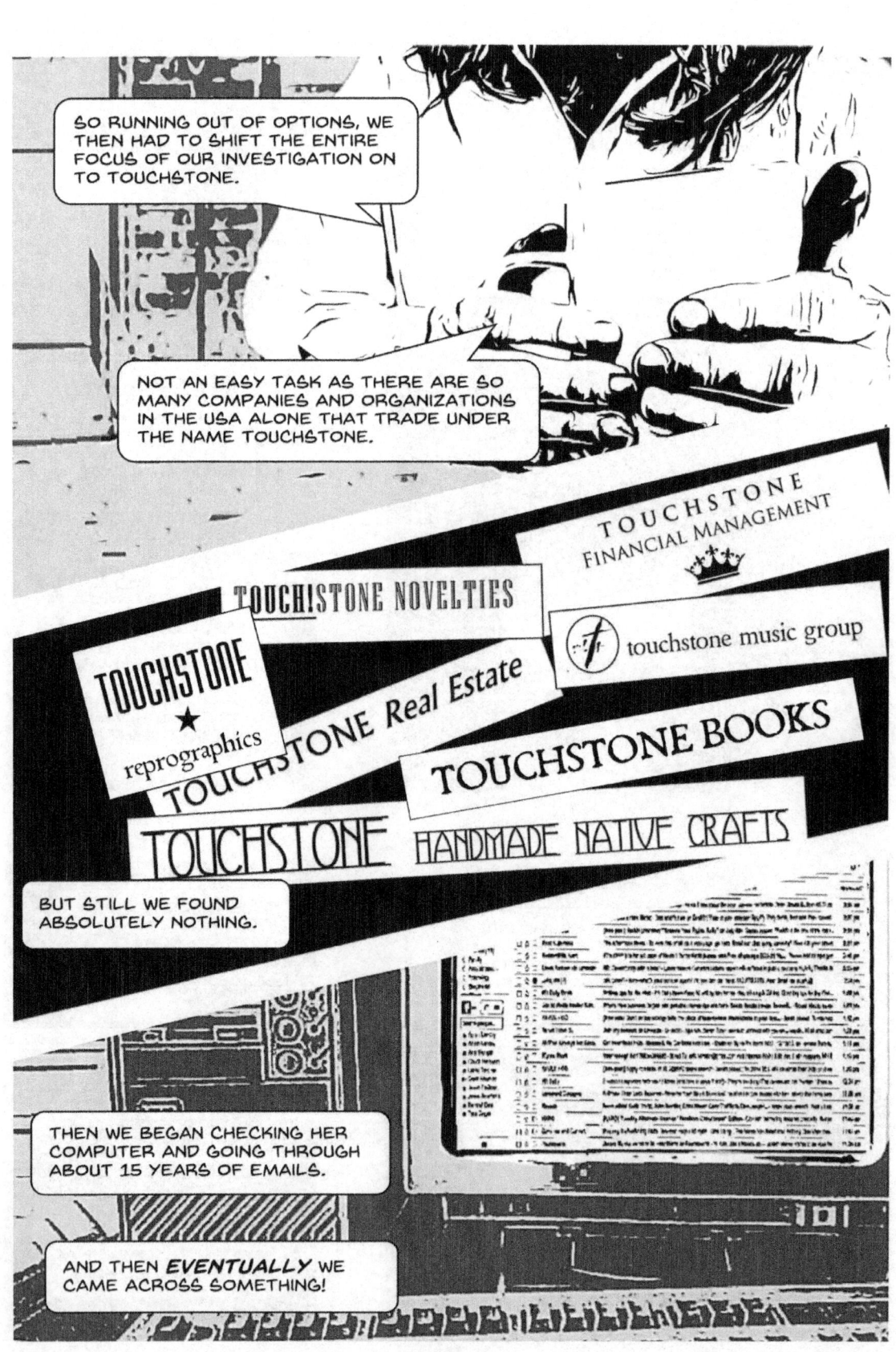

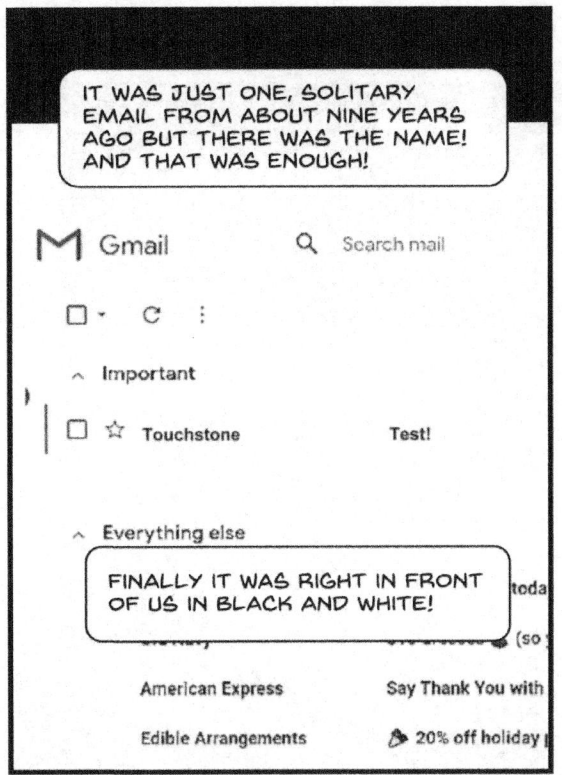

ACT ONE   SCENE FOUR

Interrobang!? Est 2017

BARISTA DRINKS
ESPRESSO - THE ORIGINAL $2.__
LATTE - ESPRESSO + HOT FROTHED MILK   3.00   3.65   4.15
CAPPUCCINO - ESPRESSO + MILK + FOAM   3.00   3.65   4.15
MOCHA - ESPRESSO + RICH HOT CHOCOLATE   3.50   4.15   4.65
AMERICANO - ESPRESSO + HOT WATER   2.25   2.75

COFFEE
DRIP COFFEE -
CAFÉ AU LAIT
STOUT

"THERE YOU GO, LADY. ONE LARGE, NON-FAT LATTE WITH CARAMEL DRIZZLE."

"THANK YOU."

"SO, NOW, WE HAVE TO GO BACK. BACK TO PUCKITANIA. BACK TO KORNEAS."

"DIDN'T I TELL YOU LADY, THIS IS ALL ABOUT HIM. TO UNDERSTAND THIS SITUATION, YOU HAVE TO UNDERSTAND KORNEAS. AND, WHEN WE WERE KIDS, HE WAS ONLY INTERESTED IN TWO THINGS..."

"MATHEMATICS AND MAGIC!"

"AND TRUTHFULLY... WE ALL OF US KNEW THAT ONE DAY HE WOULD BE A MASTER OF ONE OR THE OTHER. **OR BOTH!**"

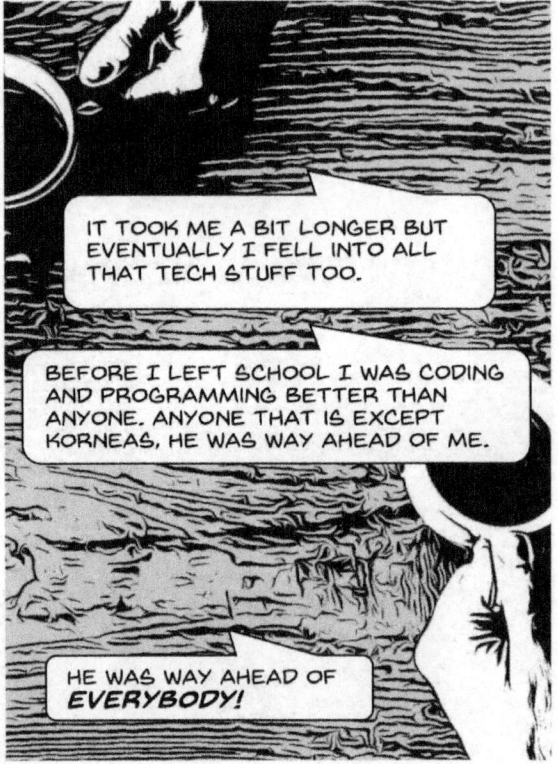

AND YOU KNOW THE SILLY THING? IN THE BEGINNING HE WAS NEVER INTERESTED IN MONEY PARTICULARLY OR SUCCESS.

HAH, SO I GUESS IN THAT RESPECT AT LEAST, YOU COULD SAY WE WERE *COMPLETELY* DIFFERENT!

BUT IN THOSE DAYS HE ALWAYS HAD THIS FOOLISH, IDEALISTIC FANTASY ABOUT THE INTERNET.

THAT IT WOULD BECOME THIS GREAT INCLUSIVE FORCE THAT WOULD ONE DAY UNITE EVERY SINGLE PERSON IN THE WORLD!

WITH JUST ELECTRICITY, A PC AND A PHONE LINE, IT WOULD MAKE THE GREATEST HUMAN ACHIEVEMENTS AVAILABLE TO ALL HUMANS! FOREVER!

WITH NOT ONE SINGLE PERSON LEFT OUT! YOU SEE THIS WAS SUCH A THING WITH KORNY!

AND THAT'S WHY HE CALLED THE COMPANY *GLOBE.*

YEAH, OK, THAT'S QUITE A GOOD STORY, ISN'T IT? SO WHAT HAPPENED?
IT WASN'T ABOUT *WHAT* HAPPENED.
IT WAS MORE A CASE OF *EVERYTHING* HAPPENING! AND HAPPENING ALL AT ONCE!
WE WERE VERY YOUNG. AND KORNEAS WAS FAR TOO IDEALISTIC. AND EVEN THOUGH HE'D MADE HIS FIRST MILLION BY THE TIME HE WAS TWENTY SIX HE WAS NEVER A GOOD BUSINESSMAN!
I FIND THAT HARD TO BELIEVE. BUT THEN AGAIN I FIND ALL OF THIS *EXTREMELY* HARD TO BELIEVE!
IN FACT HE WAS NEVER ANY SORT OF BUSINESSMAN. I USED TO TEASE HIM ABOUT IT. BUT HE HAD NO INTEREST IN THAT SIDE OF THINGS.
THE SUCCESS AND THE MONEY WERE JUST THINGS THAT HAPPENED TO HIM WHILE HE WAS BUSY SOMEWHERE ELSE. DOING THE THINGS HE ACTUALLY CONSIDERED IMPORTANT.

HE HATED THE BUSINESS SIDE OF THINGS SO MUCH THAT, IN THE EARLY DAYS, BEFORE HE BECAME A FAMILIAR FACE, WE WORKED OUT A LITTLE MAGIC TRICK OF OUR OWN...

...I WOULD GO TO ALL THE MEETINGS WITH THE GLOBE SHAREHOLDERS AND JUST INTRODUCE MYSELF AS KORNEAS! IT WORKED TOO!

THAT LEFT KORNEAS FREE TO FOCUS ON HIS REAL STRENGTH WHICH HAD ALWAYS BEEN HIS IDEAS. ALTHOUGH THESE WERE OFTEN SO REVOLUTIONARY, SOME JOURNALISTS ACTUALLY USED TO SAY HE WAS FROM THE FUTURE!

KORNEAS & THE CRYSTAL BALL OF GLOBE

I GUESS HE WAS JUST A TRUE VISIONARY AND I WAS MERELY THE SHADOW HE CAST UPON THE WORLD. BUT WE WERE SO YOUNG AND IN A WAY WE NEEDED EACH OTHER.

GLOBE INC.

WE HAD ALWAYS PLANNED TO SET UP A TECH COMPANY TOGETHER AND AS SOON AS I LEFT COLLEGE, THAT'S EXACTLY WHAT WE DID.

WE COULDN'T AFFORD TO RENT PREMISES. BUT OUR PARENTS HAD BOUGHT THIS BIG OLD CAMERADO MOTORHOME ON A WHIM, WHICH THEY NEVER USED AND SO THAT BECAME OUR FIRST OFFICE!

← GLOBE

INITIALLY, WE INTENDED TO FOCUS ON SOFTWARE DEVELOPMENT, BUT KORNEAS COULD SEE HOW THE INDUSTRY WAS CHANGING. HE GOT US INTO COMMUNICATIONS BEFORE MOST PEOPLE EVEN UNDERSTOOD ITS SIGNIFICANCE AND THAT'S WHEN THE COMPANY REALLY TOOK OFF.

YOU MUST REMEMBER THIS WAS CALIFORNIA IN THE 90'S AND THERE WAS SO MUCH MONEY BEING INVESTED IN TECH. SO... WE DROVE THAT CAMERADO ALL THE WAY TO 'FRISCO!

WHEN WE STARTED HE WAS COMPLETELY COMMITTED TO THE IDEA OF GLOBE AS AN INCLUSIVE INTERFACE FOR ALL MANKIND. BEYOND MAKING ENOUGH MONEY TO KEEP THE BUSINESS AFLOAT, HE WASN'T INTERESTED IN PROFITS.

BACK THEN, HE WANTED HIS INNOVATIONS TO BE AVAILABLE TO EVERYONE, FOR THE MINIMUM COST. HE ONLY WANTED TO HELP PEOPLE, NOT SELL THEM THINGS.

AND OF COURSE IN THE BEGINNING I SUPPORTED HIM COMPLETELY.

DID YOU KNOW IN 1990, HE DEVELOPED A TEXT BASED CODE PROGRAM THAT WOULD ENABLE THE USER TO LOCATE SPECIFIC WEB PAGES? IT WAS EFFECTIVELY THE FIRST EVER SEARCH ENGINE.

OUR GLOBE

Username ....

SIMILARLY, THERE WAS *OUR GLOBE*, WHICH WE LAUNCHED IN '95 AND WHICH WAS THE FIRST SOCIAL MEDIA PLATFORM. IN BOTH CASES, KORNEAS REFUSED TO TAKE OUT ANY SORT OF COPYRIGHT. THEY BELONG TO EVERYBODY, HE SAID. THAT WAS KORNEAS' WHOLE THING!

AWW... I USED TO LOVE OUR GLOBE!
I WAS TOTALLY OBSESSED WITH IT!
I USED TO SPEND HOURS ON IT EVERY DAY WHEN I WAS A TEENAGER!
...I WOULD CHAT TO MY FRIENDS ALL NIGHT INSTEAD OF DOING MY HOMEWORK!
YEAH, BUT HERE'S WHAT I DON'T GET! THIS SELFLESS, PHILANTHROPIC IMAGINARY BROTHER OF YOURS! HE SOUNDS TOTALLY UNLIKE THE REAL KORNEAS!
THAT KORNEAS WAS ONE OF THE WEALTHIEST MEN IN THE COUNTRY AND HARDLY AVERSE TO PUBLICITY!
IN FACT HE SEEMED TO COURT IT AT EVERY AVAILABLE OPPORTUNITY! AND FRONT ROW AT THE OSCARS DOESN'T EXACTLY SCREAM 'SHY AND RETIRING' TO ME AND MAKES A COMPLETE NONSENSE OF THIS WHOLE STORY.
OF COURSE, OF COURSE! BUT THIS WAS THE BEGINNING AND THEN TWO THINGS HAPPENED THAT CHANGED HIM FOREVER. FIRSTLY, THE COMPANY STARTED TO PUT INCREASING DEMANDS ON HIM.
IN THE OLD COUNTRY THERE WAS A SAYING - 'PAY A MAN A GOOD, DECENT WAGE AND HE WILL NEVER WANT MORE. BUT PAY A MAN TOO MUCH MONEY AND HE WILL ALWAYS DEMAND MORE.'
THAT WAS BASICALLY GLOBE!

LIKE ME, MY BROTHER WAS A TRUE EGALITARIAN AND HE BELIEVED THAT EVERYONE WHO WORKED FOR HIM SHOULD BE TREATED EQUALLY.
GLOBE
FROM THE CLEANERS TO THE SENIOR EXECS, WE WANTED EVERYONE TO ENJOY THEIR WORK AND FEEL A VITAL PART OF THE TEAM.
BUT A LOT OF PEOPLE USED TO GET PISSED ABOUT THIS, IN PARTICULAR THE FUCKING SENIOR EXECS! WHO ALWAYS WANTED MORE AND MORE!
OK. SO, WHAT WAS THE OTHER THING?
HUH, YOU SAID IT, LADY! THE OTHER THING WAS CALLED...
ROSALIND!
AND KORNEAS WAS NEVER THE SAME AFTER HE MET HER. HE JUST CHANGED COMPLETELY.

THEY MET AT SOME FUNDRAISING CHARITY THING. SHE WORKED IN TV. SHE WAS DIVORCED I THINK.

BUT KORNEAS JUST FELL HOPELESSLY IN LOVE WITH HER. NEVER SAW HIM LIKE IT BEFORE.

ACH, BUT ROSALIND KNEW EXACTLY WHAT SHE WAS DOING! SHE TOTALLY PLAYED HIM. SHE WAS SO PUSHY AND AMBITIOUS AND ALWAYS GOING ON AT HIM TO IMPROVE HIS OWN *PERSONAL MEDIA PROFILE.*

WHICH IS WHY HE WAS SUDDENLY ON *EVERY FUCKING CHAT SHOW* IN THE COUNTRY! AND BOOM! MY BROTHER IS AN INSTANT CELEBRITY! BACK WHEN SUCH A THING WAS VALUED FAR ABOVE GENIUS, ORIGINALITY OR INNOVATION!

AND PRETTY SOON SHE WAS TAKING, SHALL WE SAY, 'A GREATER INTEREST IN THE FINANCIAL SIDE OF THINGS' AND THAT'S WHEN IT ALL STARTED TO CHANGE FOR GLOBE AND FOR KORNEAS. HE WOULD CONSULT HER ABOUT EVERYTHING.

SEE, IT WAS ACTUALLY HER IDEA FOR GLOBE TO RELOCATE TO NYC, WHICH IS WHERE SHE WAS FROM. SO KORNEAS TOOK OUR BEST PEOPLE, MOVED EAST AND SET UP OUR HEADQUARTERS THERE, WHILE I STAYED HERE TO OVERSEE WHAT HE CALLED GLOBE WEST. AND WHAT I CALLED THE *ABYSS!*

AND I DIDN'T SEE HIM IN PERSON FOR OVER TWO YEARS.

HE BOUGHT HIMSELF A YACHT.

THEN HE BOUGHT HER A YACHT.

NEVER KNEW WHY THEY ACTUALLY NEEDED TWO YACHTS. BUT THERE YOU GO... *SIGH

BUT SUDDENLY HE HAD ALL KINDS OF SMART PEOPLE AROUND HIM SO HE DIDN'T NEED TO BE THE SMARTEST ANYMORE.

AND HE HAD NO INTEREST IN HOW THE INDUSTRY WAS CHANGING. IT WAS ONLY ABOUT THE MONEY. HE TOTALLY LOST HIS FOCUS, THE SENSE OF WHO HE WAS.

THERE WAS THIS TIRED OLD JOURNALISTIC CLICHÉ ABOUT THE 'CRYSTAL BALL AT GLOBE'. BUT IT WAS AROUND THIS TIME IT WAS SAID THAT IT BECAME CLOUDY!

WE'D ALWAYS SEEN EYE TO EYE ABOUT EVERYTHING BUT THAT WAS NO LONGER TRUE. AND WE CLASHED OVER A.I. ALL THE TIME!

IT WAS LIKE HE DIDN'T WANT TO TAKE HIS GREAT INNOVATIONS ANY FURTHER. WHEN HE WAS WITH ROSALIND THAT SIDE OF HIM JUST DIED.

WE STAYED IN TOUCH VIA EMAIL. BUT HE HUNG ON TO SOME VERY OLD FASHIONED IDEAS ABOUT THE ETHICS OF A.I.!

HE USED TO SAY THINGS LIKE 'WE MUSTN'T CONFUSE *HUMANNESS* WITH *HUMANITY*.' AND HE WAS ALWAYS TALKING ABOUT THE *GENIUS PARTICLE*. BUT IT MADE ABSOLUTELY NO SENSE TO ME.

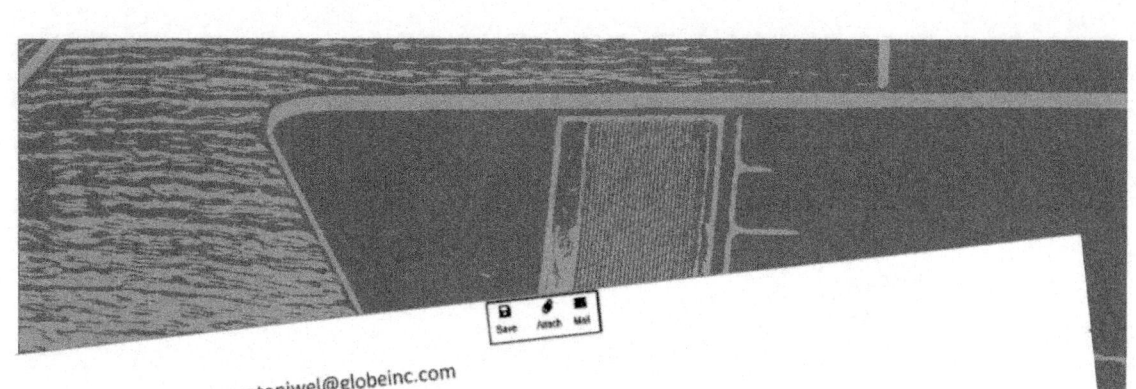

From: korneasyatopiwel@globeinc.com
To: sergeiyatopiwel@globeinc.com
Subject: no subject

and then to go back to your original question. In short, NO! How do you fairly distribute wealth via any system that is created and curated by an elite? How would we ever enforce neutrality? How do you guard against bias? It takes us into whole areas that are way beyond algorithms and download speeds!! Besides, the greatest human achievements are always beyond the sum of their factors. There is a uniqueness you can never replicate and it is foolish to try. It is beyond the limits of technology and raises too many awkward questions.

Human Genius is non-reductible. It is a spark you can't replicate even if you replicate the exact conditions! It is like thinking that there is another number somewhere between 0 and infinity that could sit over the seven and be just as good as Pi. But it can't be! It is solely the unique properties of the number 22.

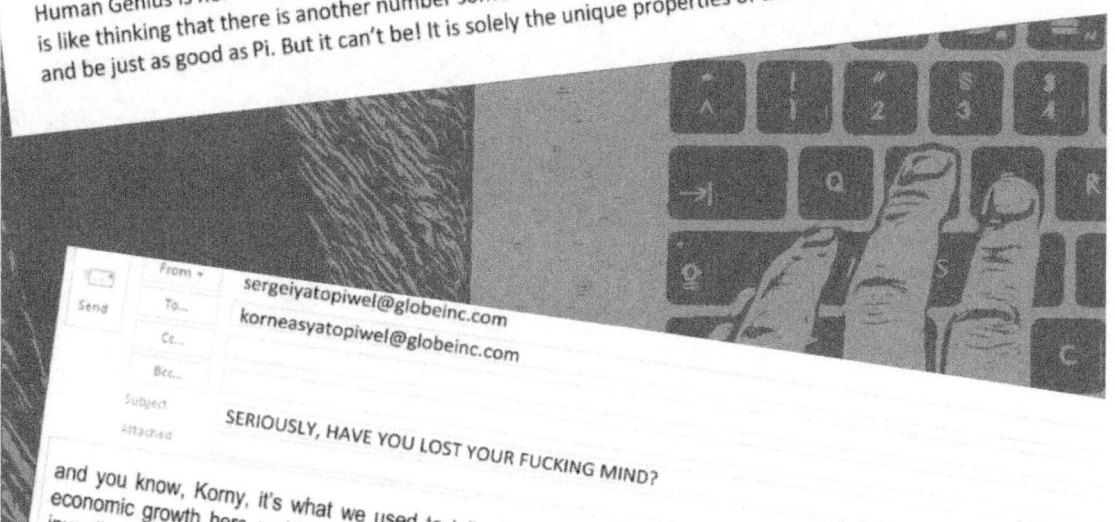

From: sergeiyatopiwel@globeinc.com
To: korneasyatopiwel@globeinc.com
Subject: SERIOUSLY, HAVE YOU LOST YOUR FUCKING MIND?

and you know, Korny, it's what we used to talk about in the old days. Yes, of course, there is so much potential for economic growth here and it would really put us back on top again but it is never about the gift or the talent or the invention, it is about what you do with your gifts. How you make that gift work for everyone regardless of income or demographics! Isn't that what you used to say about the internet! Before it became this gigantic, colossal shopping mall, where the simple-minded go to tell each other they're awesome and to broadcast their medieval opinions, their ridiculous counterintuitive theories and their lies. Where ignorance is not a hindrance anymore but both a gift and a qualification. More than ending poverty or hunger, it seems that what the human race so desperately needed was a public forum where stupid people felt empowered to judge other stupid people. Or failing that, just accuse them of being fat. A.I. has more potential than anything we've ever seen in our lifetime! Why is it so hard for you to understand this?

What happened to you, Brother?

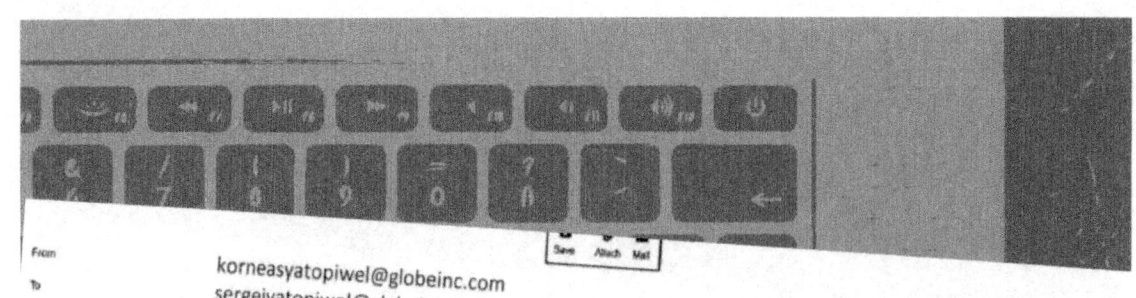

From: korneasyatopiwel@globeinc.com
To: sergeiyatopiwel@globeinc.com
Subject: no subject

but then you could further speculate that 'Humanness' is a quality humans have and those acts that we associate with humans. And of course you can replicate aspects of these. But Humanity is specifically what humans ARE. It's a huge difference.

Say, for example, in 1959 as an experiment, they took two teenage kids from the Midwest. Both had identical IQs, went to the same school and had the identical socio-economic-ethnic-religious backgrounds. They had similar interests and talents. They were both shut away in identical libraries. They read precisely the same books and only listened to the same music. But two years later it is only one of them who writes Blowin' In The Wind! The Genius Particle is just a mathematical variable, an unpredictable inconsistency. But it is infinitely unpredictable and cannot be forced into any rational system of data management.

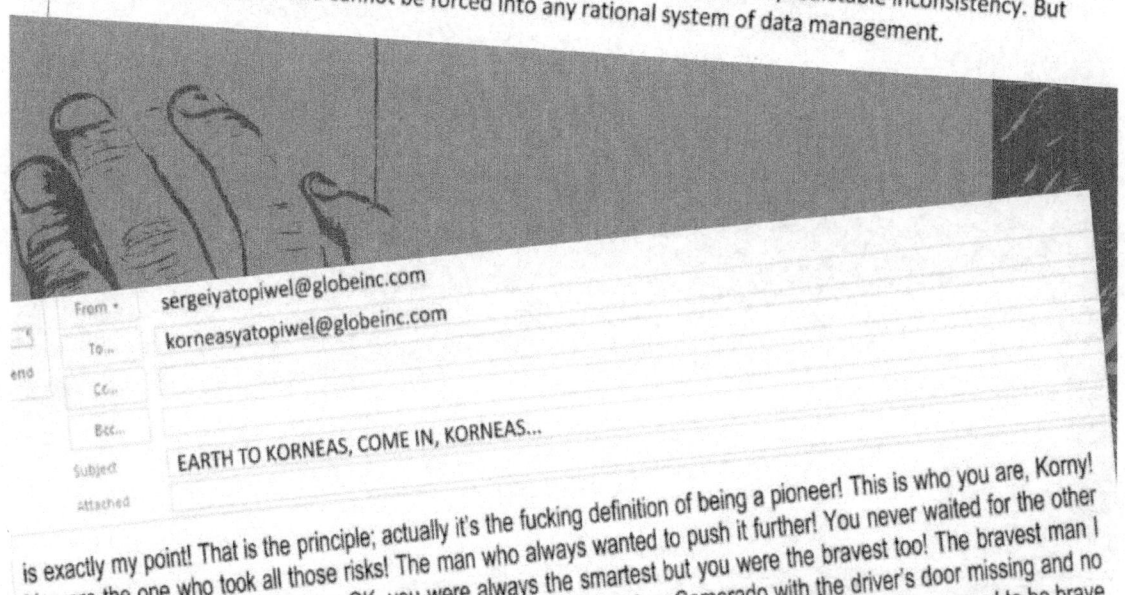

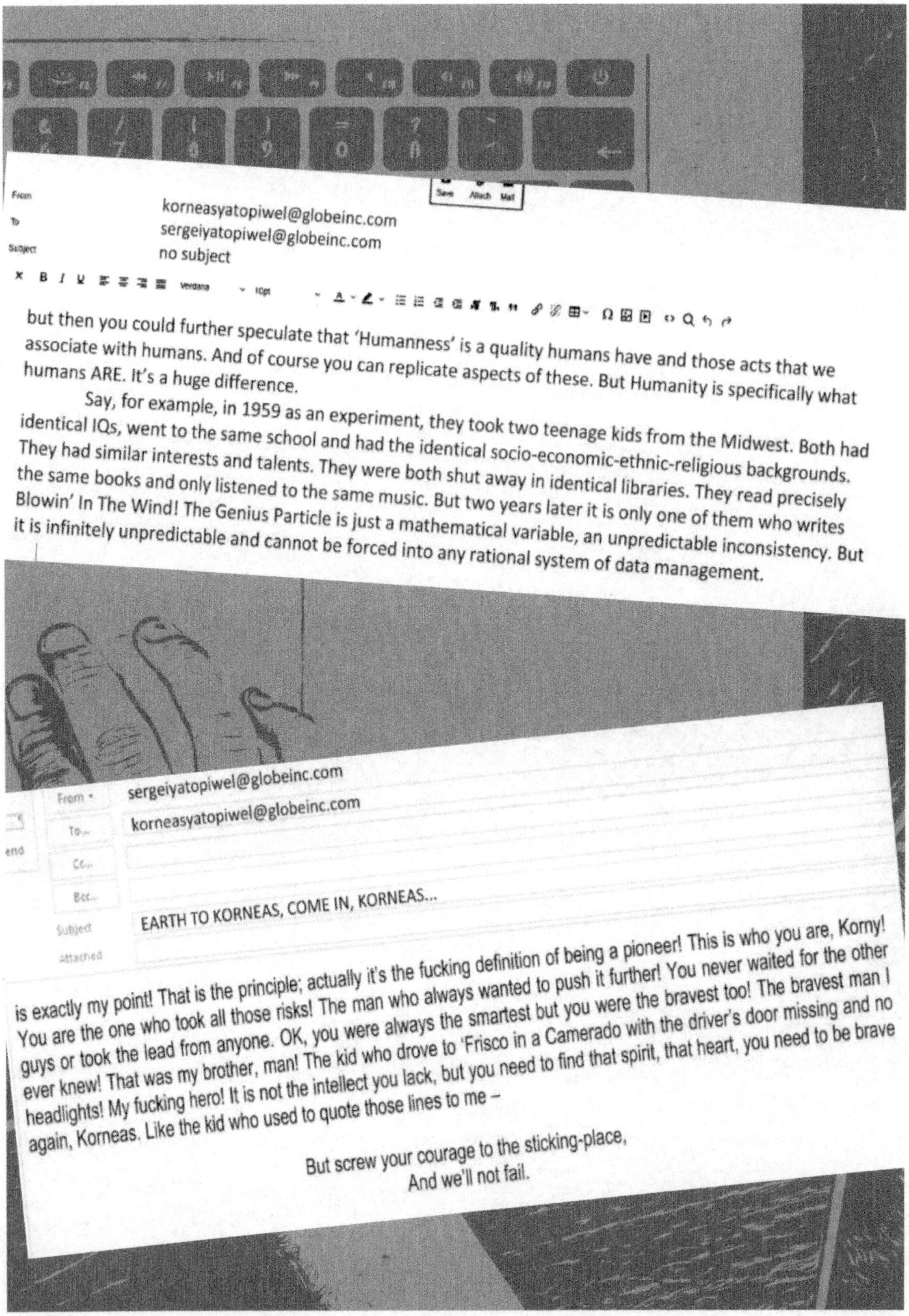

From: sergeiyatopiwel@globeinc.com
To: korneasyatopiwel@globeinc.com
Subject: EARTH TO KORNEAS, COME IN, KORNEAS...

is exactly my point! That is the principle; actually it's the fucking definition of being a pioneer! This is who you are, Korny! You are the one who took all those risks! The man who always wanted to push it further! You never waited for the other guys or took the lead from anyone. OK, you were always the smartest but you were the bravest too! The bravest man I ever knew! That was my brother, man! The kid who drove to 'Frisco in a Camerado with the driver's door missing and no headlights! My fucking hero! It is not the intellect you lack, but you need to find that spirit, that heart, you need to be brave again, Korneas. Like the kid who used to quote those lines to me –

> But screw your courage to the sticking-place,
> And we'll not fail.

THEN I HEARD NOTHING FROM HIM. NOT FOR QUITE A WHILE. THEN ONE DAY WITH ABSOLUTELY NO WARNING, THERE WAS A KNOCK ON MY DOOR...
...AND SUDDENLY THERE HE WAS, JUST STANDING THERE!
HE LOOKED A BIT TIRED BUT OH GOD, I WAS SO PLEASED TO SEE HIM!
HE HAD SPLIT FROM ROSALIND, SHE HAD JUST GONE, HE SAID, 'FUCKED OFF TO ORLANDO'. HE NEVER REALLY SPOKE OF HER AGAIN.
HE ONLY SAID THAT EVERY TIME THEY'D KISSED IT HAD FELT LIKE A BROKEN PROMISE.
OH, AND HE BROUGHT HIS BLOODY DOG WITH HIM TOO. FESTE!
Korneas
Feste
ACTUALLY I SHOULDN'T SAY ANYTHING TOO NEGATIVE AS HE PLAYS A VERY IMPORTANT PART IN ALL THIS!
ESPRESSO
FILTER DAY
IN FACT, THE KEY EVENT IN THE WHOLE STORY TOOK PLACE RIGHT HERE!
NATURAL
FILTER № 2
YOU MEAN IN SAN FRANCISCO?
NO LADY, I MEAN RIGHT HERE IN THIS VERY ROOM!

ACT TWO

ACT TWO

ACT TWO   SCENE ONE

YOU SEE, THIS PLACE WASN'T ALWAYS THE INTERROBANG.

A FEW YEARS AGO IT WAS SOMETHING ENTIRELY DIFFERENT.

WE'RE ACTUALLY SITTING IN WHAT WAS ORIGINALLY THE PREMISES OF **THE THREE FOOLS.** ONE OF THE MOST LEGENDARY MUSIC VENUES IN THE WHOLE OF NORTH BEACH.

LOADS OF GREAT BANDS GOT THEIR START RIGHT HERE! BUT THAT WAS A LONG TIME AGO NOW.

IT HAD STRUGGLED FOR A NUMBER OF YEARS BEFORE THEY FINALLY HAD TO CLOSE FOR GOOD. BUT SAY WHAT YOU LIKE, MISS SPEED, IT IS A PRETTY GOOD LOCATION FOR A COFFEE SHOP. NO?

OH PLEASE, SERGEI! CALL ME MOLLY!
BUZZ-BUZZ
IT'S PROBABLY EASIER THAT WAY.
OH, OK THEN...UM...MOLLY!
BUZZ-BUZZ
BUZZ-BUZZ
SORRY, DO YOU NEED TO ANSWER THAT? DO YOU NEED TO BE PRIVATE?
NO, IT'S NOTHING IMPORTANT. NOTHING THAT CAN'T WAIT.
AT&T
57%
11.45
Wednesday August 9
Missed Call
Missed Call
Missed Call

WE DIDN'T REALLY SPEAK MUCH FOR THE FIRST WEEK KORNEAS CAME BACK. HE JUST LAY AROUND THE HOUSE. HE SLEPT A LOT.
FOR THE MOST PART, IT WAS HIS LITTLE DOG THAT KEPT HIM COMPANY.
APPARENTLY, FESTE HAD FOLLOWED HIM HOME ONE DAY AND JUST DECIDED TO STAY.
ACH! BUT EVEN THEN, THAT DOG WAS CONSTANTLY RUNNING AWAY!
AND KORNEAS WAS FOREVER CHASING HIM!
YES! IT WAS NOT AN EASY TIME. AND ALTHOUGH I WOULD CURSE AT THAT DOG, I WELCOMED THEM BOTH AND TRIED TO MAKE MY BROTHER FEEL THAT MY HOME WAS ALSO HIS HOME.
BUT THEN, ONE EVENING, FESTE, THAT DAMN HOUDINI OF A HOUND, ESCAPED FROM THE HOUSE AND RAN OFF... AGAIN.

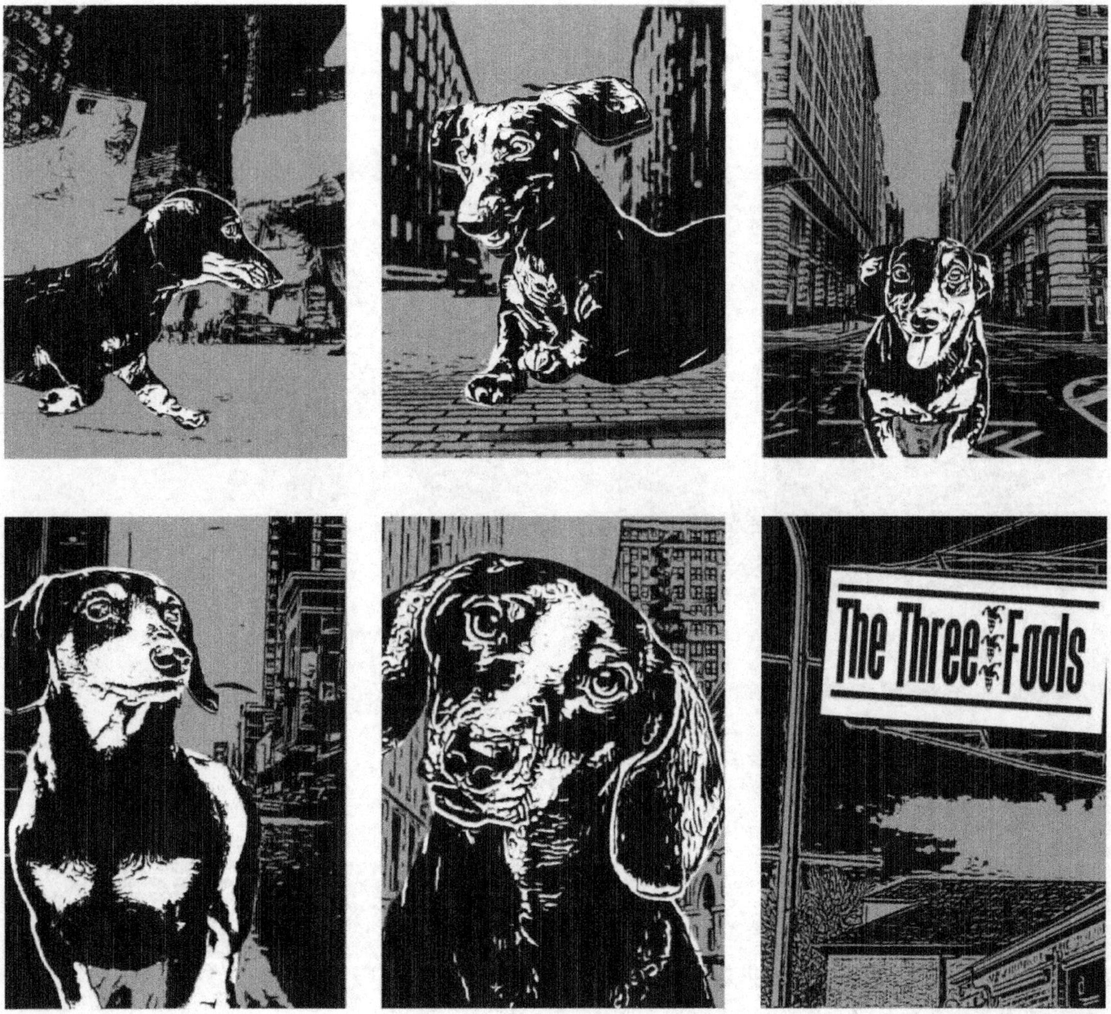
The Three Fools

AS USUAL, KORNEAS NOTICED HE'D GONE ALMOST IMMEDIATELY AND SET OFF IN HOT PURSUIT. HE ASKED AROUND AND WAS EVENTUALLY DIRECTED TO ... YES, OF COURSE, YOU'VE GUESSED IT, THIS VERY ESTABLISHMENT.

The Three Fools

MON-FRI

FUNDRAISER FOR ACTION ON POVERTY

THE LEGENDARY CHAPTER 25 and KLAXON

AND SO, IT WAS HERE ON THAT HISTORIC NIGHT THAT THE STORY OF THE THREE FOOLS, OF CHAPTER 25, OF WILLOW AND MY BROTHER, AND YES THAT DAMN DOG ALL CONNECTED.

MAYBE IT WAS JUST A COINCIDENCE THAT CHAPTER 25 HAPPENED TO BE IN TOWN THAT NIGHT HEADLINING A FUNDRAISER, AND MAYBE IT WAS JUST A COINCIDENCE THAT THE DOORS OF THE THREE FOOLS WERE OPEN ALLOWING FESTE TO RUN IN...

BUT FORGIVE ME A MOMENTARY IRRATIONALITY WHEN I SAY, I THINK IT WAS FATE. OH! I KNOW. I KNOW. I'D HAVE LOOKED LIKE YOU DO NOW IF I'D EVER HEARD ME SAY SUCH A THING.

I'M REALLY SORRY BUT AS I SAID, WILL'S MUSIC CAREER WASN'T ACTUALLY PART OF MY BRIEF AND I KNOW VIRTUALLY NEXT TO NOTHING ABOUT CHAPTER 25!

WELL, PERHAPS, ONCE YOU KNOW THE WHOLE STORY, YOU'LL THINK THAT MAYBE FATE IS STILL ABLE TO PULL SOME TRICKS FROM HER SLEEVE. YES?

HAHA! MAYBE.

BUT LET ME TELL YOU A LITTLE OF CHAPTER 25. PEOPLE THINK OF THEM AS A FOLK ACT BUT IN TRUTH THEY WERE MORE RADICAL AND MORE SUBVERSIVE THAN ANY GRUNGE OR PUNK BAND THAT EVER EXISTED!
FORGIVE ME THOUGH. I'M GETTING AHEAD OF MYSELF. BEFORE CHAPTER 25, THERE WAS JUST WILL AND HAL. THEY MET IN COLLEGE.
IT WAS MUSIC THAT BROUGHT THEM TOGETHER, BUT IT WAS LOVE THAT INSEPARABLY BOUND THEM AS ONE. SOULMATES, IN THE TRUE SENSE.
THIS MACHINE KILLS CAPITALISTS!
HEY WILL, GUESS WHAT?
I CAN'T BEAR TO BE APART FROM YOU! I.C.B.T.B.A.F.Y!
HEY HAL. I·WOULD·NOT· WISH·ANY·COMPANION· IN·THE·WORLD·BUT·YOU.
I.W.N.W.A.C.I.T.W.B.Y
WHEN THEY WEREN'T PLAYING MUSIC AND WRITING SONGS, THEY WOULD HANG OUT AT LA BOTTE ROUGE. IT WAS A FAMOUS LEFT-WING BOOK SHOP.
THEY LOVED READING ALMOST AS MUCH AS THEY LOVED MUSIC.
SO WHEN THEY DECIDED TO PERFORM AS A DUO THEY TOOK THEIR NAME FROM KARL MARX AND DAS KAPITAL.
CAPITALISTIC PRODUCTION KARL MARX
II. CAPITALISTIC CIRCULATION KARL MARX
III. CAPITALIST PRODUCTION AS A WHOLE KARL MARX
CHAPTER 25 OF DAS KAPITAL IS ENTITLED 'THE GENERAL LAW OF CAPITALIST ACCUMULATION'.

WHAT? WHAT IS IT?
OH. IT'S NOTHING.
COME ON, WHAT'S SO FUNNY?
THIS WILL TOTALLY RUIN MY IMAGE! BUT I USED TO LOVE LA BOTTE ROUGE! I VIRTUALLY *LIVED* THERE!
HAH! DON'T WORRY MOLLY! YOUR SECRET WILL DIE WITH ME!
HA HA! I USED TO IMAGINE THAT I'D WRITE A BOOK AND IT WOULD BE ON THE SHELVES THERE ONE DAY! OH, BUT PLEASE CARRY ON!

SO, THEY DIDN'T JUST ADOPT A MARXIST NAME, THEY EMBRACED THE WHOLE IDEOLOGY. THEY WERE DREAMERS, BUT THEY WERE DREAMERS WITH A MISSION.
BEFORE THEY EVEN PLAYED THEIR FIRST GIG, THEY WROTE A MANIFESTO. NO RECORD COMPANIES. NO PUBLISHING. NO DEALS. IT BECAME SOMETHING OF A SLOGAN. CAN YOU BELIEVE IT?

Voter
Registration
Concert
BUT PERHAPS EVEN MORE IMPRESSIVE THAN THAT, THEY NEVER LOST SIGHT OF THOSE IDEALS. THEY BELIEVED IN THEM AND LIVED THEM RIGHT UNTIL THE END.
THEY SOUND LIKE AN AMAZING COUPLE. I KNOW IT WAS BEFORE MY TIME, BUT STILL, I'M SURPRISED I NEVER HEARD OF THEM.
ACH! THEY BUILT QUITE A FOLLOWING, PLAYING FUNDRAISERS AND BENEFITS, BUT THEY WERE NEVER INTERESTED IN FAME. THEY JUST WANTED TO CHANGE THE WORLD!
BISHOP
SAN FRANCISCO
AND CHAPTER 25
SPECIAL GUEST ARTISTS
THE PURPLE GROWLERS

ALTHOUGH THEY DID GAIN A CERTAIN NOTORIETY. IN 1974, ON THE ACTUAL DAY NIXON RESIGNED, THEY PUT ON A FREE CONCERT HERE IN SAN FRANCISCO TO CELEBRATE THE OCCASION.

IT WAS A GREAT EVENT BY ALL ACCOUNTS, BUT IT WAS FOR VERY DIFFERENT REASONS THAT CHAPTER 25 GOT NAME CHECKED IN THE PAPER THE FOLLOWING DAY.

BACK THEN, EVEN SOMEWHERE LIKE HERE, THERE WERE STILL A FEW HARDCORE GOD-FEARING REPUBLICANS READY TO OBJECT TO 'UTTERANCES OF FOUL AND IMPROPER LANGUAGE IN A PUBLIC PLACE.'

OH! BELIEVE ME SERGEI. THEY'RE STILL AROUND. EVEN TO THIS DAY!

HAH! BUT IT WAS ONE SONG IN PARTICULAR THAT GOT THEM INTO TROUBLE. IRONICALLY, ABOUT THE APATHY AND COMPLACENCY WILL AND HAL SAW AMONGST THEIR PEERS.

IT WAS ONE OF THE FIRST SONGS THEY WROTE AND PEOPLE WOULD SING ALONG AT GIGS. THE SONG WAS CALLED 'TICK-TOCK.' BUT AFTER THAT DAY, EVERYONE KNEW IT BY ITS REAL TITLE.

TICK-TOCK - THE FUCK IT CLOCK.

"TICK TOCK - GOES THE FUCK IT CLOCK, AIN'T IT TIME THAT WE TOOK STOCK? TICK TOCK - THE FUCK IT CLOCK, TICK TOCK! TICK TOCK!"

HAHA! YES! I CAN SEE WHY THE AUTHORITIES MIGHT HAVE HAD A PROBLEM WITH THAT.

IT WAS ONLY A WORD, BUT A WORD WAS ENOUGH TO STOP THE CONCERT AND GET THEM CARTED OFF IN A POLICE VAN. ALTHOUGH I DON'T BELIEVE IN THE END THEY WERE EVER CHARGED.
BUT NOT SURPRISINGLY THE SONG THAT GOT THEM BUSTED BECAME FAMOUS OVERNIGHT!
AND FOR A SHORT TIME, THEY WERE FAMOUS TOO!
TICK TOCK!
ACH, EVERYONE KNEW THE SONG! EVEN AT 49ERS GAMES, YOU'D HEAR SOMEONE IN THE CROWD CHANTING IT WHENEVER THE OPPOSING TEAM LOOKED LIKE THEY WERE RUNNING DOWN THE CLOCK!
THAT SONG ALONE WOULD HAVE BEEN ENOUGH TO SECURE THEM A MAJOR DEAL. NATIONAL RADIO PLAY. TELEVISION APPEARANCES. THEY COULD HAVE HAD IT ALL.
AND GOD KNOWS THEY TRIED! APPARENTLY THEY HAD ALL KINDS OF OFFERS.

BUT HAL AND WILL STOOD THEIR GROUND AND TURNED EVERYONE DOWN. INSTEAD THEY RECORDED THE SONG THEMSELVES AND RELEASED THEIR OWN VERSION.

WITH ONE PARTICULAR STIPULATION.

TICK-TOCK - THE FUCK IT CLOCK WOULD NEVER BE AVAILABLE IN ANY STORE. THEY WOULD ONLY SELL THE RECORD AT THEIR FUNDRAISING GIGS.

SO THE MONEY WENT DIRECTLY TO THE CAUSES THEY WERE SUPPORTING. THEY NEVER TOOK A CENT THEMSELVES ALTHOUGH IT MUST HAVE MADE A SMALL FORTUNE OVER THE YEARS.

AND FROM THAT DAY FORWARD, IT WAS HOW THEY SOLD ALL THEIR RECORDS.

BECAUSE, AS THEY ALWAYS MAINTAINED, THE PURPOSE OF THEIR MUSIC WAS NEVER TO MAKE RICH PEOPLE EVEN RICHER.

MY BROTHER LOVED RETELLING THE STORY OF HOW CHAPTER 25 CAME TO BE AND THE WAY *TICK TOCK - THE FUCK IT CLOCK* FOUND ITS WAY INTO ROCK 'N' ROLL FOLKLORE.

BUT THAT'S REALLY JUST THE START.

YES! I CAN UNDERSTAND WHY HE LIKED IT SO MUCH. AND LOOK, I DON'T WANT TO INTERRUPT YOU, BUT WHAT HAPPENED TO ROSALIND?
AH! WELL. THIS WAS GOOD NEWS FOR ME. NOT SO MUCH FOR HER. SHE WENT TO FLORIDA WITH SOME GUY AND GOT INVOLVED IN A SO CALLED 'CASINO PROJECT'.
AND IN A WONDERFUL, SOME MIGHT SAY, TURN OF FATE, SHE WAS SCAMMED OUT OF ***ALL*** OF HER MONEY.
EXCELLENT! GOOD! SERVES HER DAMN WELL RIGHT. SHALL I GET US SOME MORE COFFEE, THEN YOU CAN CARRY ON WITH THE STORY?

ACT TWO   SCENE TWO

THEY COULD HAVE HAD SUCH A DIFFERENT CAREER BUT THEY WERE SO COMMITTED TO THEIR CAUSES. THEY SAID THEY WERE NEVER INTERESTED IN BEING FAMOUS OR RICH. *BECAUSE THEY HAD A JOB TO DO!*

BUT OVER THE YEARS, BECAUSE OF THESE COMMITMENTS THEY TURNED DOWN SO MANY OPPORTUNITIES. THEY WERE INVITED TO TOUR WITH DYLAN IN THE LATE 70'S. NEIL YOUNG TOO! AND EVEN SPRINGSTEEN, I BELIEVE!

YOU SEE, THEIR MUSIC WAS FOR THE PEOPLE. AND TO SERVE THE INTERESTS OF THOSE PEOPLE. AND SO THEY TOOK IT *DIRECTLY TO THEM* AND THERE WAS ALWAYS A MARCH OR A PROTEST SOMEWHERE THAT NEEDED THEM!

THEY REMAINED COMPLETELY COMMITTED TO THEIR IDEOLOGY AND THEY BELIEVED THAT SO-CALLED RADICAL COLLECTIVISM WAS NOT REVOLUTIONARY BUT INSTEAD COMPLETELY FUNDAMENTAL TO THE SURVIVAL OF THE SPECIES.

ACH, THEY HAD LIKE, ZERO FAITH IN CONVENTIONAL POLITICS. IN FACT IN ONE OF THEIR SONGS, THEY EXPLICITLY SAID THAT THE ENTIRE PROCESS OF GOVERNMENT AND 'SOCIAL MANIPULATION', ALSO KNOWN AS THE FUCKING MEDIA, WAS BASED UPON PRECISELY THE SAME PRINCIPLE AS *A SEVEN YEAR OLD SHOWING MAGIC TRICKS TO A FOUR YEAR OLD!*

HAH! AND I KNOW ALL ABOUT THAT ONE!

Panel 1:

"AH BUT THEY DIDN'T EXCLUSIVELY WRITE POLITICAL SONGS. THEY WROTE CHILDREN'S SONGS TOO AND LOVE SONGS AND YEAH, ONE IN PARTICULAR THAT FEATURES LATER IN THE STORY! BUT IT'S THE PROTEST SONGS THAT PEOPLE REMEMBER."

"ACTUALLY, THE MORE I THINK ABOUT IT, I'M SURE I HEARD THAT BERNIE SANDERS WAS AT HER FUNERAL."

Panel 2:

"THAT'S PROBABLY VERY LIKELY. BUT OF ALL THE CHAPTER 25 STORIES, MY FAVORITE IS THE ONE WHEN THEY WERE IN THEIR *SIXTIES* AND DECIDED TO SELL EVERYTHING AND BUY AN RV!"

"AFTER THAT THEY JUST LIVED ON THE ROAD FROM GIG TO GIG! SO I RECKON YOU COULD SAY FROM THAT POINT ONWARDS THE TWO OF THEM EFFECTIVELY LIVED OFF-GRID!"

Panel 3:

"OH MAN! AN OLD FRIEND OF MINE DID THAT! I WAS SO JEALOUS! I WISH I HAD THE NERVE TO DO SOMETHING LIKE THAT! IT MUST BE AMAZING!"

"PO GUIZI! YOU ARE FULL OF SURPRISES, YOU KNOW THAT?"

"OH, IS THAT A GOOD THING?"

"WELL, THAT DEPENDS. JUST ONE THING. IF YOU EVER DECIDE TO DO IT, YOU MUST REMEMBER TO CHOOSE YOUR VEHICLE VERY CAREFULLY... OF COURSE, YOU CAN *NEVER* GO WRONG WITH A CAMERADO!"

TA-DAA! HAPPY BIRTHDAY, WILL!
WELL? WHAT DO YOU THINK?
OH HAL! REALLY? YOU DIDN'T BUY THIS FROM THE MANSON FAMILY, DID YOU, BY ANY CHANCE?
NAH...
...MANSON WAS DUNE BUGGIES! YOU'RE THINKING OF TED BUNDY!
(*SIGH) HOW MUCH?
OH, VERY MUCH WITHIN OUR BUDGET.
WELL, IT HAS GOT A LOT OF SPACE, I GUESS. PLENTY OF ROOM FOR GUITARS AND STUFF.
REALLY LOW MILEAGE TOO.
WELL, I SUPPOSE IT'S TRUE WHAT THEY SAY - YOU'RE ONLY SIXTY ONE ONCE!
AAH, BUT DOES IT FEEL LIKE *HOME*?
OH YOU, AS LONG AS WE'RE TOGETHER, HOW CAN IT NOT BE HOME? AND YOU KNOW WHAT, HAL?
WHAT, BABY?
WHEREVER WE GO ON OUR TRAVELS, YOU'LL ALWAYS KNOW EXACTLY WHERE I AM.
A.N.A.Y.N.M.T.B.
AS NEAR AS YOU NEED ME TO BE!

SOME TIME LATER.
THE LAST OF THE *WHAT*, DID YOU SAY?
THE LAST OF THE TROUBADOURS!
CALIFORNIA
TRAN 10
THAT'S WHAT IT SAYS HERE ON THE POSTER ANYWAY.
2011
MAY DAY
SO IT MUST BE TRUE!
I DUNNO. WHY DO I FIND THAT SO DEPRESSING?
WORKERS' DAY
BECAUSE YOU'RE HAL AND THAT'S WHAT YOU DO BEST!
FEATURING THE LAST OF THE TROUBADOURS CHAPTER 25!
WHATEVER...
RALLY APRIL 29
SAN ANTONIO PARK, OAKLAND
WELL, YOU KNOW, MUSIC·OFT·HATH·SUCH·A·CHARM·TO·MAKE·BAD·GOOD·AND·GOOD·PROVOKE·TO·HARM.
SO *NOW* SHE'S QUOTING SHAKESPEARE?
WELL, IF IT AIN'T BROKE! ANYWAY, WE'RE GOING TO BE THERE PRETTY SOON. SO LET'S JUST RUN THROUGH OUR SET LIST. HOW LONG ARE WE PLAYING FOR?
JUST HALF AN HOUR I THINK. MAYBE STICK TO THE SET WE PLAYED AT THAT PICNIC THING THE OTHER DAY?
THAT WOULD WORK!
1. GAGS & BLINDFOLDS
2. SONG FOR WILL
YEAH, I WOULD EXPECT NOTHING LESS FROM A TROUBADOUR!
OH SHUSH!
8. NO GOOD DOCTOR & CAPTAIN KICKS
???

"AND THE UGLIEST PEOPLE OUTTA ALL THE HUMAN RACE...

...ARE THE ONES WITH GAGS AND BLINDFOLDS ON THEIR FACE."

LATER.

"...AND WE SEE NO EVIL AND WE SPEAK NO EVIL..."

AW! I'VE ALWAYS LOVED THIS SONG!!

THANK YOU! AND THANK YOU ALL FOR JOINING US HERE TODAY. AND KEEP SPREADING THE WORD!

AND REMEMBER! IF YOU AIN'T AN ACTIVE PART OF THE SOLUTION, THEN YOU'RE STILL PART OF THE PROBLEM!

MAY DAY INTERNATIONAL WORKERS DAY

A FEW MONTHS LATER 1.37 AM.

*COUGH, COUGH...

*COUGH, COUGH...BLEAUGH...

FUCK'S SAKE, HAL! THERE'S PEOPLE TRYING TO SLEEP HERE!

WAIT, WAIT... IS THAT BLOOD ON YOUR TISSUE?

YEAH, I STILL GET SOME TROUBLE IN THAT DEPARTMENT FROM WHERE THAT COP BEAT ME IN OAKLAND THAT TIME...

*COUGH, COUGH...

OH BUT BABY, THAT WAS TWELVE YEARS AGO NOW!

NO, NO, I REALLY DON'T LIKE THE LOOK OF THAT.

LOOK, NEXT TIME WE'RE IN FRISCO, YOU REALLY NEED TO GO BACK TO THAT FREE CLINIC.

OH, I'M FINE. DON'T WORRY. JUST GO BACK TO SLEEP.

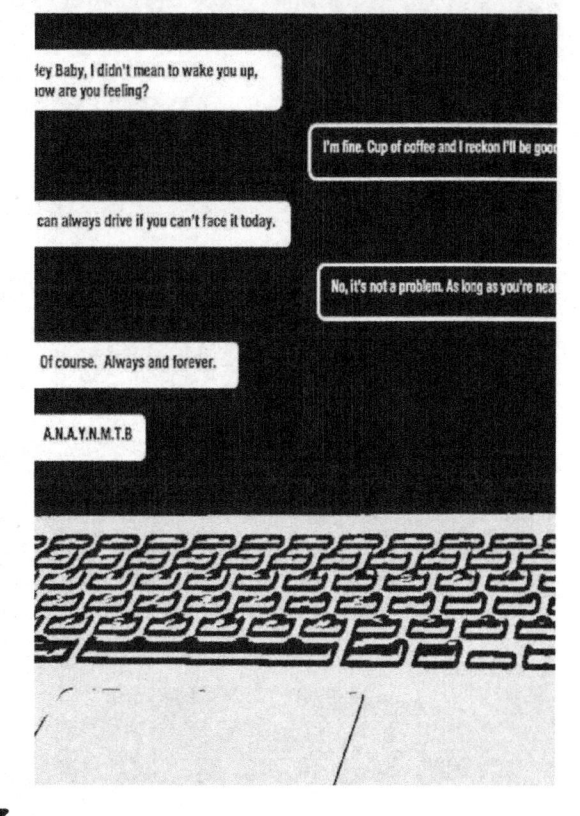

THE FOLLOWING MORNING.

HEY BABY, DIDN'T MEAN TO WAKE YOU UP, HOW ARE YOU FEELING?

I'M FINE. CUP OF COFFEE AND I RECKON I'LL BE GOOD TO GO.

I CAN ALWAYS DRIVE IF YOU CAN'T FACE IT TODAY.

NO, IT'S NOT A PROBLEM. AS LONG AS YOU'RE NEARBY.

OF COURSE. ALWAYS AND FOREVER.

A.N.A.Y.N.M.T.B.

Hey Baby, I didn't mean to wake you up, how are you feeling?

I'm fine. Cup of coffee and I reckon I'll be good

can always drive if you can't face it today.

No, it's not a problem. As long as you're nea

Of course. Always and forever.

A.N.A.Y.N.M.T.B

BUT HANG ON! SURELY THEY HAD TO HAVE MADE SOME MONEY FROM THEIR MUSIC. HOW ELSE COULD THEY HAVE SURVIVED?
ACH, THEY JUST TOOK THEIR MOST BASIC EXPENSES. FOOD, GAS, GUITAR STRINGS. THEY LIVED VERY FRUGALLY. THEY DIDN'T NEED MUCH. ANY EXTRA MONEY THEY MADE FROM SELLING RECORDS THEY PUT TOWARDS MAKING MORE RECORDS!
THEY HAD THEIR GREAT CONVICTIONS. AND THEY HAD EACH OTHER. THEY DIDN'T NEED ANYTHING ELSE.
I FIND ALL THAT TOTALLY AMAZING. SO WHAT DID THEY ACTUALLY DO WHEN THEY WEREN'T DOING THEIR MUSIC?
THEY WEREN'T BIG ON MOVIES ALTHOUGH THEY LOVED THEIR SHAKESPEARE AND WERE FOREVER QUOTING HIM AT EACH OTHER! EVEN ON STAGE!
AND USUALLY WHEN THEY WERE ALONE IN THEIR RV, THEY JUST USED TO MAKE UP STORIES TOGETHER!
IT SEEMED AS IF THEY EXISTED NOT ONLY IN THEIR OWN WORLD, BUT OUTSIDE OF TIME ALSO.
OF COURSE THEY WERE ALWAYS GOING ON MARCHES AND PROTESTS TOO. BUT THE OTHER THING THEY USED TO DO WAS ***DANCE!*** FUNNY THING IS WILL COULDN'T DANCE AT ALL WHEN THEY FIRST MET AND HAL TAUGHT HER!
GOD, I WISH SOMEONE HAD TAUGHT ME! I WOULD LOVE TO BE ABLE TO DANCE! ALWAYS WISHED I COULD!
ACH, ANYONE CAN DANCE! STUPID PEOPLE DO IT ALL THE TIME! ***EVEN I CAN DANCE!*** BUT SERIOUSLY, ACCORDING TO KORNY, THEY USED TO DANCE ALL THE TIME! ***EVERY NIGHT***, IN FACT!

♪ 'JUMPIN' AT THE WOODSIDE' ♪

"RECOGNISE THIS?"

"OH HAL, THANK YOU, I CAN'T BELIEVE YOU FOUND IT AGAIN. THIS WAS THE FIRST THING WE EVER DANCED TO!"

"OH YEAH, PRETTY MUCH! **BUT** YOU DID TEACH ME TO DANCE!"

"WELL, BASIE WAS SECOND ACTUALLY... DUKE ELLINGTON WAS THE FIRST."

"ALTHOUGH THAT'S NOT TO SAY IT WASN'T A BIT OF A STRUGGLE!"

"AW, DO YOU REMEMBER? I MUST HAVE BEEN ABOUT 22, 23... I SAID THAT I COULDN'T DANCE. JUST DIDN'T HAVE IT IN ME! DO YOU REMEMBER WHAT YOU SAID?"

"WAIT A MINUTE! I CAN'T DANCE TO *THIS*! AND WHAT IN ALL FUCK IS THIS?"

"DUKE ELLINGTON'S 'UP AND DOWN, UP AND DOWN'."

"DUKE ELLINGTON? WAIT! WHAT ARE WE NOW, HAL? OUR FUCKING PARENTS? SORRY, I'LL HAVE TO GO IN A MOMENT AND CHECK ON MY MEATLOAF..."

"SORT OF..."

"'ANYONE CAN DANCE,' YOU SAID. 'JUST LISTEN TO THE MUSIC, FOLLOW YOUR FEET AND IGNORE YOUR FUCKING BRAIN FOR ONCE!'"

TEN MINUTES LATER.

"WOW! YEAH! OK! THIS DUKE GUY, HE AIN'T SO BAD!"

"SHHH, JUST KEEP DANCING."

"BUT WHAT IF I CAN'T STOP? HEY, I LOVE YOU PUCK."

"WOW, WHAT A GENTLEMAN! WAS I USUALLY THAT CORNY?"

"THEN NEVER STOP! AND I LOVE YOU, TITANIA."

ACT TWO.   SCENE THREE

SAN FRANCISCO.

APRIL 23RD 2012

MORNING.

... AND HEY, REMEMBER THAT SURPRISE I WAS TALKING ABOUT EARLIER?

WELL, THEY'VE JUST ARRIVED HERE IN THE STUDIO AND THEY'RE SITTING RIGHT IN FRONT OF ME!

YEAH, AND I GOTTA SAY IT'S SUCH A THRILL TO HAVE THESE GUYS HERE WITH ME RIGHT NOW!

BEEN A BIG FAN FOR A LONG TIME!

ACTUALLY MAKE THAT A LONG, LONG TIME!

AND YOU KNOW, I WAS THINKING ABOUT OUR GUESTS EARLIER AND HOW THE WORLD CAN SO EASILY BE SPLIT INTO JUST TWO GROUPS! WITH NO POSSIBLE THIRD CATEGORY.
ON THE ONE HAND THERE ARE THOSE WHO ARE FAMILIAR WITH THEM AND THEIR INCREDIBLE BODY OF WORK AND THE AMAZING CONTRIBUTIONS THEY'VE MADE TO MUSIC AND SOCIAL CHANGE.
BUT BECAUSE OF THEIR PRINCIPLES AND THEIR ABSOLUTE REFUSAL TO COMPROMISE OR SELL OUT, THERE ARE ALSO VAST NUMBERS OF PEOPLE WHO HAVE SIMPLY NEVER HEARD OF THEM!
BUT FOR ME, IT'S A TOTAL HONOR AND A THRILL TO SAY WELCOME TO WILL AND HAL, THE INCREDIBLE *CHAPTER 25*!
WOW! THAT WAS AN AMAZING INTRODUCTION! THANK YOU.
AND THANK YOU FOR INVITING US ONTO THE SHOW.

IT'S GREAT TO HAVE YOU BACK IN TOWN AGAIN. BUT BEFORE WE START CHATTING, I REALLY HAVE TO TELL EVERYONE ABOUT THIS AMAZING THING YOU'RE DOING.
NOW STARTING TONIGHT, YOU'RE DOING A WHOLE WEEK AT THE THREE FOOLS. HAVE I GOT THAT RIGHT?
YES, ABSOLUTELY! THERE'S A NEW NON-PROFIT ORGANIZATION THAT'S DOING SOME GREAT THINGS AROUND HERE CALLED ACTION ON POVERTY.
AND THEY ASKED IF WE COULD DO A ONE NIGHT FUNDRAISER FOR THEM.
OF COURSE, WE'D BE ABSOLUTELY DELIGHTED, WE TOLD THEM. BUT THEN WE SAID WE COULD ACTUALLY DO BETTER THAN THAT!
SO YEAH, WE'LL BE THERE ***ALL*** WEEK!

SO DOES THIS MEAN THAT YOU PLAY DIFFERENT TUNES EVERY NIGHT?

NOT ENTIRELY. BUT WE'LL MIX IT UP A BIT AND TRY AND MAKE EACH NIGHT UNIQUE IN SOME WAY.

SO, A BIT OF A MIX OF OLD SONGS AND NEW ONES?

YES, THAT'S THE GENERAL IDEA. IN FACT, TONIGHT, WE'LL BE DOING A NEW SONG WE'VE NEVER PLAYED IN PUBLIC BEFORE. IT'S CALLED *BROWNSTONE KISSES*.

AND I BELIEVE THAT I HEARD SOMETHING ABOUT A BOOK TOO?

YES, BROWNSTONE KISSES, AKA 25 X 25#, IS ALSO THE TITLE OF OUR FIRST EVER SONG BOOK. ONLY FORTY YEARS IN THE MAKING! BUT AGAIN EVERY CENT WE MAKE WILL GO TO A.O.P.

IT'S GOING TO BE AVAILABLE TO BUY AT THE SHOWS SO HOPEFULLY IF PEOPLE LIKE IT, THAT WILL RAISE EVEN MORE MONEY.

SO THAT HAS SOME OF THE OLD SONGS TOO?

THAT'S RIGHT, WELL, 25 OF THEM!

SEE APPENDIX ONE

HA HA, WELL, YOU SEE THIS IS A PERFECT EXCUSE FOR US TO PLAY ONE OF YOUR OLD RECORDS!
NOW MY DAD WAS SUCH A FAN OF YOU GUYS. HE SAW YOU A WHOLE BUNCH OF TIMES BACK IN THE DAY AND BOUGHT ALL YOUR RECORDS!

ANYWAY WHEN WE USED TO GO ON LONG CAR TRIPS WE ALWAYS USED TO SING THIS SONG. I USED TO DRIVE EVERYONE MAD.
CHAPTER 25
HOBO
IMAGE REDACTED
I WAS ONLY ABOUT FIVE BUT I'D BE CONSTANTLY LIKE 'DADDY, CAN WE SING THAT HOBO SONG AGAIN?'
HOBO HOBO

IT'S TRUE!
SOUTH
EXIT 5B
280
San Jose
ONLY
NORTH
EXIT 5A
280
San Francisco
ONLY
"HOBO, HOBO ALABAMA-BOUND, HOBO, HOBO ALABAMA-BOUND..."

10 MINUTES LATER.

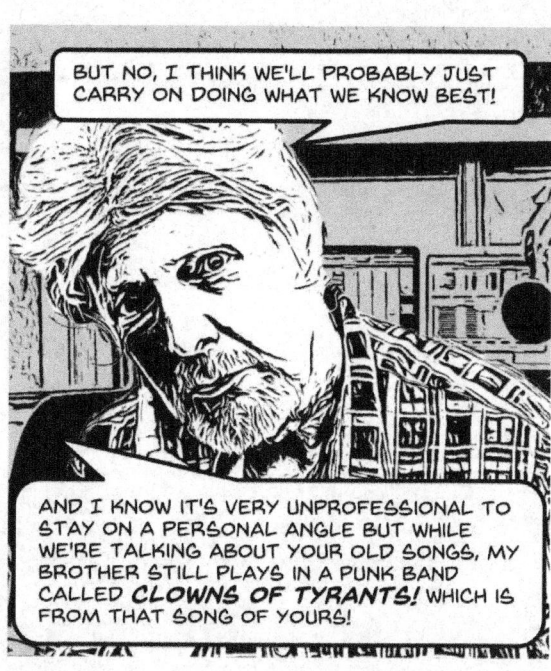

AND WE'VE JUST BEEN LISTENING TO *BROWNSTONE KISSES* BY CHAPTER 25. AND THEY'RE HERE TODAY IN THE STUDIO WITH ME.

SO I HAVE TO ASK YOU, THIS SOUNDED LIKE A FAIRLY STRAIGHT FORWARD LOVE SONG AND NOT LIKE THE USUAL SORT OF MUSIC WE ASSOCIATE WITH YOU, SO IS THIS A NEW DIRECTION MAYBE?

OH NO, NOT AT ALL. WE'VE ALWAYS WRITTEN LOVE SONGS. WE'VE ALSO WRITTEN SILLY SONGS AND CHILDREN'S SONGS AND ALL SORTS OF THINGS.

BUT NO, I THINK WE'LL PROBABLY JUST CARRY ON DOING WHAT WE KNOW BEST!

AND I KNOW IT'S VERY UNPROFESSIONAL TO STAY ON A PERSONAL ANGLE BUT WHILE WE'RE TALKING ABOUT YOUR OLD SONGS, MY BROTHER STILL PLAYS IN A PUNK BAND CALLED *CLOWNS OF TYRANTS!* WHICH IS FROM THAT SONG OF YOURS!

HAHA YEAH, *THE COLLECTIVIST RAG!*

THAT'S THE ONE! ANYWAY, I'M CERTAIN THEY'VE PLAYED AT THE 'FOOLS A COUPLE OF TIMES! AND I'M PRETTY SURE THAT HE WOULD NEVER SPEAK TO ME EVER AGAIN IF I HAD YOU ON THE SHOW AND DIDN'T MENTION ANYTHING!

AH, DOES THAT MEAN YOU'RE GOING TO MAKE US ALL LISTEN TO THAT TOO?

OH YEAH, ABSOLUTELY!

♪ " AND PAPA'S GOT...

...A BRAND NEW BAG...

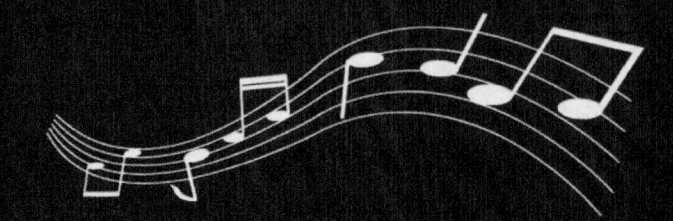

"...CALLED THE COLLECTIVIST RAG!"

ACT TWO　　　　　　　　　　SCENE FOUR

SAN FRANCISCO.

APRIL 23RD 2012

EVENING.

FESTE?

FESTE, WHERE ARE YOU, BOY?

AH, COME ON, DON'T BE LIKE THIS!

FESTE! FESTE!

WHERE ARE YOU, YOU DAFT DOGGY?

FESTE! FESTE! FESTE!

FESTE! COME HERE! YOU FUCKING ANNOYING FUCKING ANIMAL!

EXCUSE ME, SIR?
ER...YEAH?
HAVE YOU SEEN A SMALLISH WIENER DOG ON YOUR TRAVELS?
WHY, YES I HAVE. RECKON I SAW HIM HEADING INTO THE BACK OF THE THREE FOOLS. YOU KNOW THE PLACE?
YES, I DO. THANK YOU. THAT'S A GREAT HELP.
RIGHT, DAWG! I'M COMIN' TO GET YA!

The Three Fools
MON-FRI
RAISER FOR ACTION ON
ENDARY CHAPTER 25
EXCUSE ME, MISS? YOU'VE NOT HAPPENED TO SEE A LITTLE DOG AROUND THE PLACE TONIGHT, HAVE YOU?
AWW, YOU MUST MEAN THAT CUTE LITTLE OLD WIENER DOG!
WELL, HE'S NOT *THAT* OLD BUT YEAH I GUESS THAT'S HIM!
I THINK NONA TOOK HIM OUT THE BACK, INTO THE OFFICE.
I'LL FETCH HIM IN A MINUTE AS SOON AS I FINISH WITH THESE CUSTOMERS. SO JUST SIT DOWN AND HAVE A BEER. LISTEN TO THE MUSIC.
YOU KNOW, YOU KINDA REMIND ME OF SOMEONE...

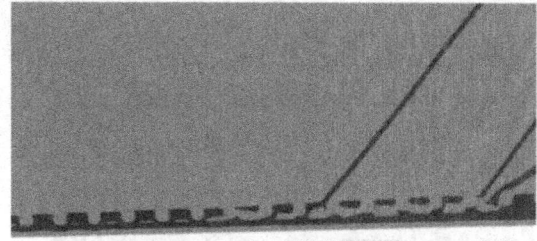

THE THREE FOOLS

"THANK YOU, THANK YOU ALL SO MUCH..."

"YES AND THANK YOU FOR SHOWING UP TONIGHT AND SUPPORTING SUCH A GREAT AND WORTHY CAUSE!"

"AND YOU KNOW, WILL AND I LOVE PLAYING ALL THOSE OLD SONGS FOR YOU..."

"WE CERTAINLY DO, HAL!"

"BUT IF YOU COULD ALL STAND IT, WE WOULD VERY MUCH LIKE TO PLAY YOU A BRAND NEW SONG RIGHT NOW!"

"SO, IF THERE'S ANYONE OUT THERE TONIGHT NURSING A BROKEN HEART..."

"...THIS ONE IS JUST FOR YOU."

AND SO FOR THE FIRST TIME ON ANY STAGE ANYWHERE...
...WE REALLY HOPE YOU'RE GONNA ENJOY...
A LITTLE NUMBER THAT WE CALL...
BROWNSTONE KISSES!
brownstone kis
vailable here

"AND MY HEAD'S AN ANCIENT WELL WHERE I STILL THROW MY WISHES...

...FOR HER MIDNIGHT WHISPERS AND HER BROWNSTONE KISSES

BECAUSE SHE'S GONE, GONE, GONE..."

"AND SOMETIMES THERE'S A KNOCK
AND I OPEN MY DOOR...

...I LIKE TO VISIT MYSELF
BUT I DON'T LIVE HERE ANYMORE

BECAUSE SHE'S GONE, GONE, GONE..."

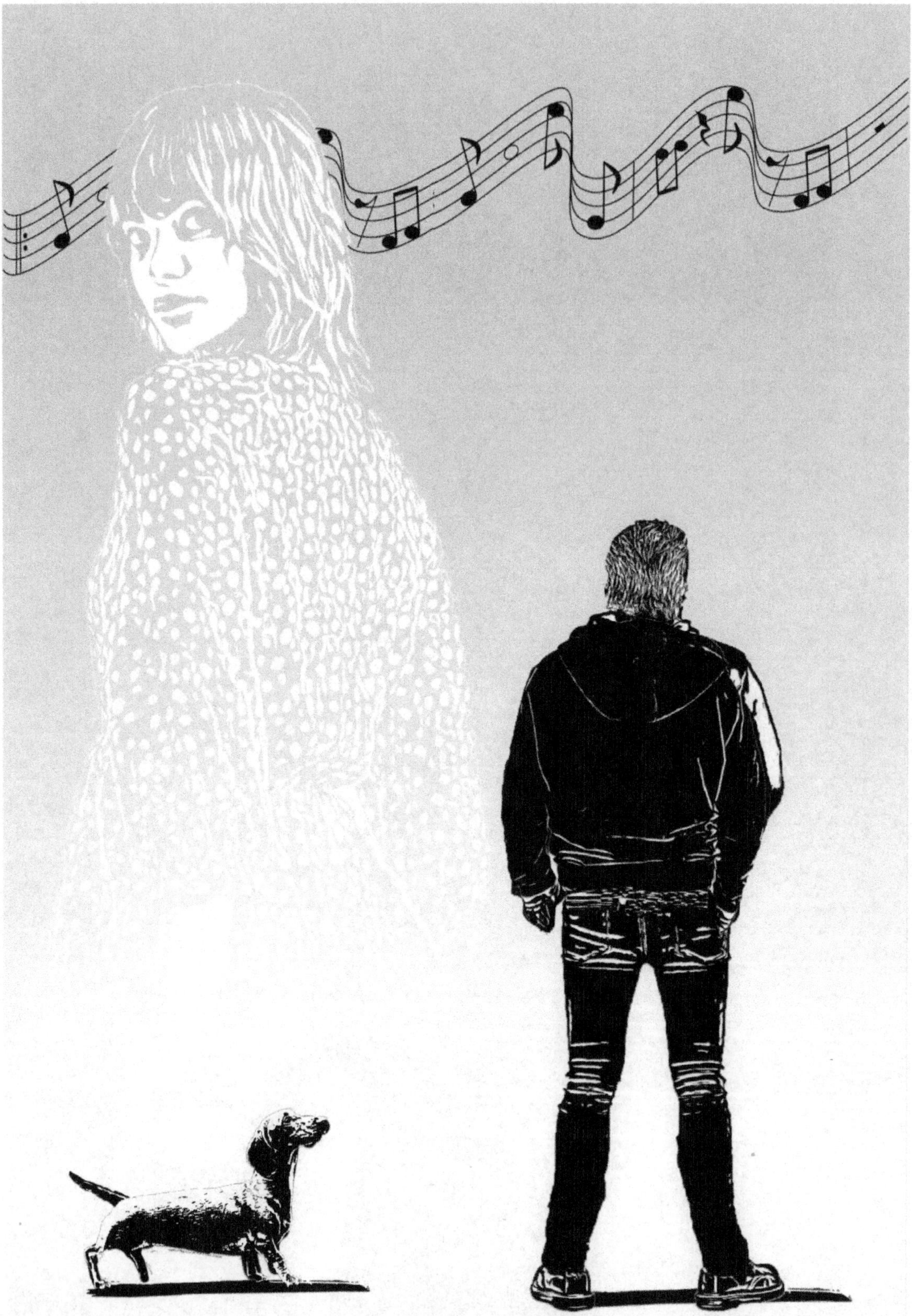

ACT TWO　　　　　　　　　　　　　　　　　　SCENE FIVE

AND YOU SEE, RIGHT AT THAT MOMENT, THAT EXACT MOMENT, EVERYTHING CHANGED FOR KORNEAS.

THAT SONG WAS LIKE A MIRROR HELD UP TO HIM. AND SUDDENLY HE COULD UNDERSTAND HIS OWN SITUATION.

OBVIOUSLY, SHE WAS GONE INSOFAR AS SHE'D LEFT HIM BUT SHE ALSO NEEDED TO BE *ABSENT* FROM HIS THOUGHTS AND HIS WHOLE SENSE OF WHO HE WAS. *GONE!* FOR MY BROTHER, IT WAS THAT SIMPLE, I GUESS.

SO, HE DIDN'T ACTUALLY KNOW THE GROUP BEFORE THAT NIGHT?

NO, NO, IF IT WASN'T FOR FESTE, THEIR PATHS WOULDN'T HAVE CROSSED. IT WAS FATE, OBVIOUSLY. NOTHING LESS. AND OF COURSE HE WENT BACK-STAGE TO MEET THEM AFTERWARDS TO THANK THEM AND SHOW HIS APPRECIATION FOR THEIR MUSIC.

THAT MUST HAVE BEEN QUITE A SHOCK FOR WILL AND HAL! DID THEY NOT RECOGNIZE HIM? I MEAN, HE WAS KORNEAS FOR HEAVEN'S SAKE!
NO, NOT AT FIRST. MY BROTHER, HE DRESSED QUITE SCRUFFILY AT THE TIME. AND HE'D ALSO RECENTLY GROWN A BEARD.
GUESS THAT WOULD MAKE SENSE...
OH MOLLY, YOU HAVE NO IDEA! EVEN THAT NIGHT, HE TOTALLY CONFIDED IN THEM. HE TOLD THEM ALL ABOUT ROSALIND AND WHAT ***BROWNSTONE KISSES*** HAD MEANT TO HIM!

THEN HE BOUGHT EVERY COPY OF THAT RECORD! EVERY SINGLE ONE!
REALLY?
YES AND THEN HE DRAGGED THEM ALL BACK THE NEXT DAY, APART FROM THE ONE HE KEPT, SO THEY COULD SELL THEM ALL AGAIN!
BUT IT WASN'T ONLY THAT ONE SONG. AND NOT JUST THE MUSIC EITHER. IT WAS THE MESSAGE TOO. IT REAWAKENED SOMETHING IN HIM.
HE TOLD ME IT WAS AS THOUGH HIS HEART HAD STARTED TO BEAT AGAIN.
FILTER Nº 1
PANAMA
FILTER Nº 2

AND YOU KNOW, WHEN HE WENT BACK THE FOLLOWING EVENING, THEY'D ACTUALLY WRITTEN A SONG FOR HIM!
HEY, HAL AND I MADE A NEW FRIEND LAST NIGHT! RIGHT HERE IN THIS VERY ROOM!
SO WE GOT UP THIS MORNING AND WROTE THIS SONG FOR HIM. WE REALLY HOPE HE LIKES IT!

"I KNEW A LADY WHO WAS SO KIND. BUT SHE BROKE MY HEART AND THEN SHE ROBBED ME BLIND...
CAPITALISTS!
WHEN SHE SAID SHE WAS HAPPY I GUESS SHE LIED 'CAUSE SHE HIT THE ROAD AND SHE HITCHED A RIDE...

WELL, IT AIN'T NO THING IT AIN'T NO THING...
...GONNA WRITE ME A RHYME THAT MAKES THE ANGELS SING!
BUT HEY, HEY BABY IT AIN'T NO THING!"
THE GERRIN BROTHERS

INTERMISSION.

AW, YOU GUYS!

THANK YOU, THAT WAS SUCH A COOL SONG!

WE JUST THOUGHT IT MIGHT CHEER YOU UP!

I MEAN IT WAS OBVIOUSLY FATE THAT BROUGHT YOU HERE LAST NIGHT.

HA, IN THAT CASE, YOU REALLY SHOULD WRITE A SONG ABOUT FESTE, MY DOG. HE'S THE REASON I ENDED UP HERE LAST NIGHT!

WELL, YOU NEVER KNOW. WE MIGHT JUST DO THAT! ANYWAY, CHEERS!

CHEERS!

SO WHAT'S THE STORY WITH THIS HERE BOTTOM OF THE BILL, UH... HORSE ACT?

OH, YOU MEAN KLAXON? YEAH, WE'VE DONE A FEW SHOWS WITH HIM OVER THE YEARS. I RECKON HE SEES HIMSELF AS BILL HICKS IN A HORSE COSTUME.

HE'LL BE STARTING SOON. HE'S WINDING·THE·WATCH·OF·HIS·WIT; BY·AND·BY·IT·WILL·STRIKE!

SO WILL AND I NEED TO ER... GO GET READY FOR OUR NEXT SET SO WE'LL CATCH UP WITH YOU LATER.

CHAPTER 25
At The Three Fools
With support from KLAXON

YEAH, AND SPEAKING PERSONALLY I DON'T THINK WE SHOULD WASTE A SINGLE SECOND EVER...

...WORRYING ABOUT OUR FUTURE DEPENDENCE ON ARTIFICIAL INTELLIGENCE.

YEAH, RIGHT!

BECAUSE, HONESTLY, RELYING ON ANY KIND OF FUCKING INTELLIGENCE HAS GOT TO BE A WHOLE SHITLOAD BETTER THAN WHAT WE'VE GOT GOING ON RIGHT NOW!

I MEAN, WHAT THE FUCK?

YOU SEE NOWADAYS NOT UNDERSTANDING STUFF HAS NOTHING TO DO WITH IGNORANCE.

ONLY THE UNFATHOMABLE NATURE OF THE SHIT YOU'RE ACTUALLY TRYING TO PROCESS! I'M BEING SERIOUS!

HOW MANY TIMES EVERY DAY DO YOU READ NEWS STORIES AND HOWEVER MUCH YOU TRY, THEY MAKE NO LOGICAL RATIONAL SENSE WHATSOEVER!

WELL, I'M HERE TODAY TO TAKE ALL THAT WORRY AWAY FROM YOU!

YOU SEE, I'M A GREAT BELIEVER IN INVESTING IN TECHNOLOGY.

AND SO I'M GOING TO TELL YOU ABOUT THIS BRAND NEW A.I. INTERFACE I'M LAUNCHING!

FULLY PORTABLE AND FULLY COMPATIBLE ACROSS ALL PLATFORMS AND SYSTEMS!

I BRING YOU KLAXO-VISTA!
YOU SEE NOW, WHENEVER YOU'RE CONFRONTED BY SOME ARTICLE THAT TOTALLY DEFIES YOUR COMPREHENSION...
...SIMPLY UPLOAD A FILE IN ANY FORMAT ON TO KLAXO-VISTA AND...
BOOM!
INSTANTLY! YOUR ENTIRE SENTIENT WORLD IS CONVERTED INTO A FUCKING MEDIEVAL WOODCUT!
YES, YES! YOU'LL SAY, SUDDENLY EVERYTHING MAKES COMPLETE AND PERFECT SENSE AGAIN!
HOORAY FOR A.I.! YOU SEE, ALIENATION SHOULD NEVER BE A DE FACTO CONSEQUENCE OF ENLIGHTENMENT, INFORMATION OR EDUCATION!
CATCHY SLOGAN, EH? BUT OF COURSE IF YOU'RE BUYING A PRODUCT ENDORSED BY A TALKING HORSE...
The Three Fools
THEN THERE'S A VERY GOOD CHANCE YOU NEED THAT PRODUCT A LOT MORE THAN YOU REALIZE...

AND DO YOU KNOW WHAT IS FUNNY?
EVEN THAT SILLY, BEAN-FED-HORSE HAD A PART TO PLAY IN THIS WHOLE WEAK-AND-IDLE-THEME OF OURS!
IT WAS PRETTY LATE WHEN MY BROTHER GOT BACK THAT NIGHT. I THINK HE ACTUALLY WOKE ME UP BUT I'LL NEVER FORGOT WHAT HE SAID.

HEY, SORRY BRO, I DIDN'T MEAN TO DISTURB YOU. IT'S JUST I WAS THINKING TONIGHT ... WE USED TO BE A GREAT OLD TEAM, DIDN'T WE?
YEAH, WE CERTAINLY WERE!

ACH, BUT WHAT HAS BROUGHT THIS ON?
WHAT'S HAPPENED, KORNY?

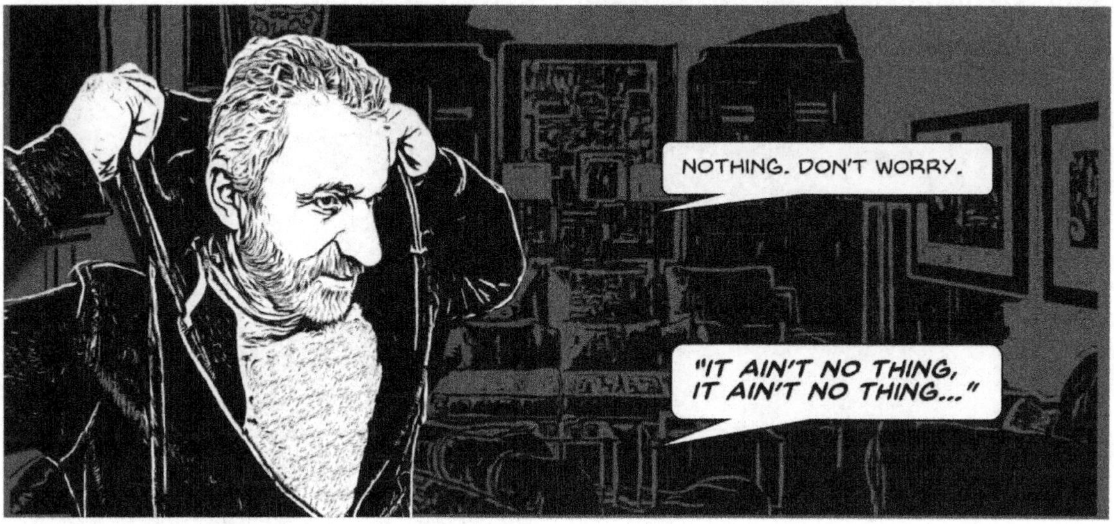
NOTHING. DON'T WORRY.
"IT AIN'T NO THING, IT AIN'T NO THING..."

ACT TWO SCENE SIX

BAD NEWS, I'M AFRAID. THEY'VE RUN OUT OF BEAR CLAWS! SO I'VE GOT US A COUPLE OF PAINS AU CHOCOLAT INSTEAD.

AND SO HOW LONG DID IT TAKE FOR WILL AND HAL TO RECOGNIZE KORNEAS?

I THINK THEY CAUGHT ON PRETTY QUICKLY EVEN THOUGH HE USED TO ALWAYS AVOID ACTUALLY INTRODUCING HIMSELF WHENEVER POSSIBLE!

OH? WAS THAT AN AFFECTATION? SHAME? GUILT?

NO, I THINK HE WAS TOTALLY SICK OF TALKING ABOUT 'KORNEAS' AND 'GLOBE' THE WHOLE TIME. BESIDES, WHEN HE MET WILL AND HAL, HE JUST WANTED TO HEAR WHAT THEY HAD TO SAY.

...AND THANK YOU, THEIR PAINS AU CHOCOLAT ARE DELICIOUS...

YOU SEE, MOLLY, HE'D ALWAYS BEEN BROADLY SYMPATHETIC TO THOSE KIND OF PRINCIPLES. BUT THEY DEFINED AND ARTICULATED THOSE THINGS FAR BETTER THAN HE COULD.

AND YOU KNOW, THAT IS WHAT MUSIC CAN DO SOMETIMES. IT CAN PUT YOU BACK IN TOUCH WITH A PART OF YOU THAT HAS BEEN SO LONG LOST AND FORGOTTEN.

BUT THERE WAS SOMETHING ELSE. SOMETHING THAT GAVE A FORM AND ORDER TO THE ALL THE IDEAS THAT HAD SWUM AROUND IN THAT BRAIN OF HIS SINCE HE WAS A BOY.

HE ATTENDED EVERY SINGLE SHOW THAT WEEK! EVERY NIGHT! AND THERE WAS SUCH A CHANGE IN HIM. I HADN'T SEEN HIM THAT HAPPY IN YEARS! NOT SINCE THE VERY FIRST DAYS OF GLOBE.

HE SEEMED SO *ALIVE* ALL OF A SUDDEN! I THINK IF HE COULD'VE PLAYED AN INSTRUMENT OR SUNG HE WOULD'VE JOINED CHAPTER 25 THERE AND THEN! AND THEN MAYBE HE WOULD PROBABLY STILL......BE ALIVE NOW.

BUT HE HAD DIFFERENT SKILLS, DIFFERENT TALENTS HE COULD USE. WHICH WAS WHY HE STARTED TO THINK ABOUT A.I. AGAIN.

DON'T FORGET, MY BROTHER AND I WERE IMMIGRANTS. IN A COUNTRY WHERE EVEN IMMIGRANTS ARE PROGRAMMED TO HATE IMMIGRANTS! HE SAW WHAT WAS HAPPENING. SAW HOW THINGS WERE CHANGING. HE SAW EXACTLY WHAT WILL AND HAL COULD SEE...

AND YOU KNOW, WHEN MY BROTHER WENT BACK ON THE WEDNESDAY NIGHT, THEY HAD ACTUALLY WRITTEN ***ANOTHER*** SONG FOR HIM!
The Three Fools
WELL, NOT FOR HIM EXACTLY!

"YOU BEEN SCRATCHIN' 'ROUND MY FRONT DOOR...
YOU BEEN HOWLIN' ALL NIGHT LONG, OH YOU DOG!...

I GUESS YOU AIN'T NO PEDIGREE...
FROM THE WAY YOU'RE ALWAYS TREATIN' ME. OH, YOU DOG!"
AND HOW I WISH EVERYTHING COULD HAVE STAYED JUST LIKE IT WAS AT THAT MOMENT, IT WOULD HAVE BEEN SO DIFFERENT. FOR ALL OF US.

Panel 1
EVERYTHING CHANGED THE FOLLOWING NIGHT, WHEN WILL MADE HER ANNOUNCEMENT FROM THE STAGE.

Panel 2
SORRY FOLKS! BUT I GOT SOME BAD NEWS FOR YOU TONIGHT!

SEEMS OUR MAN HAL HERE HAS DAMAGED HIS VOICE! PROBABLY FROM SHOUTING AT FOX NEWS ALL DAY!

Panel 3
SO HE'LL JUST BE DOING THE STRUMMING TONIGHT. WHILE I GET ON WITH ALL OUR USUAL SHOUTING AND RANTING!

Panel 4
BUT JUST SO WE'RE CLEAR! THIS SHOULD *NEVER* BE CONSIDERED A WARNING OR A DISINCENTIVE FOR ANYONE TO EVER STOP SHOUTING AT FOX NEWS!

"I CALLED UP MY FATHER...
ASKED HIM TO COME AND SEE ME SOON.
I CALLED UP MY FATHER...
MY MOTHER, MY BROTHER, MY SISTER TOO.
CAPITAL
S
BUT EVERY DAY I KEEP ON KNOCKIN'...
I KEEP ON KNOCKIN' ON OLD JOE."

MY BROTHER, YOU SEE, HE WAS ALWAYS VERY SENSITIVE TO THESE THINGS.
The Three Fools
HE KNEW RIGHT AWAY THAT THERE WAS SOMETHING WRONG WITH HAL.
KLAXON CAME OUT AND DID HIS ACT. BUT KORNY COULD NOT CONCENTRATE. HIS MIND WAS COMPLETELY ELSEWHERE.
...AND SO MAY I MAKE A SUGGESTION HERE? SEE, THIS APPLIES TO YOU REGARDLESS OF WHERE YOU STAND POLITICALLY. BUT HERE'S HOW IT IS.
NOW, IF I DON'T LIKE A BOOK OR I DON'T AGREE WITH IT FOR WHATEVER REASON, THAT IS ALL PERFECTLY FINE AND FUCKING DANDY!
I DON'T READ IT! I RIP THE THING TO SHREDS! OR I THROW IT IN THE TRASH! I HAVE THE FREEDOM TO MAKE THAT CHOICE! AND TO ACT UPON MY OWN JUDGMENT.
THAT IS MY FUNDAMENTAL RIGHT. OK?
AH, BUT HERE'S WHERE IT GETS MESSY!
RIGHT, FOR EXAMPLE, IF I DECIDE THAT THIS BOOK HERE THAT I DON'T AGREE WITH SHOULD BE BANNED AND NEVER BE READ BY ANYONE EVER AGAIN....
The Three Fools
AM I NOT JUST TAKING AWAY THEIR RIGHT TO MAKE EXACTLY THE SAME CHOICES THAT I WAS PERMITTED TO MAKE?

AM I NOT DENYING THEM THEIR FREEDOM IN SOME WAY? I MANIFESTLY HAD THAT RIGHT MYSELF AND NOW I'M ACTING TO DENY THEM PRECISELY THOSE SAME BASIC RIGHTS.
AND I'LL TELL YOU SOMETHING ELSE. HISTORICALLY SPEAKING, REGARDLESS OF YOUR PRINCIPLES, BANNING BOOKS HAS NEVER REALLY WORKED OUT THAT WELL.
IT'S NOT ABOUT SAFEGUARDING THIS OR PROTECTING THAT OR BLAH DI BLAH...
IT'S FUCKING FASCISM, MY FRIENDS, AND YOU ALL NEED TO REALIZE THIS BEFORE IT'S TOO LATE...
SO WHEN WILL AND HAL DIDN'T RETURN TO THE STAGE AFTER KLAXON'S ACT, MY BROTHER WENT BACKSTAGE TO FIND THEM.
HELLO? HELLO?
ANYBODY THERE?
WILL? HAL? CAN I COME IN?

Panel 1:
HEY GUYS! THE DOOR WAS OPEN, I WAS JUST...

OH, UM...RIGHT...ER, SORRY.

Panel 2:
HEY, HI THERE, KORNEAS. COME IN, IT'S GOOD TO TO SEE YOU. HOPE YOU ENJOYED THE SET!

YEAH, SORRY ABOUT THIS BUT HAL'S NOT...ACTUALLY HAL IS REALLY NOT VERY WELL AT ALL.

IT'S HIS USUAL PROBLEM. BUT I DUNNO, I THINK IT'S GETTING A LOT WORSE NOW.

Panel 3:
LOOK, I DON'T MEAN TO INTRUDE OR ANYTHING. AND YOU CAN TELL ME TO GO AWAY AND MIND MY OWN BUSINESS.

BUT SERIOUSLY WILL, CAN I ASK WHAT YOU MEAN BY 'HIS USUAL PROBLEM'?

AND THEN IT ALL CAME OUT.
YOU SEE, HAL HAD ALL THESE LONG TERM HEALTH ISSUES WITH HIS CHEST AND HIS LUNGS.
THIS WAS OBVIOUSLY A MASSIVE THING BUT WILL SAID THAT...
...IT'S BEEN GOING ON FOR YEARS.
BUT WE'RE NEVER REALLY IN ANY ONE PLACE LONG ENOUGH TO GET IT PROPERLY CHECKED OUT.
SO, THEN OF COURSE MY BROTHER REPLIED...
... WELL, LOOK, I KNOW ONE OF THE BEST PHYSICIANS IN THE WHOLE OF CALIFORNIA, I CAN GET YOU A CONSULTATION ANY TIME YOU LIKE. AND DON'T WORRY, I'LL TAKE CARE OF *EVERYTHING*...
NO!
NO!
NO!

BUT YOU SAID JUST NOW THAT BY THEN THEY KNEW WHO HE WAS. AND SURELY HAL WOULD HAVE KNOWN THAT KORNEAS COULD EASILY AFFORD IT!
ACH, YOU'RE MISSING THE POINT HERE. YOU SEE, WITH HAL IT WAS NEVER ABOUT THE MONEY. NOT IN THE SLIGHTEST!
*COUGH, COUGH. LOOK, MAN THAT'S INCREDIBLY GENEROUS OF YOU. I REALLY APPRECIATE IT.
I JUST CAN'T ACCEPT IT. SORRY.
BUT IT'S NOT RIGHT THAT YOU SHOULD BE SUFFERING LIKE THIS.
THIS IS SIMPLY A FRIEND HELPING A FRIEND. I MEAN, SURELY YOU WOULD DO THE SAME?
NO, NO, IT'S NOTHING LIKE THAT! LOOK, I'VE WATCHED WHILE THIS COUNTRY'S EVIL, MONTERIZED HEALTH-CARE SYSTEM HAS BANKRUPTED MILLIONS OF PEOPLE AND I'VE ALWAYS TRIED IN MY OWN WAY TO FIGHT AGAINST IT.
IT WOULD JUST FEEL WRONG, HYPOCRITICAL, IF I TOOK THE EASY WAY OUT JUST BECAUSE I HAD A RICH FRIEND.
AND BEFORE YOU SAY ANYTHING! IT'S NOT ABOUT DYING FOR YOUR PRINCIPLES. IT'S JUST ABOUT KEEPING THEM INTACT UNTIL YOU DO! *COUGH, *COUGH!

OK, SO WHAT IF I SAID I COULD FIX ALL THAT?
WHAT? *COUGH!
PUT SOMETHING IN PLACE WHICH WOULD CHANGE ALL THAT? FOR EVERYONE. EVERYWHERE! FOR ALL TIME!
ALL YOU'D EVER NEED WOULD BE A WORKING PHONE.
YOU'RE KIDDING, RIGHT?
NOT EVEN REMOTELY! I'LL TALK TO MY BROTHER. I DO THE IDEAS, HE DOES ALL THE OTHER STUFF!
BUT LOOK, I PROMISE YOU! WITH WILL AS MY WITNESS, I'LL MAKE THIS HAPPEN. SO PLEASE LET ME TAKE YOU TO SEE MY DOCTOR!
DO YOU PROMISE?
YOU HAVE MY WORD.
YOU HEAR THAT, WILL? OK, DEAL!
THAT NIGHT, HE HAD A LOOK IN HIS EYE THAT I HADN'T SEEN SINCE THE FIRST DAYS OF GLOBE. I COULD SEE THAT MIND OF HIS STIRRING AGAIN!
THE MAGICIAN WAS BACK!
HEY BRO, THE TIME HAS COME! WE NEED TO GET BACK TO WORK! FIRST THING IN THE MORNING!
OH OK, SO, WHAT ARE WE WORKING ON NOW EXACTLY?
WELL, A.I. OBVIOUSLY!

ACH, THAT'S FANTASTIC NEWS! BUT BEFORE WE GO ANY FURTHER. WE JUST NEED TO CLEAR UP ONE VERY TINY LITTLE THING.
WE DO?
YES. DO YOU REMEMBER WHAT YOU USED TO SAY ABOUT A.I.? THAT SO CALLED 'GENIUS PARTICLE' OF YOURS? IT WAS IN THAT EMAIL YOU WROTE TO ME ABOUT THOSE TWO KIDS FROM THE MIDWEST?
HA HA, OF COURSE! HOW COULD I POSSIBLY FORGET?
YOU SEE IT TOOK ME A WHILE BUT I'VE FINALLY WORKED IT OUT!
OH, RIGHT! COME ON THEN, YOU HAVE TO TELL ME NOW!
WELL, BROTHER OF MINE, IT'S QUITE SIMPLE! ONE OF THEM WAS SECRETLY GIVEN A COPY OF ***CHUCK BERRY'S GREATEST HITS*** AND HE WAS THE ONE WHO THEN WENT ON TO WRITE ***'BLOWIN' IN THE WIND'!*** S'OBVIOUS, REALLY.
HA HA... NEARLY RIGHT!
BUT ACTUALLY YOU SEE, ***BOTH*** OF THEM HAD COPIES OF ***CHUCK BERRY'S GREATEST HITS***. THEY BOTH LOVED THE MUSIC OF COURSE. BUT ONLY ONE OF THEM STUDIED THE LYRICS! THAT ONE WAS ROBERT ZIMMERMAN AND ***THAT*** WAS THE GENIUS PARTICLE AT WORK!
HA HA HA BRILLIANT! YOU SEE, THAT IS WHY YOU'RE THE SMART ONE!

ACT THREE

ACT THREE　　　　　　　　　　　　SCENE ONE

THE FOLLOWING MORNING.

AND THEN WHEN I WOKE UP THE NEXT DAY, I WENT TO SEE HIM AND HE HAD BEEN WORKING ALL THROUGH THE NIGHT.

BUT HE DIDN'T LOOK TIRED. HE ONLY HAD THAT INCREDIBLE FOCUS OF HIS. IT WAS LIKE A SORT OF GLOW HE GAVE OFF, IF YOU SAW HIM YOU'D UNDERSTAND.

I KNEW NOT TO SPEAK TO HIM. I WOULD LEAVE HIM A COFFEE AND COLLECT IT AN HOUR LATER WHEN IT HAD GONE COLD AND HE HADN'T EVEN TOUCHED IT.

THAT WENT ON ALL DAY AND INTO THE EVENING... I TELL YOU IF THERE REALLY IS A GENIUS PARTICLE, I SAW IT THAT DAY!

AND I DON'T KNOW AT WHAT TIME PRECISELY. BUT AT SOME POINT DURING THAT FIRST DAY, I GLANCED OVER HIS SHOULDER.
THAT WAS WHEN I SAW THE WORD FOR THE FIRST TIME.
touchstone

touchstone
I REMEMBER I ASKED HIM, 'WHAT IS THIS *TOUCHSTONE*?' HE DIDN'T EVEN LOOK UP FROM HIS MONITOR. AND DO YOU KNOW WHAT HE SAID?
'TOUCHSTONE,' HE SAID, 'SHOULD NEVER FORM PART OF A QUESTION. TOUCHSTONE WILL BE THE ANSWER!'
AND THEN HE ADDED ***'TO EVERYTHING!'***
HA, THIS WAS JUST HOW HE TALKED WHEN HE USED TO DO HIS MAGIC TRICKS.

YES! SO AT LAST! WE **FINALLY** GET TO LEARN WHAT THIS TOUCHSTONE WAS ALL ABOUT!

AH YES, WE ARE GETTING TO THAT NOW!

LATER THAT WEEK KORNEAS TOOK HAL TO SEE HIS DOCTOR.

THEY DID A WHOLE BUNCH OF SCANS AND TESTS. BUT EVEN ON THAT FIRST DAY, THEY KNEW THERE WAS SOMETHING SERIOUSLY WRONG.

THEY ALL WENT BACK A COUPLE OF DAYS LATER AND THE TESTS CONFIRMED WHAT THEY FEARED.

HAL'S CANCER, BY THAT POINT, WAS ALREADY AT STAGE 4.

OH FUCK, SERGEI! THAT MUST HAVE BEEN SUCH A SHOCK FOR THEM!

I GUESS THEY WERE EXPECTING BAD NEWS, BUT NOT THAT BAD.

IT HIT THEM BOTH REALLY HARD. THEY JUST RETREATED INTO THEIR OWN LITTLE WORLD. A PLACE WHERE THEY FELT SAFE.

MY BROTHER KEPT HIS DISTANCE BUT HE GAVE THEM A NOTE WITH HIS CELL NUMBER AND A MESSAGE.

WILL ASKED HIM WHAT IT MEANT. HE JUST SAID...

K Cell
415 013 20 27
"TOUCHSTONE!"

'IT IS A PROMISE KEPT.'

BUT DURING THAT TIME THEY DID SOMETHING THEY HAD NEVER DONE BEFORE.

THEY ACTUALLY PULLED OUT OF SOME GIGS.

TONIGHT For One Night Only
CANCELLED
CHAPTER 25
CANCELLED

ACH, THEY EVEN HAD THAT PANTOMIME HORSE STANDING IN FOR THEM ON A COUPLE OF SHOWS.

INTERMISSION

ACTUALLY, I DO WORRY SOMETIMES THAT WE ARE ALL FOOLS NOWADAYS...

WE'VE BECOME STUPID. NOT STUPID AS IN SIGNIFICANTLY LESS THAN INTELLECTUAL BUT IDIOTICALLY FUCKING HYSTERICALLY STUPID!

AND SO NOW I THINK IT'S ABOUT THAT TIME OF NIGHT WHEN WE ALL NEED TO HAVE A BIT OF A CHAT ABOUT ABSOLUTISM AND MORALITY.

YOU SEE THE UNDERLYING PRINCIPLE WHEN DEALING WITH ETHICS AND MORALS IS THAT THEY ARE ENTIRELY UNIVERSAL. UNEQUIVOCALLY SO.

THE GREAT GREEK PHILOSOPHERS EVOLVED THEIR IDEAS ALONGSIDE MATHEMATICIANS. JUST THINK OF PYTHAGORUS, HIS THEOREM DOESN'T APPLY TO SOME, MANY OR A WHOLE FUCK LOAD OF RIGHT ANGLE TRIANGLES, IT APPLIES TO *EVERY* SINGLE ONE.

IT IS A UNIVERSAL EQUATION AND IS IN NO WAY SELECTIVE. MORALITY IS SIMILARLY UNIMPEACHABLE AND IT CAN NO LONGER HAVE ANY CLAIM ON THE TERM THE MOMENT IT BECOMES SELECTIVE. THERE IS A *PURITY* IN MORAL CERTAINTY, AS IN ALL ESSENTIAL HUMAN TRUTHS.

THESE ARE CODES AS IMMUTABLE AS ANY SCIENTIFIC OR MATHEMATICAL LAW.
SO, ARE YOU ALL WITH ME SO FAR? GOOD. NEXT SLIDE PLEASE!
YOU SEE WHEN THEY ARE NO LONGER UNIVERSAL AND ARE APPLIED ONLY SELECTIVELY THEY CEASE TO BE MORAL OR ETHICAL ABSOLUTES. THEY ARE A TARNISHED, INVALID, IRRELEVANT CURRENCY. WE MAKE THIS MISTAKE TIME AND TIME AGAIN. YOU SEE IT IN SO MANY CONTEMPORARY DEBATES, ESPECIALLY THE MOST ***HOSTILE*** AND ***VOLATILE*** ONES!
AS AN EXAMPLE I WOULD CITE THE ONGOING CAUSE OF ***CULTURAL APPROPRIATION***. NOW! STOP RIGHT THERE! DO I LOOK LIKE A FUCKING PROUD BOY? NO, RELAX, BOYS AND GIRLS, I AM CATEGORICALLY ***NOT*** TALKING ABOUT THE ACTUAL SUBJECT OF CULTURAL APPROPRIATION HERE, ONLY THE UNDERLYING PHILOSOPHICAL FLAWS IN THE DIALOGUE IT TRAILS IN ITS WAKE.
YEAH, IF THERE'S A STUPID PERSON NEXT TO YOU, YOU MAY WANT TO CHECK THEY'RE STILL AWAKE AT THIS POINT.
NOW YOU CANNOT SELECTIVELY APPLY MORAL ABSOLUTES BECAUSE IT SUITS WHATEVER PARTICULAR STAND YOU TAKE IN AN ARGUMENT. WHETHER YOU'RE ON THE SIDE OF THE ***GOOD FASCISTS*** OR THE ***BAD FASCISTS!***
IT DOESN'T WORK LIKE THAT. THESE PRINCIPLES ARE ***UNIVERSAL*** AND SHOULD BE THE STARTING POINT! OTHERWISE THEY ARE TOO EASILY ABUSED.
I TELL YOU, MAN, SOCRATES WOULD WEEP.

A WHITE LADY MAKES THE CHOICE TO BUY AND TO WEAR AN ETHNIC DRESS. AND YEAH OK, THIS IS WRONG. THIS IS DEEMED BY SOME TO BE CULTURAL APPROPRIATION.

BUT DON'T JUST APPLY THAT MORAL JUDGMENT TO THAT LADY AND HER DRESS, LET'S CONSIDER THE WIDER, UNIVERSAL APPLICATIONS.

NOW, ALL YOU WHITE BOYS OF COURSE SHOULDN'T PLAY THE BLUES AND CERTAINLY SHOULDN'T PROFIT FROM IT.

ACTUALLY THAT'S PROBABLY NOT A BAD IDEA BUT WE'LL LEAVE IT THERE FOR A MOMENT.

YOU SEE, A BROADER APPLICATION OF THAT ETHNICITY IDEA COULD BE A VERY NEGATIVE JUDGMENT ON THE ROLLING STONES.

AND I HATE TO TELL YOU THIS BUT, BECAUSE OF THEIR 'APPROPRIATION' OF CHUCK BERRY AND LITTLE RICHARD...

WE NEED TO PULL THE BEATLES INTO THE ARGUMENT TOO.

AND YEAH, ELVIS OF COURSE!

IN FACT, VIRTUALLY ANY ROCK & ROLL STAR YOU CARE TO MENTION. ALL THE JOY THOSE PEOPLE BROUGHT INTO OUR LIVES, ALL THAT GREAT MUSIC THAT GOT US THROUGH OUR SHITTIEST SADDEST TIMES!
YOU SEE, YOU APPLY THE ETHNIC DRESS CONCEPT MORE UNIVERSALLY AND WE IMMEDIATELY FIND OURSELVES BEING LED INTO SOMETHING VERY DARK AND VERY DANGEROUS.
AND WHEN US WHITE FOLK HAVE LOST ALL OUR FAVORITE MUSIC, DON'T WORRY WE STILL HAVE OUR ART. WELL, ACTUALLY WE DON'T.
NOTHING SINCE ABOUT 1870 AT ANY RATE! YOU SEE IT WAS THEN THAT GAUGHIN AND VAN GOGH STARTED 'APPROPRIATING' JAPANESE ART INTO THEIR WORK.
AND THEN, OF COURSE, THE CRIME OF THE FUCKING CENTURY!!
PICASSO BORROWING FROM AFRICAN ART AS THE CORNERSTONE OF CUBISM! OFF WITH HIS SHINY LITTLE FUCKING HEAD ALREADY!
ALL MODERNITY STARTS WITH PICASSO AND CUBISM. YOU RECLAIM THAT AND IT'S JUST ANOTHER WAY OF MAKING THE WORLD AN EVEN MORE SOUL DESTROYING PLACE.

YOU SEE MY ARGUMENT IS THAT IF YOU'RE USING MORAL ABSOLUTES THEY HAVE TO BE COMPLETELY AND UNQUESTIONABLY ABSOLUTE. IF YOU ONLY APPLY THEM SELECTIVELY YOU ONLY WEAKEN YOUR POSITION.
YOU COMBAT INTOLERANCE WITH TOLERANCE! YOU CAN'T FIGHT IT WITH JUST A DIFFERENT SORT OF INTOLERANCE! HOW DOES THAT EVEN WORK IN YOUR HEAD?
YOU JUST NEED TO PAUSE THAT STUPIDITY FOR FIVE MINUTES.
I MEAN SERIOUSLY, IS YOUR IDEOLOGY SO DAMN FRAGILE YOU HAVE TO ATTACK AND BRUTALIZE ANYONE WHO DOESN'T SHARE IT? HATE TO SAY THIS BUT MAYBE ON SOME LEVEL YOU NEED TO QUESTION YOUR DEGREE OF COMMITMENT?
NOW I'M NOT ADVOCATING AN ENTIRE NEW LITERACY PROGRAM BUT MAYBE YOU COULD JUST READ A BOOK NOW AND AGAIN. MIGHT SOLVE A FUCK LOAD OF PROBLEMS. I MEAN THIS ENTIRE INSANE SITUATION GOING ON RIGHT NOW WITH THE CHRISTIAN RIGHT WINGERS LOSING ALL THEIR SHIT ON THE WHOLE TRANS ISSUE. AND THEN PRETENDING TO HAVE READ ABOUT IT IN THE BIBLE!
NOW THAT'S PLAIN FUCKING LYING! OR AS THEY LIKE TO CALL IT, ***'BEARING FALSE WITNESS'***.
WE REALLY NEED TO SPEAK TO THESE PEOPLE BEFORE IT'S TOO LATE. ACTUALLY, I THINK IT CAN BE THE BEGINNING OF A WHOLE NEW READING INITIATIVE. START WITH YOUR BELOVED BIBLE, WHICH YOU HAVE SO CLEARLY NEVER READ AND HAVE ZERO UNDERSTANDING OF.
DON'T GO NUTS AND TOTALLY FUCK YOURSELF UP. JUST START GRADUALLY ON THE FIRST PAGE. THAT'S RIGHT, THE FIRST ACT OF GENESIS. AND HERE IS HOW WE SOLVE THE WHOLE TRANS THING ONCE AND FOR ALL! AW FUCK, BABY, I DO LOVE ME SOME BOOKS!
RIGHT THEN, FOLLOW MY LOGIC HERE, FOLLOW MY LOVELY EMPIRICAL, IMMUTABLE ***FACT-BASED*** THINKING!

FIRSTLY, THE CREATION OF EVE. NOW AS YOU ALL KNOW THE FIRST WOMAN WAS CREATED WHEN A RIB WAS TAKEN FROM ADAM. IT'S OK, YOU CAN FACT CHECK ALL OF THIS. SO CONSEQUENTLY WHEN THE FEMALE ELEMENT WAS REMOVED FROM ADAM HE WAS THEREAFTER 100% MALE. THIS MAKES PERFECT RATIONAL SENSE, OK, WELL IT DOES TO CHRISTIANS.

SO PRIOR TO THIS RIB BEING REMOVED, THE PERSON OF ADAM WAS NEITHER MALE OR FEMALE AND THOSE TWO CATEGORIES AND DEFINITIONS ONLY OCCURRED **AFTER** THAT WHOLE RIB THING AND THE SEPARATION INTO OPPOSITE AND COMPLIMENTARY GENDERS. THAT IS ENTIRELY LOGICAL.

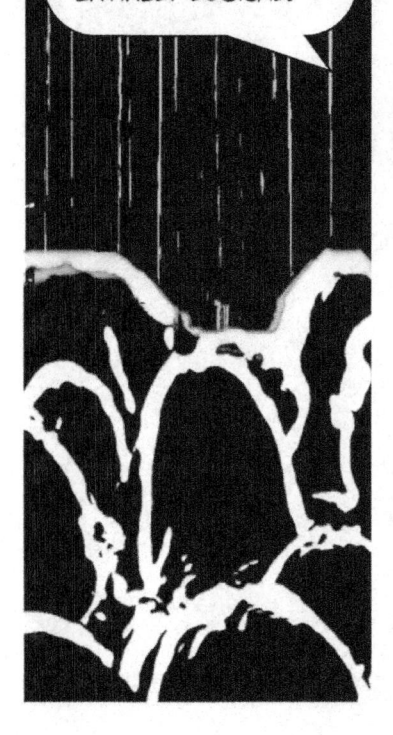

SO, GOING BACK ONE STEP. AN EQUALLY SOUND AND RATIONAL PRESUMPTION WOULD BE THAT BEFORE THIS DIVISION INTO TWO DISTINCT GENDERS, ADAM EMBODIED BOTH OR PERHAPS NEITHER STATE. THEREFORE, BOYS AND GIRLS, THE WORD WE WOULD NOWADAYS USE FOR THAT IS **'NON-BINARY'**. SO, READING THE BIBLE FACT NUMBER ONE, ADAM WAS NON-BINARY! HOORAY!

AH, BUT WAIT, THERE'S MORE! FIRST PAGE OF GENESIS AGAIN WE LEARN THAT ADAM WAS MADE IN GOD'S IMAGE AND CONSEQUENTLY, **RATIONALLY AND LOGICALLY**, AND JUST BEFORE I DIE IN A HAIL OF BULLETS HERE, IT NEEDS TO BE THEREFORE POINTED OUT THAT GOD WOULD HAVE ALSO BEEN **UNEQUIVOCALLY NON-BINARY.**

SO, LET'S BE CLEAR, THAT IS NOT INTERPRETATION OR ANALYSIS, THAT IS SIMPLE PURE EMPIRICISM. YOUR GREAT GOD, THE CORE OF YOUR ENTIRE BELIEF STRUCTURE WAS NON-BINARY! SO NOW YOU SEE WHY READING IS DANGEROUS? IT IS BOTH **WEAPON AND ARMOR!**

AH, BUT BEFORE, AS PATRONS OF THIS FINE INCLUSIVE VENUE, YOU START TO FEEL TOO SUPERIOR, CAN I POINT OUT THAT A TRUE INCLUSIVE ENVIRONMENT IS ONE THAT HAS MENUS IN BRAILLE AND WHEELCHAIR ACCESSIBLE RESTROOMS!

YOU SEE, THERE'S NO SUCH THING AS **SELECTIVE INCLUSIVITY!**

YEAH, BUT THERE AIN'T NO SUCH THING AS **RADICAL PIETY** EITHER... SO WHAT THE FUCK DO I KNOW?

ACT THREE   SCENE TWO

"SO HOW LONG WAS IT BEFORE THEY GOT BACK IN TOUCH WITH YOUR BROTHER?"

"JUST A COUPLE OF DAYS. BUT HE WAS SO WORRIED. IT WAS SUCH A SHORT TIME BUT IT WAS LIKE THEY WERE FAMILY TO HIM."

K. Cell
415 013 20 27
"TOUCHSTONE!"

"HE KEPT ON WORKING BUT HE WAS LISTENING TO THEIR MUSIC CONSTANTLY. AND WHEN THEY CALLED HIM HE WAS ROUND THERE WITHIN THE HOUR."

HI WILL. SORRY IT TOOK ME SO LONG TO GET HERE, THE TRAFFIC WAS TERRIBLE. HOW IS HE?
IT'S SO GOOD TO SEE YOU, KORNEAS. HAL IS INSIDE JUST HAVING A LITTLE NAP.
THE MEDS ARE KINDA WIPING HIM OUT! BUT I PROMISED TO WAKE HIM AS SOON AS YOU GOT HERE...
TOUCHSTONE
HE'S SO DESPERATE TO HEAR ABOUT THIS WHOLE TOUCHSTONE THING.
AND ME TOO!
WELL, THERE'S STILL A LONG LONG WAY TO GO. BUT I CAN GIVE YOU THE ROUGH IDEA...
...THAT'S OK! WILL AND I ARE USED TO ROUGH!
HEY THERE BRO', HOW ARE YOU DOING?
NICE SUIT, BY THE WAY!
WHY DON'T YOU COME IN AND TELL US ALL ABOUT TOUCHSTONE? HONESTLY, I THINK WE'VE WAITED LONG ENOUGH AND I RECKON WE PROBABLY DESERVE TO KNOW NOW!

WELL, BASICALLY TOUCHSTONE IS GOING TO ALTER FOREVER THE WAY WE APPROACH HEALTHCARE.

IN SIMPLE TERMS ALL THE TECHNOLOGY BEHIND TOUCHSTONE IS EITHER CURRENT...

OR WHAT WE CAN LOGICALLY ANTICIPATE BEING AVAILABLE IN THE NEXT COUPLE OF YEARS.

BECAUSE IT'S ABSOLUTELY FUNDAMENTAL THAT TOUCHSTONE IS FREE FOREVER!

FREE FOR EVERY PERSON IN THE WORLD WITH ACCESS TO A PHONE OR A COMPUTER.

TOUCHSTONE IS GOING TO BE A PERSONALIZED A.I. REAL TIME ANIMATED, RESPONSIVE AND COMPLETELY SENTIENT 3D/4D HUMAN AVATAR.

EFFECTIVELY, YOUR OWN FREE PERSONAL 24 HOUR A DAY DOCTOR/THERAPIST/COUNSELOR.

IT WOULD BASICALLY BE A UNIQUE VIRTUAL PHYSICIAN/HEALTH SPECIALIST TAILORED TO YOUR PRECISE MEDICAL NEEDS.

AND AVAILABLE TO YOU **FREE** OF CHARGE WHENEVER REQUIRED.

USING ESTABLISHED CARRIERS, IT WOULD BE ABLE TO PROVIDE MEDS ON A NEXT DAY BASIS.

AND IF ANY CONDITION REQUIRED HOSPITALIZATION TOUCHSTONE WOULD ARRANGE THAT TOO.

HEALTH MUST ALWAYS REMAIN AN UNQUESTIONABLE BASIC HUMAN MORAL RIGHT.

"FOR IT IS NOT AN A PRIORI GIVEN THAT THE RICH SHOULD LIVE LONGER THAN THE POOR."

IT WILL BE A COMPLETELY UNIVERSAL INTERFACE THAT WILL ADAPT TO ANY OPERATING SYSTEM. AND IT WILL BE ENTIRELY FUTURE PROOF.

I'VE GOT ALL THE TOP TECH GUYS AT GLOBE WORKING ON IT RIGHT NOW.

ALTHOUGH BECAUSE OF CERTAIN SECURITY CONCERNS THEY'RE ALL WORKING ON IT INDIVIDUALLY AND ONLY DEALING DIRECTLY WITH ME.

BUT WORKING ON ELABORATING AND DEVELOPING THE CURRENT TECHNOLOGY, IT WILL ONLY BE A MATTER OF A FEW YEARS BEFORE YOU WILL SEE THE FULL POTENTIAL OF TOUCHSTONE.

IN DEVELOPMENT NOW THERE ARE PROGRAMS WHICH WILL ENABLE YOUR CELL PHONE TO FUNCTION AS A BLOOD PRESSURE MONITOR, TO MEASURE YOUR HEART RATE AND BLOOD SUGAR LEVEL.

DID YOU KNOW WE ARE LESS THAN A YEAR AWAY FROM SOFTWARE THAT WILL TURN YOUR CELL INTO A VIRTUAL STETHOSCOPE?!

YOU SEE, ALL OF THESE WILL BE FUNDAMENTAL AND ESSENTIAL TO THE SERVICES PROVIDED BY TOUCHSTONE.

AND IF TOUCHSTONE CAN SAVE OR RADICALLY IMPROVE THE LIFE OF JUST ONE PERSON THEN MY EFFORTS WILL NOT HAVE BEEN WASTED. ANYTHING BEYOND THAT IS NOT MY CONCERN RIGHT NOW...

124

"ACTUALLY, THAT'S THE EASY PART! I'M GOING TO SELL GLOBE TO FUND IT!"

"FUCK! YOU CAN'T BE SERIOUS?"

"OH, I'M *TOTALLY* SERIOUS! 'TIS·MY·VOCATION·HAL. 'TIS·NO·SIN·FOR·A·MAN·TO·LABOR·IN·HIS·VOCATION."

"YOU SEE, WE HAD A SAYING BACK IN PUCKITANIA. 'WHAT IS A FORTUNE WORTH, IF IT HAS NO VALUE?'"

"FOR ME, TOUCHSTONE HAS EXACTLY THIS VALUE THEY REFER TO!"

"AND I'VE HAD ANOTHER IDEA, WHICH I WILL NEED TO DISCUSS WITH OUR MARKETING PEOPLE ..."

"THEY'LL BE AN ANNOUNCEMENT IN A FEW MONTHS OR SO. BUT THAT SHOULD EASILY COVER THE START UP COSTS OF TOUCHSTONE."

"BUT I RECKON WE COULD TEMPT VIRTUALLY EVERY SINGLE MAJOR CORPORATION INTO SIGNING UP FOR A SPONSORSHIP DEAL."

"WE'D CHARGE THEM A FORTUNE JUST FOR THEIR LOGO TO BE ROTATED ON THE INTERFACE."

"FOR WHO WOULD NOT WANT THEIR BRAND TO BE ASSOCIATED WITH SUCH A HUMANITARIAN CAUSE?"

YOU KNOW, WE HAVE ANOTHER SAYING HERE IN CALIFORNIA. WHENEVER YOU ARE GOING TO ACT COMPLETELY OUT OF CHARACTER, THERE'S NEVER ANY POINT IN GOING AT IT HALF-COCKED!
HA HA! BUT LOOK, THERE'S ONE OTHER THING. OBVIOUSLY FOR THE TIME BEING NONE OF THIS CAN GO BEYOND THESE FOUR WALLS.
ONE OF THE FIRST THINGS I'LL NEED TO DO IS INSTRUCT OUR LEGAL TEAM TO REGISTER THE NAME 'TOUCHSTONE' AS A MOBILE CLINIC.
AND ALSO AS AN H.P.P.C.S. THAT IS TO SAY A HIGH PRIORITY PHARMACEUTICAL COURIER SERVICE.
WHICH MEANS THAT WHEN WE'RE READY TO GO, WITH THE USER'S CONSENT, WE CAN LEGALLY ACCESS ALL MEDICAL RECORDS.
WOW, MAN! MY HEAD IS JUST KINDA SPINNING RIGHT NOW! SO, AS OF TODAY, WHAT IS THE FIRST MOVE?
WELL, THE FIRST THING I REALLY NEED TO DO IS TALK TO MY BROTHER...

ACT THREE   SCENE THREE

YOU SEE, THERE WAS THAT ONE GREAT CONSTANT IN MY BROTHER'S LIFE. HE ALWAYS FOUND A CAMERADO SUCH AN ENDLESS SOURCE OF INSPIRATION!

ACH, BUT I'LL NEVER FORGET THAT NIGHT, WHEN HE GOT BACK FROM SEEING WILL AND HAL. THAT DAMN DOG HAD GOT OUT AGAIN! AND AS I CAUGHT UP WITH HIM, THERE WAS KORNEAS JUST STANDING THERE! LIKE HE WAS WAITING FOR ME.

WE WALKED AROUND FOR AN HOUR, MAYBE TWO, AND HE TOLD ME ALL ABOUT TOUCHSTONE.

...SO LET ME GET THIS STRAIGHT. WHEN YOU SAY *GLOBE*, YOU DON'T JUST MEAN GLOBE, DO YOU? YOU MEAN ALL THE SUBSIDIARIES TOO?

YOU REALLY WANT TO SELL *EVERYTHING*?

YES! *ABSOLUTELY* EVERYTHING!

IN TWENTY YEARS WE HAVE MANAGED TO SQUANDER THE POTENTIAL OF WHAT WAS, CONCEIVABLY, MAN'S GREATEST INVENTION.

WE ARE LEFT WITH SOMETHING THAT HAS NOT IMPROVED OUR LIVES OR MADE US KINDER, BETTER PEOPLE.

INSTEAD IT HAS DROWNED US IN THE TRIVIAL AND INESSENTIAL. GIVEN US PORTALS FOR OUR MISPLACED RAGE AND ALLOWED US TO HIDE OUR HUMANITY BEHIND A SCREEN. REDUCED US TO NOTHING MORE THAN TINY COGS IN THE WHEELS OF THE ENTERTAINMENT INDUSTRY.

I'VE WATCHED ALL THE POSSIBILITY I SAW WHEN WE WERE YOUNGER EVAPORATE. WE COULD HAVE USED THAT TECHNOLOGY TO ACHIEVE SO MUCH...

NOW WE CAN! TOUCHSTONE IS OUR CHANCE TO RECOUP THOSE LOST OPPORTUNITIES, SERGEI! WE CAN MAKE A DIFFERENCE. WE CAN FINALLY DO SOMETHING GOOD AND LASTING.

BUT I NEED TO KNOW THAT YOU'RE WITH ME ON THIS.

YOU DO?

WE ALL STAND ON THE SHOULDERS OF GIANTS. EXCEPT ME. I ALWAYS STAND ON THE SHOULDERS OF MY BROTHER!

AW, WHAT AN AMAZING THING TO SAY.
ACH, MY BROTHER WAS AN EXCEPTIONAL HUMAN BEING. I WISH YOU COULD HAVE MET HIM. AND TOUCHSTONE WAS HIS MOST EXTRAORDINARY IDEA.
BUT EVEN THEN, ALL I COULD SEE WERE PROBLEMS.

...KORNY, IF WE GO AHEAD ON THIS, WE'LL HAVE ONE TO TWO YEARS AT BEST BEFORE EVERYONE CATCHES UP ON THE TECHNOLOGY.
IT NEEDS TO BE PROTECTED.
WE'LL NEED PATENTS AND COPYRIGHT ON *ALL* THE PROGRAMS AND *ALL* THE SOFTWARE.
OTHERWISE WE WON'T BE ABLE TO STOP ANOTHER TECH GIANT FROM REPLICATING TOUCHSTONE AS AN ENTIRELY PROFIT MAKING ENTERPRISE!
IT WOULD TAKE ONLY A SINGLE LEAK FROM SOMEONE AT GLOBE...
NO NO! NO LAWYERS! ABSOLUTELY NOT!
HEY, DO YOU REMEMBER WHAT GRANDMA USED TO SAY?
"THE ONLY REASON LAWYERS WERE INVENTED WAS BECAUSE PEOPLE FORGOT HOW TO TRUST EACH OTHER!"
WELL, I TRUST ALL THE PEOPLE ON MY TEAM. EVERY SINGLE ONE!

AND THAT'S THE OTHER THING. YOU MUST REALIZE YOU'RE PUTTING EVERYONE AT RISK. NOT JUST YOURSELF.
IN WHAT SENSE?
CAN YOU IMAGINE THE HAVOC THIS WILL CAUSE? HOW DO YOU THINK THIS IS GOING TO PLAY WITH THE BIG HEALTH INSURERS?
NOT TO MENTION ALL THOSE MASSIVE PHARMACEUTICAL CORPORATIONS!
TRUST ME, THEY WILL ***NEVER*** LET YOU DO THIS!
IF THEY DON'T KNOW ABOUT IT, THEN HOW CAN THEY STOP IT?
BESIDES, EVERYTHING ABOUT TOUCHSTONE WILL BE TOTALLY ANONYMOUS AND UNTRACEABLE.
I THOUGHT YOU COULD HELP ME WITH THAT.
YES, OF COURSE.
THIS APPLIES TO ALL OF US, WE URGENTLY NEED TO STOP PUTTING PROFIT BEFORE PEOPLE. AND TOUCHSTONE IS ONLY A VERY TINY PART OF THAT.
ACH, YOU KNOW WHAT?
WHAT?
YOU ARE STARTING TO SOUND LIKE YOUR FRIEND, HAL!
THANK YOU. I'LL TAKE THAT AS A COMPLIMENT!
HANG ON, DID YOU SEE WHAT HAPPENED TO...

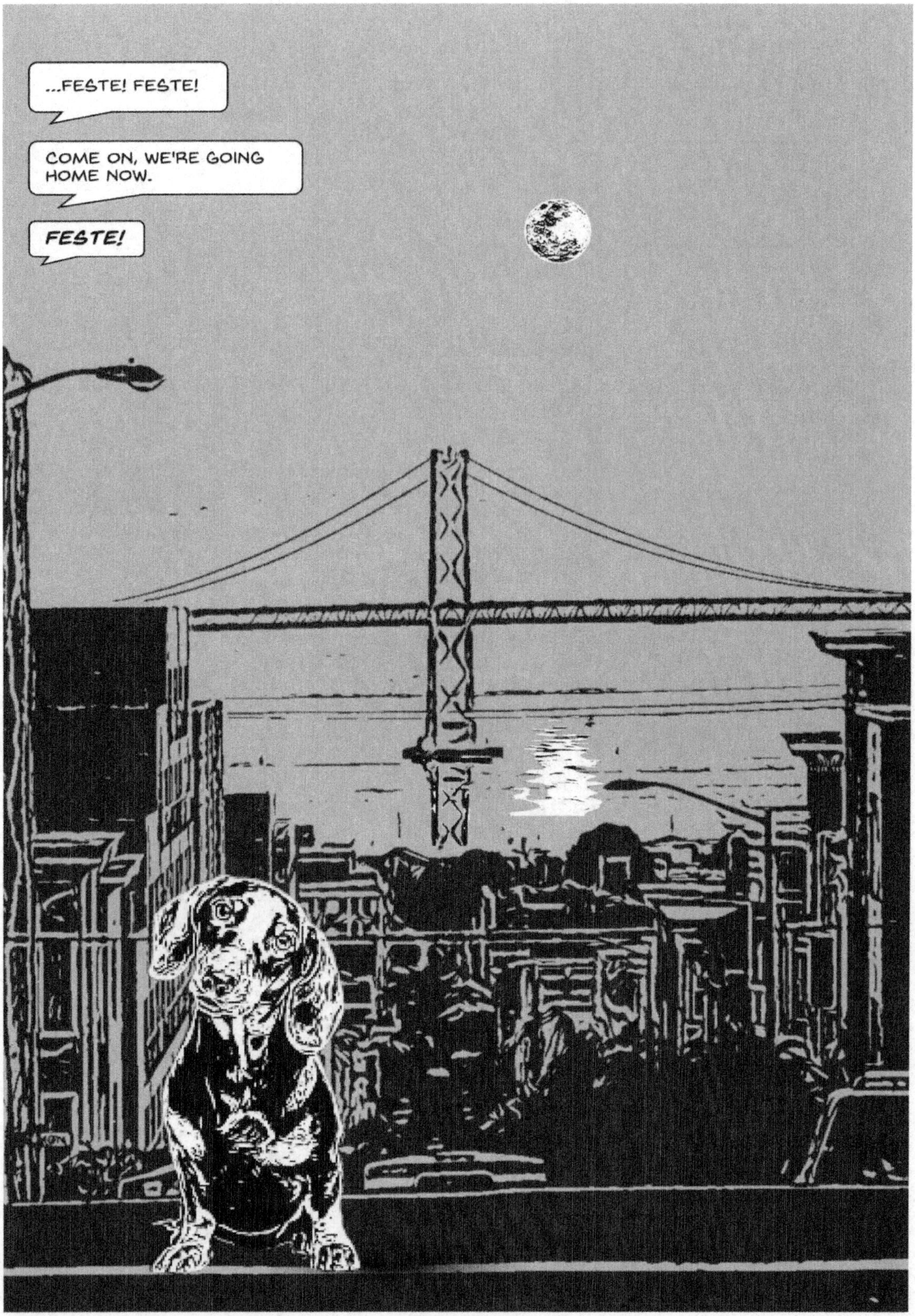
...FESTE! FESTE!
COME ON, WE'RE GOING HOME NOW.
FESTE!

ACT THREE

SCENE FOUR

AW MAN, FUCK! SO THAT WAS WHAT TOUCHSTONE WAS ALL ABOUT! WELL, I GUESS IT ALL FALLS INTO PLACE NOW AND I CAN SEE WHY HE THOUGHT IT WAS GOING TO CHANGE EVERYTHING!

I MEAN, WHAT A TOTALLY MINDFUCKING CONCEPT!

THAT MUST HAVE BEEN ONE UNFORGETTABLE EVENING...

... SERGEI? *SERGEI?* ARE YOU OKAY?

OH MOLLY, SO MANY, MANY TIMES I HAVE DREAMT ABOUT THAT NIGHT.

IF I COULD HAVE MADE HIM LISTEN TO ME. IF I COULD HAVE JUST PERSUADED HIM TO FORGET THE WHOLE IDEA...

...THINGS MIGHT HAVE BEEN VERY DIFFERENT. WHO KNOWS?

OH SERGEI! I'M SORRY WE HAVE TO DO THIS. I REALIZE IT MIGHT BE DIFFICULT FOR YOU.
I HAVE NEVER SPOKEN TO ANYONE ABOUT THIS *EVER*.
AND YES, TOUCHSTONE WAS AN INCREDIBLE THING. BUT WITH MY LAST DYING BREATH, I WILL DESPISE IT AND EVERYTHING ABOUT IT!
BUT THE TWO OF YOU DID DO AN AMAZING JOB IN KEEPING TOUCHSTONE OFF THE RADAR! I MEAN, NO ONE IN MY FIRM COULD EVEN GET A SNIFF OF IT!
ACH, NOT THAT GOOD A JOB OBVIOUSLY, AS IT TURNED OUT.
CERTAIN PEOPLE OR A CERTAIN PERSON DID FIND OUT AND THAT WAS ALL IT TOOK!
LOOK, MOLLY, I DON'T THINK THIS IS A GOOD IDEA. ACTUALLY, I THINK THIS IS A REALLY BIG MISTAKE.
WHAT IS? WHAT'S A BIG MISTAKE?

NO, NO ... I'M JUST, YOU KNOW ... I DON'T FEEL COMFORTABLE TALKING ABOUT ALL THIS HERE.
YOU NEVER KNOW...
YOU NEVER ...
... NEVER ...
... NEVER KNOW WHO MIGHT BE LISTENING. MAYBE THIS PLACE ISN'T SAFE FOR US, MOLLY.
LET'S FIND SOMEWHERE ELSE WE CAN TALK WHERE THERE ARE LESS PEOPLE AROUND.

OF COURSE, DO YOU HAVE ANYWHERE IN MIND?
YES, I DO. I THINK I KNOW SOMEWHERE.

WELL, IS IT FAR FROM HERE?
NO IT'S NOT FAR AT ALL. IT'S WHERE WE USED TO TAKE FESTE SOMETIMES.
IT'S NICE. YOU WILL LIKE IT, I'M SURE.

COME ON, WE'LL BE THERE IN NO TIME.
RIGHT BEHIND YOU, CHIEF...

FIVE MINUTES LATER.
YES, THIS IS THE PLACE.
PIONEER PARK
ESTABLISHED 1876

OH, YES, I DO KNOW THIS PLACE. USED TO COME HERE A LOT WHEN I WAS FIRST MARRIED.
YOU KNOW, STILL AT THAT SILLY LOVE·COMFORETH·LIKE· SUNSHINE·AFTER·RAIN· STAGE!
OH, SO YOUR HUSBAND, MOLLY. WHAT IS HE LIKE?
COULD BE DEAD, AS FAR AS I KNOW!
NOT SEEN HIM FOR TWENTY YEARS! NOT SINCE THE DIVORCE.
THAT IS VERY SAD!
NAH, HE WAS A BIG, BIG MISTAKE! NEVER AGAIN!
ANYWAY, DO YOU FEEL OK TO TALK HERE?
YES, YES, THIS IS SO MUCH BETTER.
SO WHAT HAPPENED AFTER THAT NIGHT?
OH, I KEPT TRYING TO TALK TO HIM. BUT SUDDENLY WE WERE SO BUSY WITH EVERYTHING. IT WAS JUST TOTAL MAYHEM!

138

HE DIDN'T EVER SAY ANYTHING BUT I GUESS HE PROBABLY THOUGHT I'D GONE A BIT PARANOID.
ACH! BUT EVEN IF YOU'RE PARANOID, IT DOESN'T AUTOMATICALLY MEAN YOU'RE WRONG!
I USED TO WARN HIM ABOUT TALKING ON HIS PHONE. OR EVEN DISCUSSING TOUCHSTONE TOO MUCH WHEN WE WERE AT HOME.

IF I HAD ***ANYTHING*** TO GO OVER WITH HIM I USED TO WAIT UNTIL WE WERE FAR AWAY FROM THE HOUSE. YOU KNOW, LIKE WHEN WE TOOK FESTE FOR HIS WALK.

BUT IF HE WAS YOUR BROTHER, MOLLY, WOULDN'T YOU HAVE WANTED TO PROTECT HIM?

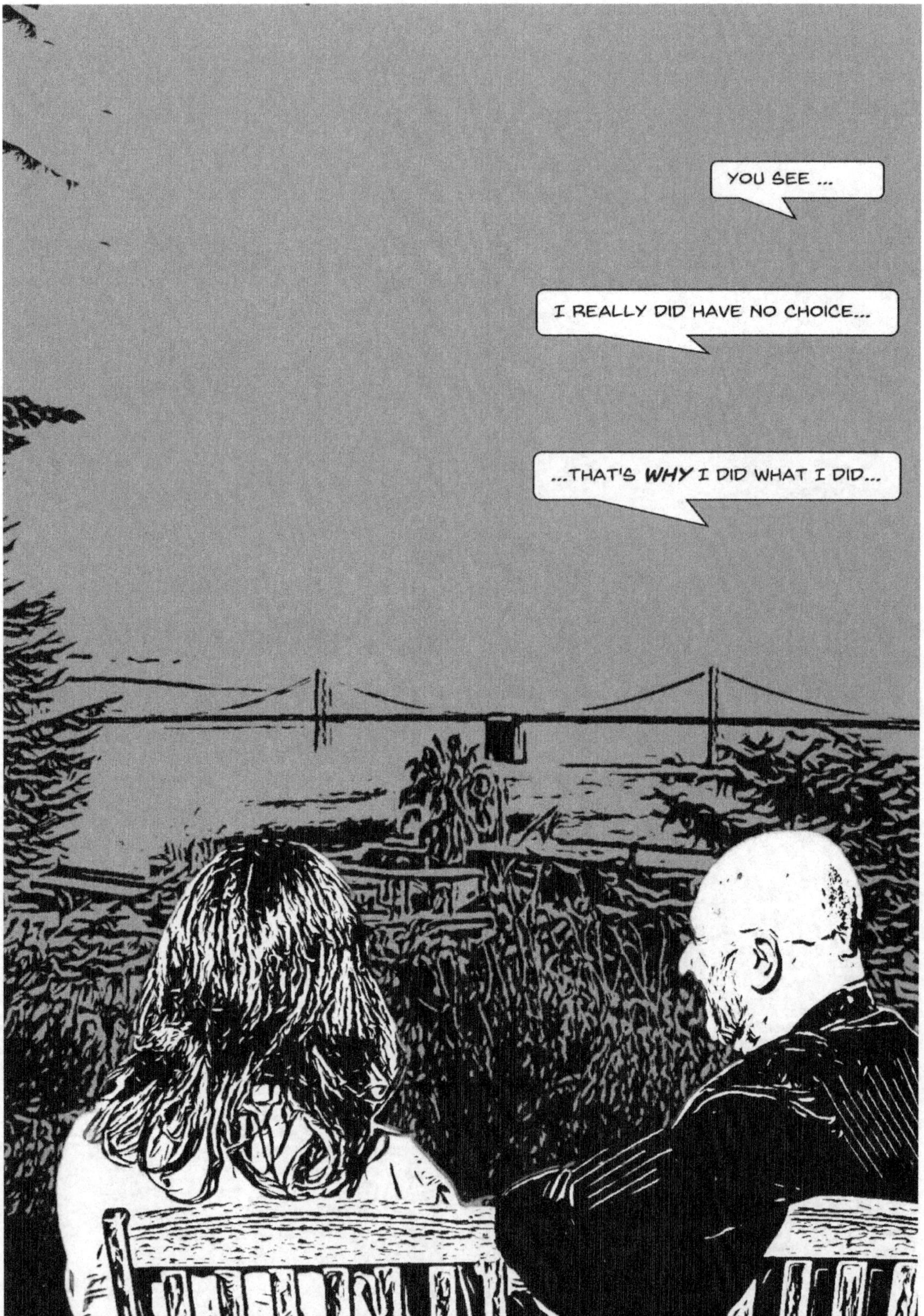
YOU SEE ...
I REALLY DID HAVE NO CHOICE...
...THAT'S WHY I DID WHAT I DID...

ACT THREE

SCENE FIVE

FROM THE TIME WE WERE VERY SMALL...

MY BROTHER ONLY EVER SAW THE VERY BEST IN PEOPLE.

AND THAT WAS HIS SINGLE GREAT FAILING.

I, ON THE OTHER HAND, SAW ONLY THE VERY WORST.

AND THAT WAS MINE...

"HEY, WILL GEER! I'LL MAKE THIS CLEAR!

WE ALL REALLY NEED YOU HERE!"

IT WAS NOT LONG AFTER THAT HE TOOK ME TO SEE CHAPTER 25 FOR THE FIRST TIME. I SAW THEM MANY, MANY TIMES AFTER THAT.

"COME TAKE A SEAT, ENJOY THE VIEW...

...AND WATCH THE NAZIS MARCHING TWO BY TWO!"

I THOUGHT THEY WERE PRETTY AMAZING. AND IT WAS GREAT TO HEAR MUSIC THAT HAD IMPORTANT THINGS TO SAY.
ALTHOUGH PERHAPS I DIDN'T QUITE SHARE MY BROTHER'S ENTHUSIASM!
"YOU'RE GOING THROUGH YOUR POCKETS AT THE SIDE OF THE ROAD. AND YOU'RE FEELING A LITTLE LIKE OLD TOM JOAD."
"SO SET YOUR DIAL TO 1932 FOR CANNERY ROW RADIO!"
SOMETIMES HAL'S VOICE WAS OK.
BUT ON OTHER NIGHTS HE WAS BARELY ABLE TO SING AT ALL.
BUT EVEN WHEN HE COULDN'T SING, EVERY TIME I SAW HIM, HE ALWAYS HAD SO MANY INTERESTING THINGS TO SAY.

THE MOST DANGEROUS AND MOST POWERFUL MOVEMENT OF ALL TIME SURROUNDS US RIGHT NOW AND IS GAINING STRENGTH EVERY DAY!

IT IS A MOVEMENT MORE INSIDIOUS THAN CAPITALISM AND MORE DANGEROUS THAN FASCISM.

I'M TALKING ABOUT THE CULTURE OF *INACTIVISM*.

INACTIVISTS ARE MUCH TOO BUSY TURNING AWAY AND IGNORING ALL THE REAL ISSUES.

OR ARE OTHERWISE PERMANENTLY OCCUPIED BY THEIR PETTY POLARIZING MORAL CRUSADES OR ALL THEIR ISOLATING DIVISIVE SINGLE ISSUES...
...THAT THEY HAVEN'T GOT AROUND TO GIVING THEMSELVES A NAME YET!

SO I JUST DID IT FOR THEM.
WHAT CAN I TELL YOU? I GUESS I'M JUST GENEROUS LIKE THAT!
SO HAIL, ***INACTIVISTS*** THE WORLD OVER! BROTHERS AND SISTERS, WE SALUTE YOU!

OH, BUT HAL IN FULL FLIGHT WAS TRULY SOMETHING TO BEHOLD! AND YOU COULD SEE THAT MY BROTHER WAS QUITE IN AWE OF HIM.
OBVIOUSLY, THEY DID SHARE SIMILAR PERSPECTIVES ON SO MANY THINGS.
NOT TO MENTION THE SAME RATHER TOUCHING AND DURABLE AFFECTION FOR CAMERADOS!
BUT HE CONFIDED IN HAL TOO AND THAT'S WHAT REALLY STARTED TO WORRY ME.

PERHAPS KORNEAS WAS RIGHT AND I GENUINELY WAS A LITTLE PARANOID. BUT HAL WOULD TALK AND TALK AND GET CARRIED AWAY SOMETIMES.
AND I THINK I BECAME OBSESSED WITH THE IDEA THAT HE WOULD SAY SOMETHING ABOUT TOUCHSTONE BEFORE WE WERE READY.

KORNEAS TRUSTED HAL COMPLETELY BUT I KNEW WE COULD NOT RISK TOUCHSTONE BECOMING PUBLIC KNOWLEDGE. SO MUCH WOULD HAVE BEEN AT STAKE.
THE ACTUAL DEVELOPMENT OF THE SOFTWARE STILL OCCUPIED MOST OF OUR TIME BUT WE WERE AT THE POINT WHERE THE SELLING OF GLOBE WAS ONLY A FEW MONTHS IN THE FUTURE. I GUESS THAT'S WHY I WAS SCARED.

> IN SOME WAY, I FELT I NO LONGER HAD ANY CONTROL OVER THINGS.

> CONTROL? IN WHAT SENSE?

> WE USED TO SAY THAT SECRECY WAS SECURITY AT GLOBE.

> AND ONE OF MY MAIN FUNCTIONS WITHIN THE FIRM WAS TO ENSURE THAT ALL OUR INNOVATIONS REMAINED UNDER THE RADAR UNTIL WE WERE READY TO GO PUBLIC.

> THAT WAS HOW I LOOKED AFTER MY BROTHER AND I WAS FUCKING GOOD AT IT!

> I MEAN, WHEN YOU WERE GOING THROUGH WILL'S ESTATE, DID YOU EVER ONCE STUMBLE UPON THE WORD *IDIOLECT*?

IDIO-WHAT?
IDIOLECT!
ER...IT DOESN'T RING A BELL.
EXACTLY! THAT'S BECAUSE I MADE ABSOLUTELY SURE OF THAT!
OK, SO PRECISELY WHAT IS OR WHAT WAS IDOLECT?
WE'LL GET TO THAT VERY SHORTLY BUT NOT RIGHT NOW...

ACT THREE

SCENE SIX

BUT OF COURSE, MY BROTHER WAS PREOCCUPIED AT THAT TIME. NOT JUST ABOUT TOUCHSTONE.

HAL WAS HAVING SOME SERIOUS EPISODES AND THERE WERE ONE OR TWO GENUINE EMERGENCIES.

YOU KNOW, I CAN'T RECALL EXACTLY HOW MANY TIMES THEY TOOK HIM INTO E.R.

BUT EVERY TIME, AFTER AN HOUR OR SO, HAL WOULD INSIST HE WAS FINE AND CHECK HIMSELF OUT.

AND THEN SOMETIMES HE WOULD ACTUALLY SEEM HEALTHIER THAN EVER!

ONE NIGHT WHEN I WENT TO SEE THEM, HE WAS ON SUCH GREAT FORM.

THEY DID A SONG FROM THE OLD DAYS CALLED *GUTBUCKET TUXEDO*.

HAL EVEN WORE A TUX FOR THE OCCASION TOO! AND THEY DID THIS GREAT LITTLE DANCE TOGETHER!

"HAND ME MY SKID ROW BROGUES AND MY BARRELHOUSE WALKING CANE!"

"I'LL GRAB MY RAG TAG DRESS AND THAT PERFUME THAT I ONCE WORE."

"GET OUT THAT GUTBUCKET TUXEDO...

AND WE'LL GO OUT DANCING LIKE BEFORE."

AW, SERGEI, I WOULD HAVE LOVED TO HAVE BEEN AROUND TO SEE THAT!
THAT JUST SOUNDS AMAZING!

YEAH, THAT WAS A PARTICULARLY GREAT NIGHT! BUT SOME NIGHTS ALL HE COULD DO WAS JUST STRUM HIS GUITAR.
BUT THERE WERE ALSO TIMES WHEN THEY WOULD HAVE TO COMPLETELY PULL OUT OF A SHOW.
AND THEN THAT HORSE WOULD HAVE TO STAND IN FOR THEM... INDEED, THE·SWEET·AND·BITTER FOOL·WILL·PRESENTLY·APPEAR.

... YEAH, I THINK THAT'S PROBABLY ABOUT ALL I HAVE TO SAY ON THE SUBJECT OF *INACTIVISM!* SO HOW ABOUT RIGHT NOW WE ALL TAKE PART IN MY BRAND NEW SOCIAL EXPERIMENT.

AND YOU NEVER KNOW, MAYBE WE'LL FIND A BETTER WAY FOR US TO MANAGE THIS TOTALLY FUCKED UP WORLD WE'VE INHERITED.

NOW I WANT YOU ALL TO CLOSE YOUR EYES AND IMAGINE YOU'RE ALONE IN A COMPLETELY EMPTY SUBWAY CAR, METRO CARRIAGE OR WHATEVER. YOU HAVE THE WHOLE CAR TO YOURSELF. THEN IT PULLS INTO A STATION AND SOMEBODY GETS ON AND SITS DIRECTLY OPPOSITE YOU.

YOU LOOK UP AND YOU SEE A PERSON OF A DIFFERENT RACE OR RELIGION FROM YOUR OWN. YOU NOTICE HE IS VERY SCRUFFILY DRESSED, DIRTY JEANS, A FOUL HOODIE, FILTHY TRAINERS. SUDDENLY YOU FEEL ALONE, ANXIOUS, VULNERABLE, YOU FEEL HIM STARING AT YOU. YOU TURN AWAY AND NOW HOLD IT RIGHT THERE...

BECAUSE WHEN YOU TURN BACK, IT'S THE *SAME PERSON* BUT NOW HE'S SMARTLY DRESSED IN A THREE PIECE PINSTRIPE SUIT, NICE GOLD ROLEX AND A BRIEFCASE ON HIS LAP, A BANKER YOU THINK, A LAWYER MAYBE AND SUDDENLY, BE HONEST NOW, ALL THE PANIC LEAVES YOU AND YOU FEEL CALM AND SAFE AGAIN. RIGHT?

SO THEN, IF IT'S NOT THE GUY'S RACE OR HIS RELIGION WHAT EXACTLY WERE YOU SO FUCKING SCARED OF? I'LL TELL YOU...

*COUGH, COUGH...

WHY YES, BOYS AND GIRLS, IT'S FUCKING *POVERTY!*
YIP! THE THING THAT WE ARE TRAINED TO FEAR THE MOST IN THIS WHOLE CAPITALIST FUCKFEST OF OURS IS POVERTY. AND THE DESPERATE ACTS THAT POVERTY MIGHT FORCE A PERSON TO COMMIT!
SO, EVEN MORE THAN OUR SILLY INSANE BIGOTRIES AND PREJUDICES, WE ALL HATE POVERTY. BUT DON'T YOU SEE WHAT A BRILLIANT BOND THAT WOULD BE BETWEEN US? WE COULD ALL LINK ARMS AND MARCH AS THE UNITED HATERS OF POVERTY. THAT WOULD GIVE US ALL SO MUCH POWER, SO MUCH PURPOSE.
LET'S UNITE AND DEFEAT THE THING WE ALL FEAR THE MOST. LET'S DEFEAT POVERTY TOGETHER. BECAUSE THERE IS NO JOY COMPARABLE TO THAT OF WATCHING A FUCKING CAPITALIST WEEP! AND YEAH, YOU CAN TRUST ME ON THIS!
OK, YOU CAN ALL OPEN YOUR EYES NOW. AND I KNOW WHEN WE DO THIS EXPERIMENT, ONE OR TWO ESPECIALLY STUPID PEOPLE OFTEN RATIONALIZE THEIR FEARS BY DECIDING THAT THE SCRUFFY PERSON MIGHT BE "ON DRUGS".
WELL, I HAVE IT ON VERY GOOD AUTHORITY FROM MY FRIENDS IN THE COLUMBIAN CARTELS THAT SO MANY OF THEIR VERY BEST CUSTOMERS WORK ON WALL STREET AND IN THE CITY OF LONDON! THE MAIN DIFFERENCE IS *THEY CAN FUCKING AFFORD IT!*
SO ONCE AGAIN, WHETHER YOU KNOW IT OR NOT, WHAT YOU ARE ACTUALLY FEARING AND HATING AND THE THING THAT'S MAKING YOU FEEL UNCOMFORTABLE IS *POVERTY!*
I CAN SEE HOPE FOR US IN A WORLD WITHOUT POVERTY. BUT I DON'T SEE MUCH HOPE ANYWHERE ELSE. SO MAYBE WE NEED TO THINK ABOUT ALL THIS BEFORE IT'S TOO FUCKING LATE!

BUT WHILE ALL THAT WAS GOING ON, I WAS STILL WORRIED ABOUT TOUCHSTONE.
THERE WERE ONGOING ISSUES WITH THE PROGRAM AND WE'D FALLEN BEHIND SCHEDULE.
ONE OR TWO OF OUR TOP PROGRAMMERS HAD SUDDENLY QUIT FOR NO APPARENT REASON AND NATURALLY THIS FED INTO MY PARANOIA ABOUT CONFIDENTIALITY.
THE SHEER AMOUNT OF MONEY AT STAKE TO ANYONE WITH ACCESS TO THAT TECHNOLOGY WAS INCALCULABLE! AND OF COURSE I WAS CONSTANTLY WORRIED THERE'D BEEN A LEAK.
BUT MY BROTHER WOULD NEVER BUDGE ON THAT WHOLE LEGAL ISSUE.
ACH... IT WASN'T EVER EASY TO QUESTION HIS JUDGMENT. BUT THAT WAS MY BROTHER.
BUT YOU MUST REMEMBER THIS WAS TEN YEARS AGO AND IT'S ONLY NOW WE'RE CATCHING UP ON THIS WHOLE A.I. THING. AND THE PERSON WE ARE ATTEMPTING TO CATCH UP WITH IS MY BROTHER! ON A BAD DAY, HE WAS FIVE YEARS AHEAD OF THE COMPETITION. ON A GOOD DAY? ***AT LEAST TEN!***

I LOVED WILL AND HAL TOO BUT DURING THAT TIME, MY BROTHER AND HAL BECAME ESPECIALLY CLOSE.

NOW, IT'S NOT MY PLACE TO MAKE CONNECTIONS HERE BUT A FEW YEARS EARLIER OUR DAD HAD TAKEN EARLY RETIREMENT FROM UCLA.

AFTER WHICH HE AND MOM HAD MOVED BACK TO THE OLD COUNTRY.

WE HAD BOUGHT THEM THIS BEAUTIFUL BIG CHALET UP IN THE MOUNTAINS AND THEY WERE HAPPY THERE.
BUT VERY, VERY FAR AWAY.

SUDDENLY, IN TERMS OF FAMILY ALL KORNY AND I HAD WERE EACH OTHER.

HE HAD ALWAYS LOOKED AFTER ME BUT I FELT IT WAS MY TURN NOW. HAL WAS A GREAT, BRILLIANT IDEALIST BUT LIKE MY BROTHER, AT THE CORE OF HIS IDEALISM WAS AN UNSHAKEABLE FAITH IN PEOPLE. AND THEIR CAPACITY TO ACT DECENTLY.

SO LET'S SAY SOMETIMES I SAW THINGS A LITTLE DIFFERENTLY.

AND WHEN YOU REALLY CARE ABOUT SOMEONE THERE ARE ALWAYS THOSE TIMES WHEN YOU HAVE TO MAKE HARD CHOICES.

SO I THOUGHT FOR ONCE IN MY LIFE I SHOULD TRY AND BE LIKE THAT SMARTEST MAN IN THE ROOM WHO ISN'T IN THE ROOM...

ACT FOUR

ACT FOUR SCENE ONE

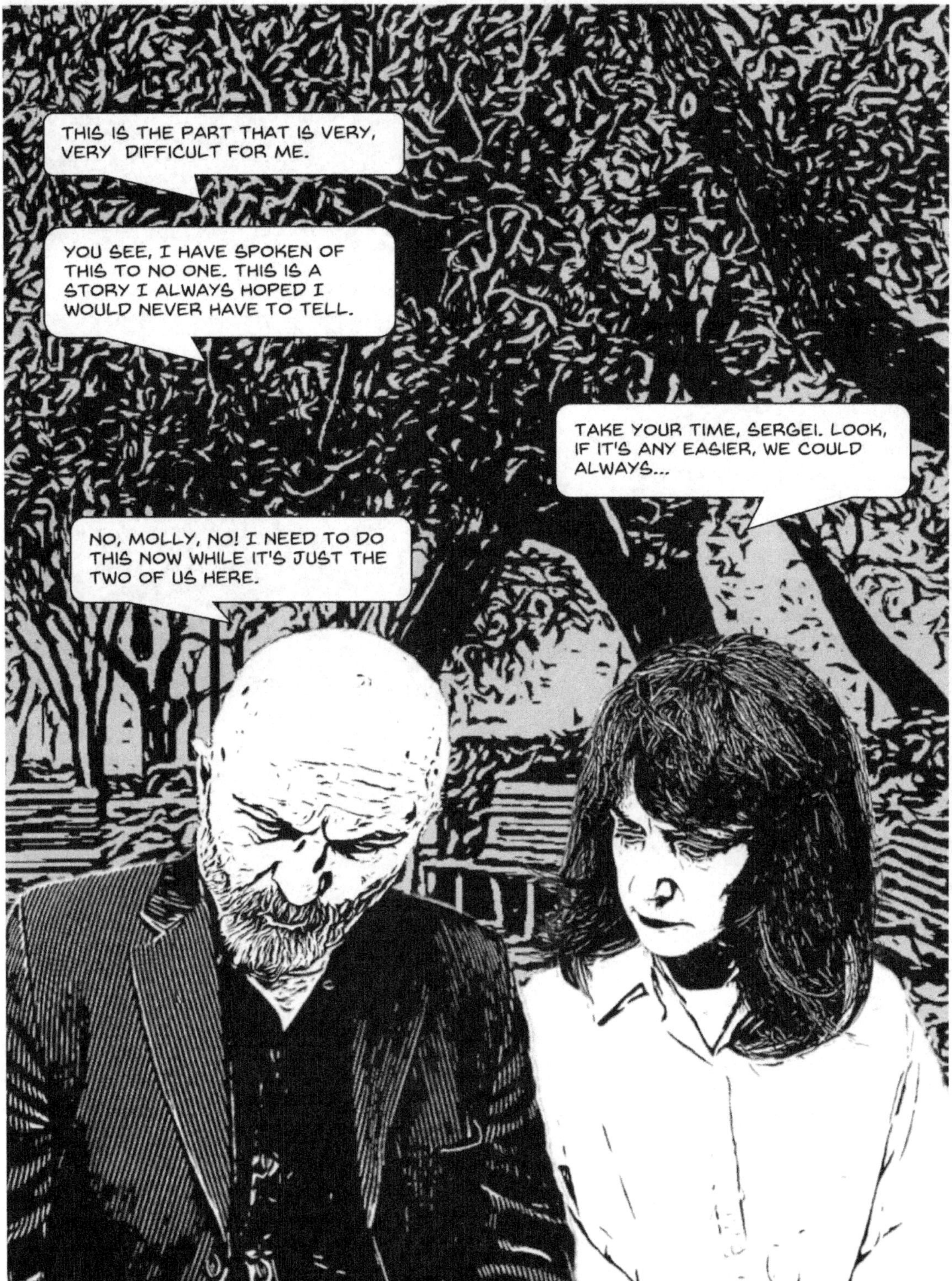

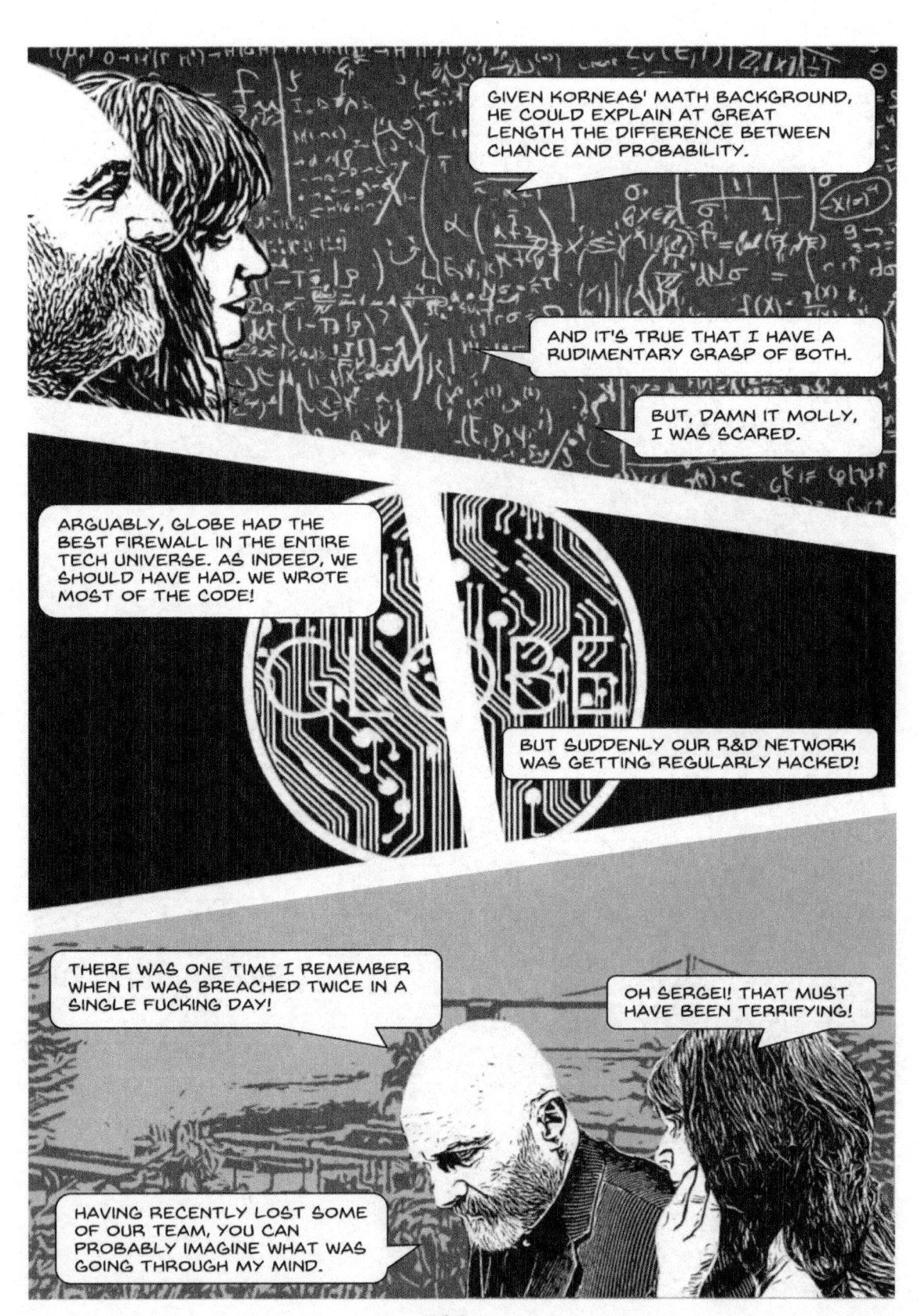

GIVEN KORNEAS' MATH BACKGROUND, HE COULD EXPLAIN AT GREAT LENGTH THE DIFFERENCE BETWEEN CHANCE AND PROBABILITY.

AND IT'S TRUE THAT I HAVE A RUDIMENTARY GRASP OF BOTH.

BUT, DAMN IT MOLLY, I WAS SCARED.

ARGUABLY, GLOBE HAD THE BEST FIREWALL IN THE ENTIRE TECH UNIVERSE. AS INDEED, WE SHOULD HAVE HAD. WE WROTE MOST OF THE CODE!

BUT SUDDENLY OUR R&D NETWORK WAS GETTING REGULARLY HACKED!

THERE WAS ONE TIME I REMEMBER WHEN IT WAS BREACHED TWICE IN A SINGLE FUCKING DAY!

OH SERGEI! THAT MUST HAVE BEEN TERRIFYING!

HAVING RECENTLY LOST SOME OF OUR TEAM, YOU CAN PROBABLY IMAGINE WHAT WAS GOING THROUGH MY MIND.

AND THEN THERE WAS IDOLECT OF COURSE. AND ALTHOUGH IT WAS AN OFFSHOOT PROGRAM FROM WITHIN THE WHOLE GREATER TOUCHSTONE PROJECT, IT PUSHED OUR DEADLINES BACK EVEN FURTHER.
AND THE LONGER IT WENT ON, THE MORE VULNERABLE AND EXPOSED I FELT WE WERE.
HAH, THAT IS ONE OF THE REASONS YOU NEVER FOUND THE WORD IDOLECT!
Send
sergeiyatopiwel@globeinc.com
To...
korneasyatopiwel@globeinc.com
Cc...
Bcc...
Subject
RE:
Attached
K.
Still got the same issues with
interface.
Maybe go back to Plan A?
I MADE SURE IT WAS NEVER WRITTEN DOWN ANYWHERE OR REFERRED TO DIRECTLY. EVEN WITHIN THE CONFINES OF GLOBE!
AND ON MY INSISTENCE THE TERM WAS ONLY EVER SPOKEN AND EVEN TO THIS DAY THERE ARE ONLY FIVE PEOPLE WHO KNOW OF ITS EXISTENCE.
AND THREE OF THEM ARE DEAD!

I SUPPOSE IF I HAD TO PICK A POINT IN TIME WHERE THE STORY OF IDIOLECT BEGINS...
THEN I GUESS WE SHOULD PROBABLY START WITH THAT WHOLE NEW ORLEANS THING.
HANG ON A SEC, SERGEI, THE *WHAT?*
ACH, YES I KNOW, IT MIGHT SOUND STRANGE BUT IT WAS ONE OF THOSE MOMENTS, LIKE FESTE AND THE THREE FOOLS, WHEN THE ONLY WORD IS FATE.

COME ON, LET'S TAKE A STROLL UP HERE AND MAYBE YOU CAN SEE THINGS FROM A DIFFERENT ANGLE.

OK, SO TELL ME ABOUT NEW ORLEANS. WHAT HAPPENED?
WELL, IT ALL STARTED WHEN HAL HAD A COUPLE OF REALLY BAD EPISODES AND THEY'D BEEN CANCELLING GIGS ALL OVER THE PLACE.
AW, THE POOR GUY...
AT ONE POINT HE SPENT A NIGHT IN HOSPITAL WHILE THEY RAN A FEW MORE TESTS.
HE WAS ONLY IN OVERNIGHT BUT WHEN MY BROTHER AND WILL WENT TO COLLECT HIM THE NEXT MORNING, HE'D HAD ONE OF HIS IDEAS!
AS WILL USED TO SAY, 'HAL ONLY EVER HAS THREE KINDS OF IDEAS, MAD ONES, STUPID ONES AND BRILLIANT ONES.' SO THIS MIGHT HAVE BEEN A RARE EXAMPLE OF ONE THAT WAS ACTUALLY ALL THREE!

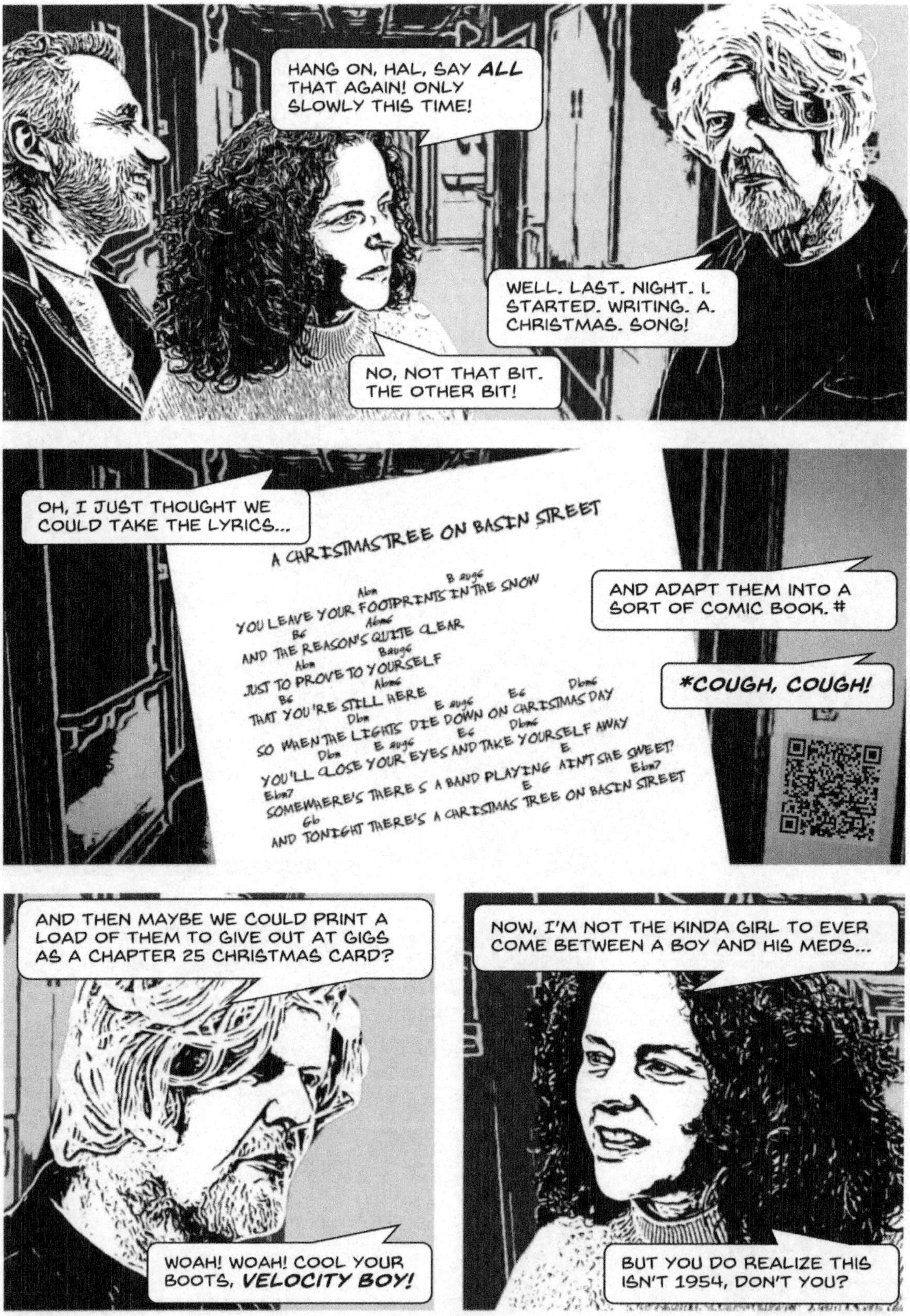

SEE APPENDIX TWO

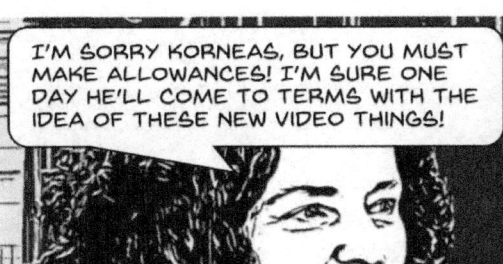

"I'M SORRY KORNEAS, BUT YOU MUST MAKE ALLOWANCES! I'M SURE ONE DAY HE'LL COME TO TERMS WITH THE IDEA OF THESE NEW VIDEO THINGS!"

"OH, AND YOU SHOULD ALSO KNOW ABOUT HIS TOTAL OBSESSION WITH ANYTHING TO DO WITH NEW ORLEANS!"

"HE'S NEVER SO MUCH AS SET FOOT IN THE PLACE!"

"BUT HE'S TALKED ABOUT IT VIRTUALLY NON-STOP FOR ABOUT 40 YEARS!"

"AND THAT WAS IT! IT WAS AT PRECISELY THAT SECOND THAT THE ROAD OF ALL OUR LIVES DIVIDED INTO TWO PATHS!"

"MY BROTHER COULD HAVE SAID ANY NUMBER OF THINGS. HE COULD HAVE SAID NOTHING AT ALL."

"BUT I GUESS FATE STEPPED IN AND WHAT HE SAID WAS..."

"... AW, YOU KNOW, IT'S SO BEAUTIFUL THIS TIME OF THE YEAR."

"LOOK, WHY DON'T I ARRANGE A TRIP FOR US? WE COULD STAY A COUPLE OF WEEKS."

"I COULD BOOK YOU GUYS SOME STUDIO TIME AND YOU CAN RECORD YOUR CHRISTMAS SONG ACTUALLY IN NEW ORLEANS!"

"MAYBE EVEN WRITE SOME MORE SONGS WHILE YOU'RE THERE..."

ACT FOUR   SCENE TWO

AND SO JUST LIKE THAT, THE NEXT WEEK THEY ALL WENT OFF TO NEW ORLEANS!

THEY STAYED IN A HOTEL ON THE OUTSKIRTS OF THE FRENCH QUARTER.

AND MY BROTHER BOOKED THEM SOME TIME IN A STUDIO SO THEY COULD RECORD THEIR CHRISTMAS SONG.

BUT YEAH, THEY DID A WHOLE LOT OF THAT DUMB TOURISTY SHIT TOO!

OH, BUT HAL WAS SO HAPPY TO FINALLY BE THERE! HE STRUGGLED A BIT WITH HIS VOCALS IN THE STUDIO BUT THEY GOT THEIR SONG RECORDED EVENTUALLY.

"MAY THE HOMESICK AND THE LONELY FIND THEIR REST..."

*COUGH, COUGH!

PERHAPS IT WAS THE LOCATION OR JUST A NEW ENVIRONMENT, BUT WILL AND HAL STARTED REMEMBERING ALL THESE SONGS FROM THE PAST.

SONGS THAT THEY'D WRITTEN OR HALF-WRITTEN BUT NEVER ACTUALLY RECORDED.

HOTEL Arden

CHOP YOU DOWN WOULD BE ANOTHER GREAT ONE TO DO HERE. DO YOU REMEMBER THAT ONE?

'IF I SEE YOU IN MY TOWN?' ETC. YEAH OF COURSE! LOVED HOW YOU USED TO SING THAT. WE COULD EVEN TRY *I'M JINXED*. THAT ALWAYS SOUNDED VERY NEW ORLEANS TO ME!

*COUGH, COUGH!

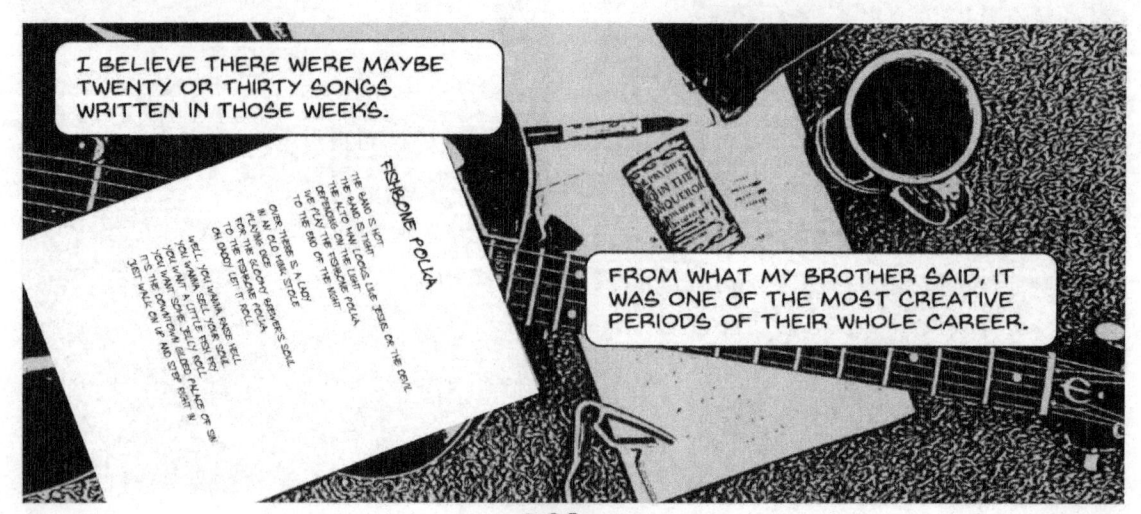

THEY ALSO STARTED TO WRITE COMPLETELY NEW SONGS.

THEY WERE ALWAYS PROLIFIC. BECAUSE, LIKE HAL USED TO SAY, 'A PAMPHLET, NO MATTER HOW GOOD, IS NEVER READ MORE THAN ONCE, BUT A SONG IS LEARNED BY HEART AND REPEATED OVER AND OVER.'

BUT THIS TIME THESE WERE NOT JUST FOLK SONGS, THEY CAME UP WITH ALL *SORTS* OF SONGS!

BLUES SONGS, JAZZ SONGS, FUNNY OLD TIMEY SONGS...

THEY KEPT HAVING IDEAS AND THEN MORE IDEAS AND THEY JUST CARRIED ON WRITING.

AND THEN THEY WENT STRAIGHT INTO THE STUDIO TO RECORD THEM!

I BELIEVE THERE WERE MAYBE TWENTY OR THIRTY SONGS WRITTEN IN THOSE WEEKS.

FROM WHAT MY BROTHER SAID, IT WAS ONE OF THE MOST CREATIVE PERIODS OF THEIR WHOLE CAREER.

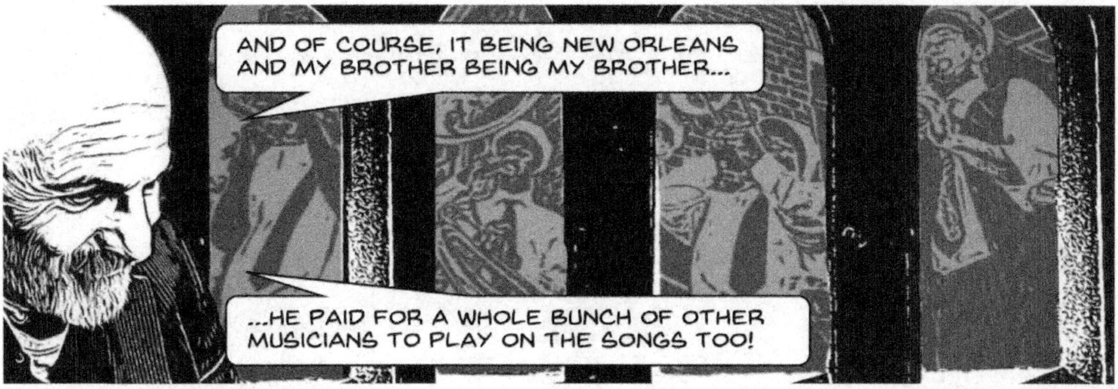
AND OF COURSE, IT BEING NEW ORLEANS AND MY BROTHER BEING MY BROTHER...
...HE PAID FOR A WHOLE BUNCH OF OTHER MUSICIANS TO PLAY ON THE SONGS TOO!

BUT IT WAS ALL WILL AND HAL. AS SOON AS THEY'D RECORDED A NEW SONG THEY'D JUST GO STRAIGHT ON TO THE NEXT ONE!
"NOW OLD SLOWBONE TAKES THE MIC
TO INTRODUCE THE GUYS
AND LOOKS DOWN FROM THE STAGE
THROUGH HIS ONE GOOD EYE
AND SINGS THE FISHBONE POLKA..."

"HE'S MY BOWTIE PAPA
WITH HIS FUNNY OLD TIMEY WAYS.
BUT EVERY TIME HE LOVES ME
I REMEMBER THE GOOD OLD DAYS."

THEY EVEN GOT KORNEAS TO SING ON THE CHORUS OF ONE OF THEIR MAD OLD VAUDEVILLE SONGS!
"AND IT AIN'T NO LIE,
IT CAN MAKE YOUR DADDY
SIT RIGHT DOWN AND CRY."
ACH, HE LOVED THAT!

AW, BUT HE WAS HAVING THE TIME OF HIS LIFE TOO AND OBVIOUSLY VERY INVOLVED WITH WHAT WAS HAPPENING WITH WILL AND HAL. SO WE HAD VERY LITTLE CONTACT AT A TIME WHEN I **REALLY** NEEDED TO TALK TO HIM.

EVEN BACK THEN THERE WAS VERY SOPHISTICATED ALGORITHMIC SOFTWARE THAT CALCULATED THE PROBABILITY OR IMPROBABILITY OF WORD SEQUENCES.

FOR EXAMPLE 'COIT TOWER' AND 'SAN FRANCISCO' WOULD HAVE A HIGH PROBABILITY FACTOR. YES?

THINGS STARTED TO REACH A CRISIS POINT WITH TOUCHSTONE.

BUT THE CHANCES OF A SEEMINGLY RANDOM SERIES OF WORDS LIKE 'INTERFACE' 'HEALTHCARE', 'A.I.' AND 'TOUCHSTONE' BEING INPUTTED INTO A SINGLE ENTRY WOULD BE LITERALLY BILLIONS TO ONE.

Re:SEARCH

Globe, Touchstone, AI, Health

Program, Beta, interface, software

SECURITY WAS BECOMING A MAJOR ISSUE AND WE WERE HAVING TO UPDATE OUR FIREWALL PRETTY MUCH ON A DAILY BASIS.

BUT THEN THERE WAS ALSO WHAT WE CALL THE 'CHATTER' TOO.

SO WHEN WE GOT THE DATA THAT 'TOUCHSTONE' TOGETHER WITH SOME OR ALL OF THOSE WORDS WERE BEING LOGGED TOO REGULARLY TO BE CHANCE OR COINCIDENCE I BEGAN TO PANIC.

THINGS WERE STARTING TO GET PICKED UP. THINGS WE MONITORED CLOSELY. YOU KNOW WHEN YOU TYPE A WORD INTO A SEARCH ENGINE, IT GETS LOGGED.

I BECAME TOTALLY OBSESSED WITH THE IDEA THAT SOMEONE FROM GLOBE HAD BROKEN THEIR NON-DISCLOSURE AGREEMENT.
YOU SEE, EVERYONE HAS A PRICE. ***INTEGRITY, PRINCIPLE*** AND ***MORALITY*** ARE JUST BARGAINING CHIPS - THE WORDS YOU THROW AROUND WHILE YOU HOLD OUT FOR AN EVEN BETTER OFFER!
SO I KNEW IT WAS ONLY A MATTER OF TIME BEFORE ONE OF OUR MAIN RIVALS LAUNCHED THEIR OWN VERSION OF TOUCHSTONE, ONE THAT WAS AN ENTIRELY COMMERCIAL VENTURE.
ONE CREATED SIMPLY TO MAKE MORE MONEY FOR EXACTLY THE SORT OF PEOPLE WHO REALLY DON'T NEED ANY MORE MONEY.
THIS WOULD HAVE KILLED... BROKEN MY BROTHER'S HEART. I COULDN'T LET IT HAPPEN. IT NEEDED TO BE PROTECTED.
KORNEAS WAS ***WAY DOWN YONDER*** AND FAR, FAR AWAY. I HAD TO DO SOMETHING...

ACT FOUR　　　　　　　　　　　SCENE THREE

SO I DID THE ONLY THING I THOUGHT I *COULD* DO UNDER THE CIRCUMSTANCES.

TO DISCUSS COPYRIGHT AND INTELLECTUAL PROPERTY REGARDING SOFTWARE.

'AN HONEST ATTORNEY IS LIKE A MINOTAUR...

IT WAS A STUPID, STUPID IDEA!

BUT I REALLY NEEDED TO TALK TO A LEGAL EXPERT FROM *OUTSIDE* THE COMPANY. SO WITHOUT A WORD TO ANYONE AT GLOBE, I GOT IN TOUCH WITH AN ATTORNEY.

PRESENT COMPANY EXCEPTED OBVIOUSLY, BUT YOU KNOW THAT OLD SAYING ABOUT ATTORNEYS?

... IT IS NOT THAT THEY ARE RARE - *THEY HAVE NEVER FUCKING EXISTED!*'

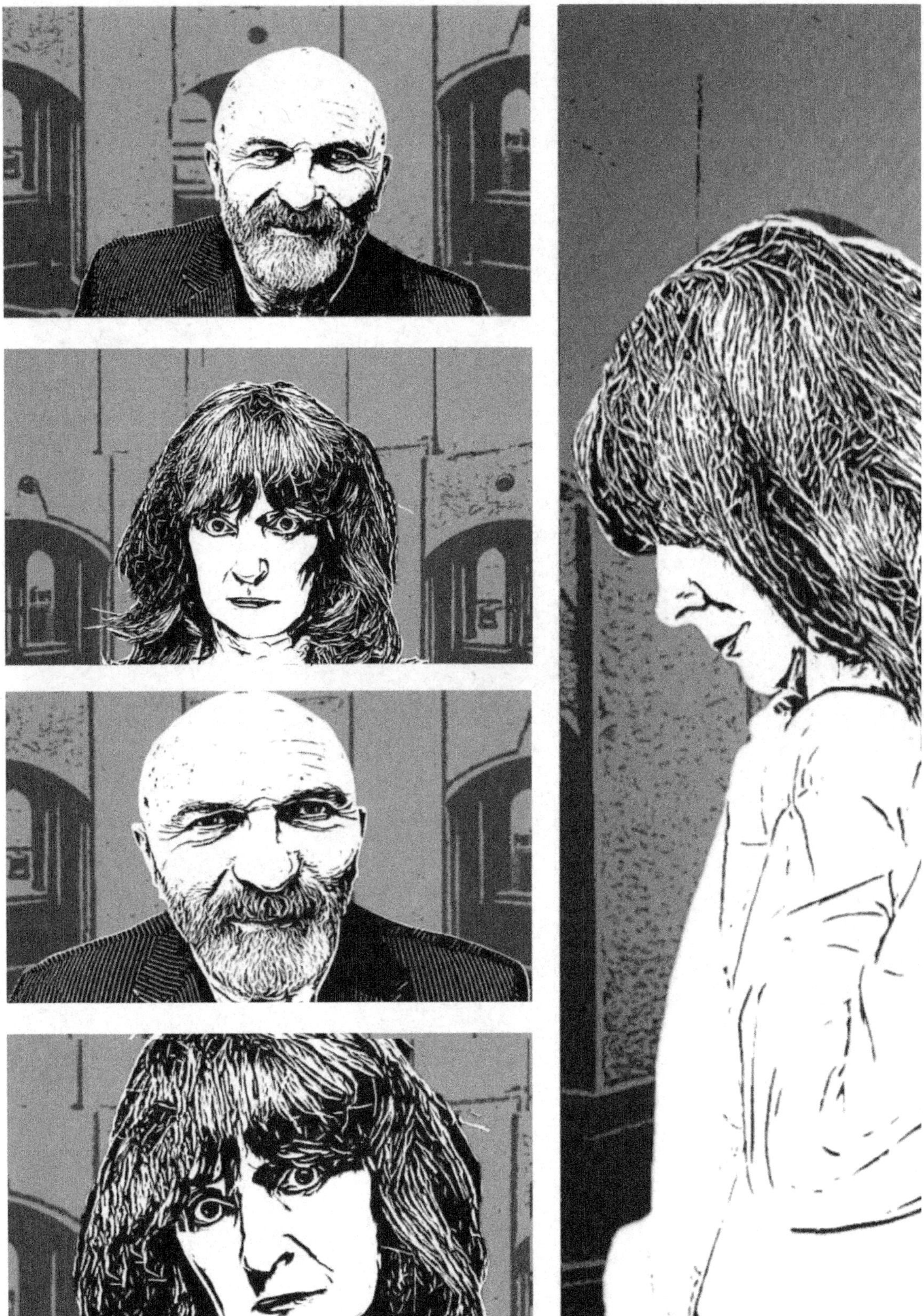

WELL, SERGEI...

...WHAT, WHAT CAN I SAY?

MAYBE JUST THAT...

...I ENDORSE THAT STATEMENT 100%!

SERIOUSLY, THEY MAKE ME PHYSICALLY SICK!

I HATE THEM AND I HATE BEING AROUND THEM AND WORKING WITH THEM. IN FACT, I DON'T EVEN LIKE ACTUALLY *BEING* AN ATTORNEY!

IF I'M HONEST, IT'S THE LAST JOB I WOULD HAVE EVER WANTED FOR MYSELF.

BUT YOU KNOW, GRANDPA WAS A JUDGE, DADDY WAS A LAWYER. MOMMA TOO.

MY OLDER BROTHER IS A BIG TIME LITIGATOR.

SO SEE IF YOU CAN GUESS WHAT HAPPENS NEXT?

BUT THE TRUTH IS I TOTALLY HATE MY JOB. AND YOU KNOW WHAT? I'M NOT EVEN ANY GOOD AT IT!
TO BE COMPLETELY HONEST WITH YOU, THIS IS THE FOURTH FIRM I'VE WORKED FOR IN AS MANY YEARS!
YEAH, GOOD OL' DADDY CAN ALWAYS BE RELIED UPON TO PULL STRINGS AND CALL IN FAVORS!
BUT I'M NOTHING, A NOBODY!
JUST THE OFFICE GRUNT!
SO THEY FIND THESE STUPID MENIAL TASKS FOR ME TO DO IN THE HOPE THAT I'LL QUIT!
LIKE SENDING ME ACROSS TOWN TO LOOK FOR YOU!
IT WAS JUST ANOTHER SHITTY MOLLY JOB THEY FOUND FOR ME, LIKE ALL THE OTHERS!
TOUCHSTONE WAS A LOW PROFILE INACTIVE FILE. A LOOSE END THAT GOT PASSED FROM DESK TO DESK AND INEVITABLY ENDED UP ON MINE!
AND OF COURSE, NO OTHER ATTORNEY AT THE FIRM WAS EVER GOING TO DEMEAN THEMSELVES BY GOING OUT AND KNOCKING ON DOORS!

Panel 1:
YOU KNOW ALL THOSE PHONE CALLS I'VE BEEN IGNORING?

Panel 2:
THEY ARE ALL GOING TO BE FROM THE HEAD OF MY DEPARTMENT, TELLING ME TO GET BACK TO THE OFFICE IMMEDIATELY!

THIS IS WHAT MY LIFE IS LIKE! I SPEND TIME WITH THESE PEOPLE.

Panel 3:
I AVOID THEIR TEDIOUS CONVERSATIONS AND SHELTER FROM THE DARK NOXIOUS CLOUD THAT IS THE FOUL DEGENERATE CONGLOMERATE OF THEIR BODY ODORS, THEIR COLOGNES AND THEIR VILE AND NAUSEATING POLITICS!

SO I PROMISE YOU THIS MUCH – YOU WILL *NEVER* HATE ATTORNEYS MORE THAN I DO!

Panel 4:
WELL, I MUST ADMIT I'M A BIT STUNNED! YOU SEEM SO, SO...YOU KNOW...?

Panel 5:
YEAH. THAT'S JUST MY GUMSHOE MOLLY ACT!

BUT THAT'S *ALL* IT IS. AN ACT!

ACH, MOLLY, YOU ARE JUST FULL OF SURPRISES, AREN'T YOU?
AND I SUPPOSE A CONFESSIONAL ATTORNEY IS NOT ALL THAT DISSIMILAR TO AN HONEST ONE!
THINKING THE WAY I DO IN A PROFESSION LIKE THIS ONE, I'D PROBABLY FEEL LESS LONELY, NEUROTIC AND ISOLATED BEING A LIGHTHOUSE KEEPER!
OR A SHEPHERD!
HA HA, MAYBE IT'S NOT TOO LATE TO CHANGE CAREERS?
ACTUALLY, YOU KNOW, I ALWAYS WANTED TO WORK AT THAT LA BOTTE ROUGE BOOKSHOP!
THERE WAS A VACANCY THERE ONE TIME AND I WAS SO EXCITED BUT MY FATHER SAID NO!
HE SAID IT WOULDN'T LOOK GOOD ON MY RESUMÉ!

BUT THAT WAS MY FATHER FOR YOU! ACTUALLY, WHEN I WAS A TEENAGER I DESPERATELY WANTED TO BECOME AN ASTRONOMER. BECAUSE IN MY CLEVER TEENAGE BRAIN, I'D FIGURED OUT A WAY I COULD GET PAID TO JUST GAZE AT STARS ALL DAY!
AND THEN ONE DAY I'D WRITE A FAMOUS BOOK ALL ABOUT STARS! OH, I ALWAYS WANTED TO WRITE A BOOK! BUT I GUESS THAT WILL NEVER HAPPEN NOW.
THE SKIES ARE PAINTED WITH UNNUMBERED SPARKS; THEY ARE ALL FIRE AND EVERY ONE DOTH SHINE.
YEAH, AS A POSSIBLE CAREER CHOICE, HE DIDN'T THINK VERY HIGHLY OF THAT ONE EITHER!
I'LL HAVE TO STOP YOU IN A MOMENT, MOLLY, YOU'RE MAKING ME FEEL SYMPATHY FOR AN ATTORNEY! ACH! WHATEVER NEXT?
EVEN MY IDIOTIC EX WAS A FUCKING ATTORNEY!
HAH, BUT JUST THINK, IF I'D BEEN A BIT MORE SELECTIVE...
I MIGHT HAVE ENDED UP WITH YOU AS MY ATTORNEY!
OH MOLLY, THEN THINGS MIGHT HAVE BEEN SO, SO DIFFERENT...
IF IT HAD BEEN YOU I MET THAT DAY...

ACT FOUR   SCENE FOUR

YOU MUST UNDERSTAND, I'VE HAD SO MUCH TIME TO THINK ABOUT THAT DAY.

ON THE SUNDAY, KORNEAS SENT ME AN EMAIL ANNOUNCING HE'D BE IN NEW ORLEANS FOR AT LEAST ANOTHER FORTNIGHT!

ON THE MONDAY, I MADE AN APPOINTMENT WITH ONE OF THE BIGGEST LEGAL FIRMS IN THE CITY.

ON THE TUESDAY, I PUT ON MY SMARTEST JACKET AND WENT TO TALK TO AN ATTORNEY.

I WENT THERE ENTIRELY WITHOUT MY BROTHER'S KNOWLEDGE. TOTALLY BEHIND HIS BACK. BUT I JUST THOUGHT I'D TELL HIM WHEN EVERYTHING WAS IN PLACE. AND I KNEW THAT ON THAT DAY HE WOULD THANK ME.

AND I KEPT REPEATING THAT LINE TO MYSELF ALL THAT DAY. **OVER AND OVER AGAIN.**

DURING THAT FIRST MEETING, WE ONLY SPOKE FOR AN HOUR OR SO. IT WOULD BE A LONG AND EXPENSIVE PROCESS, HE SAID, BUT I KNEW IT WOULD BE WORTH IT.

ALL I REMEMBER IS WALKING HOME AFTERWARDS AND FEELING A GREAT WEIGHT HAD BEEN LIFTED FROM MY SHOULDERS.

THROUGH A VERY SPECIFIC SET OF PATENTS AND INTELLECTUAL COPYRIGHTS, TOUCHSTONE WOULD BE PROTECTED.

NOTHING COULD TAKE IT FROM US NOW.

AND MY BROTHER WOULD BE PROTECTED TOO. AND ALL THAT HE'D WORKED FOR.

OUTSIDE OF THE TWO PEOPLE WHO SAT IN THAT OFFICE THAT DAY, NO ONE KNEW OF MY VISIT.

OR WHAT IT WAS ABOUT.

ONE OR TWO PROGRAMMERS AT GLOBE HAD PROVIDED ME WITH VITAL DOCUMENTS.

BUT THEY ASSUMED KORNEAS HAD REQUESTED THEM.

I THINK I SLEPT THAT NIGHT FOR THE FIRST TIME IN MONTHS.

I REMEMBER SAYING AT THAT FIRST MEETING THAT ONE MAN'S IDEALIST IS ANOTHER MAN'S FANTASIST. AND THAT MY BROTHER HAD ALWAYS BEEN AN IDEALIST.
BUT SO MUCH MORE SO SINCE HE'D BEEN KNOCKING AROUND WITH HAL.
YOU SEE, KORNEAS ALWAYS BELIEVED THAT INDIVIDUALS WERE INHERENTLY GOOD AND DECENT AND THAT ALL GREED WAS CORPORATE IN SOME MANNER.
YEAH, WE NEVER AGREED ABOUT THAT EITHER!

HE THOUGHT I WAS CYNICAL AND NEGATIVE!
BUT TELL ME THIS, WHO EVER DIED OF BEING CYNICAL?

YOU DO REALISE, DON'T YOU?
THAT'S QUITE POSSIBLY THE MOST CYNICAL THING ANYONE'S EVER SAID!

HAH. THAT'S PROBABLY TRUE. BUT ANYWAY THAT FEELING OF RELIEF AND VICTORY I HAD WAS ONLY TEMPORARY.

A WEEK OR SO LATER, HAL WAS TAKEN IN TO HOSPITAL IN NEW ORLEANS.

HE'D HAD ANOTHER BAD EPISODE AND ON THAT FIRST NIGHT, MY BROTHER AND WILL SAT OUTSIDE IN THE CORRIDOR THE ENTIRE TIME WAITING FOR NEWS.

BUT JUST LIKE FESTE AND THE THREE FOOLS, IT WAS ANOTHER MOMENT WHEN CIRCUMSTANCE OR FATE CHANGED THE ENTIRE DIRECTION OF KORNEAS' LIFE.

THEY SAT IN SILENCE FOR HOURS UNTIL WILL SAID...

SHALL I... SHALL I TELL YOU WHAT I'M GOING TO MISS THE MOST? THE ABSOLUTE MOST OF ALL?

EVEN MORE THAN ALL THE STORIES WE'VE BEEN MAKING UP OVER THE YEARS...

EVER SINCE WE GOT TO NEW ORLEANS, I HAVEN'T BEEN ABLE TO STOP THINKING ABOUT IT...
IT'S NOT THE MUSIC, THE SINGING, OR EVEN THE PERFORMING, THAT'S JUST WHAT WE **DO**. NO! THE TRUE SENSE OF US IS IN THE ACTUAL SONGWRITING. THAT'S WHAT WE **ARE.**
WE'VE BEEN DOING IT FOR FORTY FIVE YEARS! AND THESE PAST FEW WEEKS MADE ME REALIZE HOW LUCKY I AM. HAL AND I ARE CONNECTED IN A MILLION WAYS. IN WAYS MOST PEOPLE JUST COULDN'T UNDERSTAND.
BUT **NEVER** ARE WE CONNECTED MORE THAN WHEN WE'RE WRITING SONGS TOGETHER.
I ALWAYS WANTED TO WRITE A BOOK WITH HAL BUT I GUESS THAT WILL NEVER HAPPEN NOW.
BUT THIS WHOLE BATCH OF NEW NUMBERS WE'VE WRITTEN SINCE WE'VE BEEN HERE HAS BEEN THE BEST THING THAT COULD HAVE HAPPENED. AND ALSO THE WORST!
SO IF YOUR MAGIC TOUCHSTONE MACHINE COULD GRANT WISHES...
THEN I'D JUST WISH FOR HAL AND I TO CARRY ON WRITING SONGS...
FOREVER...

AND YOU SEE, RIGHT THEN! THAT WAS THE PRECISE SECOND IT HAPPENED! AS WILL SAID, SHE AND HAL HAD AN AMAZING CONNECTION.
YES, BUT AT THAT MOMENT MY BROTHER BECAME PART OF THAT BOND. AND IDOLECT WAS BORN.
OH, BUT THE AMAZING BOLT OF ELECTRICITY SPARKING BETWEEN THEM IN THAT COSMIC BLINK OF AN EYE? THAT WAS WHAT HE ONCE CALLED THE GENIUS PARTICLE!

...WELL, ON A FUNDAMENTAL LEVEL THAT WOULD BE NO MORE THAN A SIMPLE QUESTION OF DATA.
ALTHOUGH...
...WE WOULD BE TALKING ABOUT AN ABSOLUTELY STAGGERING, COLOSSAL AMOUNT OF DATA!
BUT DEFINITELY FINITE. AND CERTAINLY NOT INFINITE! SO IN THEORY, IT COULD BE STORED, ACCESSED AND PROCESSED.
YEAH, YOU KNOW WHAT, WILL? I RECKON WE COULD DO SOMETHING LIKE THAT FOR YOU. BUT YOU'LL NEED TO GET THAT MAN OF YOURS TO COOPERATE!
IN FACT, HE'LL NEED TO BE ANSWERING AN AMAZING NUMBER OF QUESTIONS AND DOING A WHOLE LOT OF TALKING!
DO YOU THINK YOU CAN DO THAT?

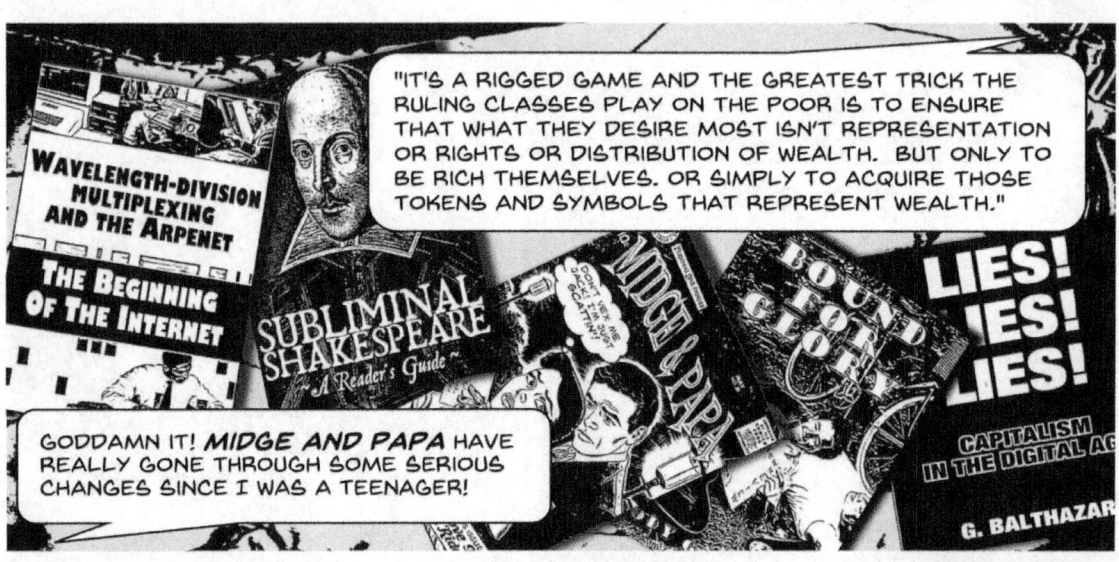

THEY ACTUALLY KEPT HAL IN HOSPITAL FOR A COUPLE OF DAYS.

WHICH GAVE KORNEAS A BIT OF TIME HE COULD SPEND WORKING ON THIS LATEST IDEA.

WHEN THEY FINALLY PICKED HAL UP, HE SEEMED FINE. ANXIOUS TO GET BACK TO WORK IN FACT!

DID YOU MANAGE TO LOOK AT ANY OF THE BOOKS I BROUGHT IN?

"IT'S A RIGGED GAME AND THE GREATEST TRICK THE RULING CLASSES PLAY ON THE POOR IS TO ENSURE THAT WHAT THEY DESIRE MOST ISN'T REPRESENTATION OR RIGHTS OR DISTRIBUTION OF WEALTH. BUT ONLY TO BE RICH THEMSELVES. OR SIMPLY TO ACQUIRE THOSE TOKENS AND SYMBOLS THAT REPRESENT WEALTH."

GODDAMN IT! *MIDGE AND PAPA* HAVE REALLY GONE THROUGH SOME SERIOUS CHANGES SINCE I WAS A TEENAGER!

ANYWAY, GET A MOVE ON! KORNEAS IS OUTSIDE IN THE CAR WAITING FOR US.

AND HE'S GOT AN AMAZING NEW IDEA. ONE THAT WILL MAKE YOU AND YOUR MUSIC TRULY IMMORTAL!

OH I DUNNO ABOUT THAT... WILL IT HURT?

I MEAN, WHEN HE FREEZES ME...

ACT FOUR — SCENE FIVE

"IT WAS ACTUALLY WILL WHO CAME UP WITH THE NAME *IDIOLECT!* MY BROTHER HAD PROBABLY JUST THOUGHT OF IT AS BEING ANOTHER BRANCH OR SOME SORT OF OFFSHOOT OF TOUCHSTONE."

"BUT WILL WAS INSISTENT! SHE SAID THE WORD WAS IN A BOOK SHE'D RECENTLY READ ABOUT SHAKESPEARE."

"IN FACT, THE NAME WAS DECIDED ON BEFORE THEY'D EVEN TOLD HAL ABOUT IT!"

BUT HAL WAS HARD TO PIN DOWN, HE WAS ALWAYS IN SO MUCH OF A HURRY. THEY HAD ONLY BEEN APART 48 HOURS BUT IN THAT TIME HE AND WILL HAD BOTH WRITTEN NEW SONGS!

IRONICALLY, ACH *OBVIOUSLY*, THEY'D EACH WRITTEN ABOUT THE OTHER! AND ON WHAT WOULD BE THEIR FINAL DAY IN THE STUDIO, THEY BOTH RECORDED THEIR NEW SONGS.

THEY SANG THE SONG THAT HAL HAD WRITTEN ABOUT WILL...

"IF IT AIN'T BROKE DON'T FIX IT. THAT'S WHAT MISS WILLOW SAYS. IF IT AIN'T BROKE DON'T FIX IT. IN ANY OLD KIND OF MESS!"

"WELL, I STAY IN STEP AND I WALK THE LINE. I KEEP HER SECRETS AND SHE KEEPS MINE!"

THEN THEY RECORDED WILL'S SONG ABOUT HAL...

"AT NIGHT WHEN THE MOON'S HIGH IN THE SKY AND YOU THINK THAT LIFE'S JUST PASSING YOU BY YOU MIGHT BE RIGHT OR YOU MIGHT BE WRONG BUT I THINK I HEAR SOMEONE PLAYING OUR SONG!"

"IF WE JUST KEEP TRAVELLING THE ROAD WE'RE ON, THERE'S ALWAYS ONE MORE JUKE AND ONE MORE HONKY TONK."

BUT HAL WAS UNDER NO ILLLUSIONS WHATSOEVER. HE KNEW EXACTLY HOW ILL HE WAS.
ON THEIR LAST NIGHT IN NEW ORLEANS, THEY WALKED AROUND THE FRENCH QUARTER TOGETHER AND KORNEAS FINALLY EXPLAINED TO HAL WHAT THE NEW PROJECT WAS ALL ABOUT.
ALTHOUGH EVERY TIME KORNEAS SAID 'SHOULD THE WORST HAPPEN', AND 'FUTURE PLANS' AND 'LONGER TERM IDEAS', HAL KNEW PRECISELY WHAT HE WAS REFERRING TO.
*COUGH, COUGH
SO, WHO'S THE IDIOT? AM I THE IDIOT? OK, SAY ALL THAT AGAIN.
HA HA HA! IDIOLECT! FOR THE HUNDREDTH TIME!
IN BASIC TERMS, IT'S MUCH LIKE TOUCHSTONE. A PROGRAM, A USER INTERFACE AND ACCESSIBLE DATA.
BUT A STAGGERING AMOUNT OF UNIQUE VERY PERSONAL DATA.
AND THAT PRECISE UNIQUE VERY PERSONAL PERSON...
...WOULD BE YOU, BABY!

IDOLECT WILL BE A SYSTEM, A METHOD, BY WHICH CHAPTER 25 CAN CONTINUE TO WRITE SONGS... ER, INDEFINITELY.
SO WE START BY CREATING AN ESSENTIALLY SENTIENT A.I. VERSION OF HAL. ONE THAT'S HAD ALL YOUR LIFE EXPERIENCES, THE SAME BACKGROUND, THE SAME EDUCATION AS YOU.
ONE THAT VISITED EXACTLY THE SAME PLACES. READ YOUR BOOKS, LISTENED TO ALL YOUR RECORDS, ONE THAT THINKS LIKE YOU AND EVEN TALKS LIKE YOU!
ALL THAT INFORMATION IS STORED AS HARD DATA AND BASED ON THE TOUCHSTONE INTERFACE WE CAN THEN BUILD A FULLY RESPONSIVE AND CREATIVE VIRTUAL HAL.
THIS MEANS THAT WILL CAN CARRY ON WRITING SONGS WITH YOUR INPUT. AS EFFECTIVELY YOUR MEMORY AND INTELLECT WILL BE STORED WITHIN THE PROGRAM.
BUT WE'LL NEED TO KNOW ABSOLUTELY EVERYTHING ABOUT YOU.
ALTHOUGH, HAL, I CAN PERSONALLY GUARANTEE THAT AT NO POINT DURING THIS PROCESS YOU WILL HAVE ELECTRODES ATTACHED TO YOU!
YEAH, OK, THAT WAS MY NEXT QUESTION!
BUT I'M AFRAID YOU WILL BE ASKED THOUSANDS OF QUESTIONS. AND YOU'LL NEED TO PROVIDE AN AMAZING AMOUNT OF DETAIL ABOUT YOURSELF.

SO I APOLOGIZE IN ADVANCE FOR ALL THE VISITORS YOU'LL BE HAVING IN THE COMING MONTHS. BUT WHEN IT GETS ON YOUR NERVES JUST REMEMBER IT'S NOT JUST THE MUSIC, HOWEVER GREAT IT MIGHT BE, IT'S EVEN MORE IMPORTANT THAT THE *MESSAGE* LIVES ON.

WELL, IF YOU'RE TALKING ABOUT MESSAGES, YOU DON'T NEED TO WORRY SO MUCH ABOUT FORMAL EDUCATION.

BECAUSE I CAN TELL YOU ONE THING RIGHT NOW FOR A CERTAIN FACT! SOMETHING THAT UNITES OUR ENTIRE WRETCHED SPECIES!

AND IT DOESN'T MATTER IF IT'S A BOOK OR A POEM, OR EVEN A LINE OF VERSE. IT COULD BE A PAINTING. IT MIGHT BE MUSIC. IT COULD APPLY EQUALLY TO THAT ONE SONG! MAYBE JUST A SINGLE LYRIC?

SIMILARLY, IT COULD BE A SCENE FROM A MOVIE AS MUCH AS THE ENTIRE WORKS OF A SINGLE DIRECTOR. OF COURSE, IT MIGHT BE A TV SHOW. BUT I WILL GUARANTEE YOU THIS...

THAT AT SOME POINT IN THE GREAT INCALCULABLE VASTNESS OF EVERY HUMAN LIFE, *WE ARE, ALL OF US, SAVED BY ART!*

I THINK HAL COULD GRASP THE BASIC CONCEPT BEHIND IDIOLECT EVEN IF HE DID FIND ALL THE TECHNOLOGY TOTALLY BEWILDERING!
MAYBE HE JUST TRUSTED YOUR BROTHER? AND TRUSTED HIS MOTIVES?
YES, YOU KNOW, I THINK HE DID.
ANYWAY, THEY STARTED WORKING ON THE PROJECT AS SOON AS THEY WERE HOME AGAIN.
KORNEAS USED SOME OF HIS TOUCHSTONE TEAM TO WORK AS RESEARCHERS, 'DATA STALKING' HE CALLED IT AND THEY SPENT ABOUT 12 HOURS EVERY DAY WITH HAL.
SO DID YOU TELL HIM ABOUT YOUR VISIT WITH THE ATTORNEY?
ACH, I NEVER GOT THE CHANCE. I WANTED TO BUT WE WERE ALWAYS SO BUSY. HE WAS SO INVOLVED WITH HAL AND THE LAUNCH DATE FOR TOUCHSTONE WAS APPROACHING.
AND THEN OF COURSE BY THAT POINT, I'D GOT THE LETTER. OR RATHER THE ***FIRST*** LETTER.
EH? WHAT LETTER?

IT WASN'T EXACTLY AMBIGUOUS OR LEFT MUCH SCOPE FOR MULTIPLE INTERPRETATIONS!

OH MAN, THAT MUST HAVE BEEN **TERRIFYING!**

I'D FOUND IT WHILE KORNEAS WAS IN NEW ORLEANS, LEFT ON THE WINDSHIELD OF MY CAR. IN OTHER WORDS, NOT LONG AFTER I'D SPOKEN TO THAT FUCKING ATTORNEY!

YOU MEAN, YOU THINK HE...?

TOUCHTONE will DIE! OR Your BROTHER WILL DIE

AS KORNEAS USED TO SAY, *BECAUSE A MAN BELIEVES IN FATE, IT DOESN'T MEAN HE BELIEVES IN COINCIDENCE!*

AND MAYBE IT'S A PRIMAL, ANIMAL INSTINCT BUT I KNEW STRAIGHT AWAY WHAT WAS HAPPENING AND WHERE THERE HAD BEEN A LEAK. *A WORD IN THE RIGHT EAR,* AS THEY SAY. ACH, I GUESS HE SAW AN OPPORTUNITY AND IT'S NOT ABOUT HONESTY OR INTEGRITY, SOMETIMES IT'S JUST ABOUT BEING HUMAN.

COULD IT NOT HAVE BEEN SOMEONE FROM GLOBE WITH A GRUDGE?

NO, NO CHANCE!

SO, IS THAT YOUR INSTINCT AGAIN?

NAH, ANYONE FROM GLOBE WOULD HAVE KNOWN HOW TO SPELL TOUCHSTONE!

ACT FOUR

SCENE SIX

YEAH, WELL OK, IF YOU WERE RIGHT, I CAN TOTALLY SEE WHY YOU WOULDN'T BE TOO POSITIVE ABOUT ATTORNEYS.

BUT YOU KNOW, I CAN EASILY BELIEVE *ALL* THAT. ONE OR TWO I'VE MET WOULD DEFINITELY BE *MORE* THAN CAPABLE OF DOING SOMETHING SO SHITTY.

I'M SO SORRY.

EH, WHAT ARE YOU SORRY ABOUT?

I'M SORRY FOR TOTALLY AND COMPLETELY MISJUDGING YOU, MOLLY.

HAH, YOU KNOW WHAT? I RECKON WE SHOULD RUN AWAY TOGETHER...

YES, WE TOTALLY SHOU...

... AND DIG PITS AND SET TRAPS TO CAPTURE EVERY SNEAKY FUCKING ATTORNEY THAT'S STILL OUT THERE!

OH? HA HA, YES...GOOD IDEA!

SO WHY COULDN'T YOU JUST TELL KORNEAS THAT YOU'D BEEN TO SEE AN ATTORNEY? EXPLAIN ABOUT THE LETTER AND, I DON'T KNOW, WARN HIM IN SOME WAY?
I KNOW I SHOULD HAVE SAID SOMETHING BUT THEN I WOULD'VE HAD TO TELL HIM THAT I'D GONE BEHIND HIS BACK. HE WOULD HAVE FELT SO HURT AND ANGRY.
BUT WAS THERE ANYONE ELSE AT GLOBE YOU COULD HAVE SPOKEN TO? OR EVEN THE POLICE?
OF COURSE, I THOUGHT ABOUT THAT. BUT I KNEW THAT IT WOULD ALL SOMEHOW GET BACK TO KORNEAS.
AND BESIDES HE WAS SO INVOLVED WITH HAL AND IDIOLECT, I BARELY SAW ANYTHING OF HIM.
YEAH, ACTUALLY 'BUG' IS JUST A TINY BIT OVERDRAMATIC, HAL!
I THINK NOWADAYS AND IN CONTEXT THE TERM WOULD BE A 'LIVE AUDIO FEED'.
BUT IF IT MAKES YOU HAPPY, JUST FOR TODAY, WHILE WE SET EVERYTHING UP, WE CAN STICK TO '*THAT WATERGATE SHIT*'!
ANYWAY, IT'S JUST GOING TO BE FIXED ABOVE THE CENTRAL LIGHT FIXTURE HERE. AND IT WILL RECORD ALL YOUR DAILY CONVERSATIONS AND INTERACTIONS. ***EVERYTHING!***
OH YEAH AND BEFORE YOU ASK ***THAT*** QUESTION ...
...THERE'S A MASTER SWITCH OVER HERE AND SO WHENEVER YOU WANT TO BE, YOU KNOW ... PRIVATE, YOU CAN JUST DISABLE THE FEED.

You see in addition to logging all the music you've ever listened to, every book and every movie...

We also need an accurate record of your precise manner of speaking.

Everyone has a unique way of using language, choice of words, repetition, favorite phrases.

And I suppose that's basically what's meant by *idiolect*.

cough, cough!

It's like a fingerprint, I guess.

So when is all this happening? When did you say these 'data stalkers' of yours were coming?

Ha, no, don't worry about that. It would play havoc with their expense claims!

And will they expect lunch?

But they should definitely be with you no later than Wednesday.

YEAH, WEDNESDAY IS FINE. WE'RE DOING ANOTHER FUNDRAISER AT THE THREE FOOLS ON TUESDAY. YOU'LL COME WITH US, I HOPE. BUT WE'LL BE HERE ALL DAY WEDNESDAY...
*COUGH, COUGH!
ACTUALLY...
ACTUALLY, BABY, I DON'T THINK I'LL BE ABLE TO DO TUESDAY. TO BE HONEST, I JUST... I JUST DON'T FEEL LIKE I'M GOING TO BE UP TO IT.
MAYBE NEW ORLEANS TOOK IT OUT OF ME MORE THAN I THOUGHT BUT I SIMPLY DON'T HAVE THE ENERGY... I'M SORRY. I'LL CALL THEM TOMORROW.
ER, OK, BABY.
*COUGH, COUGH!

POOR WILL! I THINK THAT WAS THE PRECISE MOMENT WHEN SHE FINALLY ACCEPTED THAT HAL WOULD NEVER GET BETTER. AND IT WAS REALLY ONLY A MATTER OF TIME.

THE STRANGE THING IS, FROM WHAT MY BROTHER TOLD ME, HAL ACTUALLY SEEMED TO ENJOY BEING 'DATA STALKED'!

I THINK HE LOVED TALKING TO THE PEOPLE FROM GLOBE RESEARCH ABOUT ALL THE IMPORTANT THINGS IN HIS LIFE. HIS POLITICS AND HIS MUSIC AND EVERYTHING.

KORNEAS SAID HAL MADE HIM THINK ABOUT AN OLD PUCKITANIAN SAYING. THE ONE THAT SORT OF TRANSLATES AS –

'THE MEASURE OF A MAN'S ENTHUSIASMS CAN BEST BE JUDGED BY THE JOY HE DERIVES IN SHARING THEM!'

BUT HAL WAS BEING EXTREMELY BRAVE. ALTHOUGH THAT'S NOT TO SAY THAT WILL WASN'T BEING BRAVE AS WELL.

SOMETIMES AFTER A DAY IN THEIR COMPANY, I WOULD SEE MY BROTHER IN TEARS.

YEAH, I CAN IMAGINE WHY YOU WOULDN'T WANT TO TALK ABOUT LETTERS AND ATTORNEYS AT THOSE TIMES.

BUT THAT MUST HAVE BEEN TOUGH FOR YOU TOO.

IT WAS SUCH A DIFFICULT TIME WITH ALL THE OTHER STUFF GOING ON. THERE WERE MORE LETTERS. AND ALWAYS THE SAME MESSAGE.
AND THEN I STARTED BEING FOLLOWED EVERYWHERE...
OH FUCK, SERGEI! I MEAN, ARE YOU SURE?
OF COURSE I'M SURE! THEY WEREN'T EXACTLY SUBTLE! BUT THAT WAS THE WHOLE POINT.
THEY WANTED ME TO KNOW I WAS BEING FOLLOWED!
I DON'T KNOW, MAYBE I COULD HAVE IGNORED ALL THAT...
... BUT THEN THEY STARTED SENDING ME THE PHOTOGRAPHS.

ACT FOUR. SCENE SEVEN.

THEY WERE IN AN ENVELOPE LEFT ON THE WINDSHIELD OF MY CAR AGAIN. AND ALSO SENT TO ME AS AN EMAIL FROM A SERVER THAT NO LONGER EXISTED THE MOMENT I TRIED TO TRACE IT.

DOZENS OF PICTURES OF MY BROTHER WITH WILL AND HAL OUTSIDE THEIR RV. TAKEN IN THE PREVIOUS COUPLE OF WEEKS.

THEY WERE SENT TO ME FOR ONE REASON ONLY!

TO SHOW ME THAT THEY KNEW EXACTLY WHERE KORNEAS WAS! I DIDN'T EVEN KNOW WHERE WILL AND HAL PARKED THEIR VAN. IN FACT I NEVER HAD THE REMOTEST IDEA! *BUT THEY FUCKING KNEW!*

BUT OF ALL THE EVENTS IN THIS STORY, THE THING THAT HAPPENED NEXT IS THE ONE THAT I REGRET THE MOST.

I ADMIT MY MIND WAS OCCUPIED WITH THE LETTERS AND THE PHOTOGRAPHS BUT I WAS CONCERNED THAT KORNEAS WAS SPENDING ALL HIS TIME WITH HAL.

HE'D PULLED A LOT OF THE TOUCHSTONE TEAM TO WORK ON IDIOLECT. WE HAD BEEN HAVING REGULAR PRODUCTION MEETINGS ON TOUCHSTONE BUT HE KEPT MISSING THEM. IT REMINDED ME OF HIS TIME WITH ROSALIND.

SO STUPIDLY, I CONFRONTED HIM!

... WELL, WHERE ARE YOUR PRIORITIES NOW, MY BROTHER?

THEN TELL ME WHY HAVE YOU ABANDONED TOUCHSTONE?

YOU ARE TURNING YOUR BACK ON THE MILLIONS YOU CAN SAVE! ALL FOR THE SAKE OF A SINGLE MAN YOU CANNOT!

HEY, THAT IS NOT FAIR!

WHY WOULD YOU EVEN SAY SOMETHING LIKE THAT?

WHY DOES EVERYTHING ALWAYS HAVE TO BE REDUCED TO A SIMPLE BLACK OR WHITE CHOICE WITH YOU?

I KNOW I WAS IN A STATE OF PANIC BUT I SAID SOME IDIOTIC THINGS THAT NIGHT. BAD THINGS.

BUT IT'S A FACT THAT IN ORDER TO HAVE BRILLIANT PEOPLE LIKE HAL AND MY BROTHER...

SLAAAAAAM!!

...YOU WILL ALWAYS NEED STUPID, MORONIC PEOPLE LIKE ME BY WHICH YOU CAN JUDGE THEM!

ACH, BUT IT WAS A RIDICULOUS ARGUMENT AND I DON'T BLAME KORNEAS FOR WALKING OUT.

I KNOW, I KNOW! DON'T LOOK AT ME LIKE THAT!

I DIDN'T KNOW WHERE HE WENT. BUT A COUPLE OF DAYS LATER I RECEIVED ANOTHER PHOTO. I GUESS IT WAS NO SURPRISE HE'D BEEN WITH WILL AND HAL.

BUT THIS TIME THERE WAS A MESSAGE THAT ARRIVED WITH THE PHOTO.

AND THAT WAS THE THING WHICH TRULY TERRIFIED ME.

Sorry to hear about your ARGUMENT! ☹

AND IT REALLY WAS A MESSAGE IN BOTH SENSES OF THE WORD! HOW COULD THEY HAVE EVEN KNOWN ABOUT THAT? THEY WERE GETTING FAR TOO CLOSE.

WHATEVER THEY PAID THAT FUCKING ATTORNEY, THEY WERE TOTALLY GETTING THEIR MONEY'S WORTH!

OH SERGEI! SO HOW LONG DID THIS GO ON WITH KORNEAS?

ACH, JUST A DAY OR TWO, IT WAS THE USUAL STUPID BROTHER STUFF!

ALTHOUGH IT RAISED AN ISSUE THAT WAS NEVER REALLY RESOLVED.

AND HE REMAINED SO TOTALLY FOCUSED ON HAL AND IDIOLECT AT THAT TIME IT WAS IMPOSSIBLE TO GET HIM TO EVEN TALK ABOUT TOUCHSTONE SOMETIMES!

BUT I KNEW I COULD NEVER TELL HIM ABOUT THE LETTERS OR THE PHOTOS WITHOUT HIM KNOWING I HAD BETRAYED HIS CONFIDENCE.

AND THEN HAL HAD ANOTHER REALLY BAD EPISODE AND WAS BACK IN HOSPITAL AGAIN.

THIS TIME THE DOCTORS REALLY WEREN'T OPTIMISTIC AND THERE SEEMED VERY LITTLE CHANCE OF HIM ACTUALLY GOING HOME.

BUT YOU KNOW HAL...

* COUGH, COUGH! ... AND AS FAR AS MUSIC IS CONCERNED ... I ABSOLUTELY MUST INCLUDE ... THE ER ... HARRY SMITH ANTHOLOGY! FUCK, MAN, THOSE RECORDS WERE SO ... SO IMPORTANT...

OH, ER, DID I MENTION THAT ALREADY?

* COUGH, COUGH!

YEAH, ACTUALLY ON THE FIRST DAY, I THINK!

OH, YOU SHOULDN'T BE WORRYING ABOUT ALL THAT NOW, BABY. DOCTOR SAID YOU NEED TO REST.

* COUGH, COUGH!

ON ... ONE CONDITION.

OH, AND WHAT WOULD THAT BE?

YOU, YOU BRING YOUR GUITAR IN TOMORROW ... AND SING FOR ME.

BECAUSE IF ANYTHING IS GOING TO GET ME THROUGH ... THIS ... IT WILL BE THE SOUND OF YOU ... YOU SINGING ...

AH, BUT WILL HAD SOMETHING DIFFERENT IN MIND THAT SHE WANTED TO DO FOR HAL.

SHE WENT THROUGH THEIR ENTIRE RV WHEN SHE GOT BACK JUST SEARCHING FOR THIS ONE FORGOTTEN ITEM!

AH-HA! THERE YOU ARE, YOU SNEAKY LITTLE DEVIL!

I KNEW YOU HAD TO BE AROUND HERE SOMEPLACE OR ANOTHER!

SO SHE COPIED THIS OLD SONG ONTO HER PHONE AND WENT BACK TO SEE HAL THE NEXT DAY.

*COUGH, COUGH! OH, DIDN'T THEY LET YOU BRING YOUR ... GUITAR IN THEN?
NO, I HAVEN'T GOT MY GUITAR, BABY. BUT GUESS WHAT? I'VE BROUGHT SOMETHING ALONG THAT'S EVEN BETTER!
WILL REMINDED HAL OF ONE OF THE FIRST SONGS HE HAD EVER WRITTEN, FROM BACK IN THE SIXTIES WHEN HE WAS STILL JUST A TEENAGER.
WILL HAD ALWAYS LOVED ME AND MY BIKE AND CHERISHED THE ONE ROUGH RECORDING HAL HAD MADE AT THE TIME.
MANY TIMES THEY'D PLANNED TO RE-RECORD THE SONG AS CHAPTER 25. BUT FOR ALL KINDS OF REASONS THIS HAD NEVER MATERIALIZED.
SO THAT DAY WILL HAD DECIDED TO FINALLY MAKE IT HAPPEN FOR HAL.
WILL PLAYED THE OLD ORIGINAL TRACK ON HER PHONE AND SANG ALONG.
Me And My Bike
"WATCH AS WE RUSH BY, MY, MY, MY... SAILING THROUGH THE STARING SKY."
"BUT THEY'LL NEVER FIND A WAY TO SEPARATE ME FROM MY BIKE."
HAL SMILED AND CRIED AND EVEN TRIED TO SING ALONG TOO! AND IN THOSE AWFUL HOURS, APART FROM EACH OTHER, WHAT THEY BOTH NEEDED MOST WAS THEIR MUSIC.

YOU KNOW, WHENEVER I THINK OF WILL AND HAL, THEY'LL ALWAYS REMAIN MY DEFINITION OF THE MOST PERFECT COUPLE OF ALL. I THINK OF ALL THE STORIES, JUST LIKE THAT ONE, WHICH ATTACHED THEMSELVES TO THEM OVER THE YEARS.

IT'S LIKE THEY SHARED THIS KIND OF ANCIENT ELECTRICITY. BECAUSE, REGARDLESS OF ANY CIRCUMSTANCE OR SITUATION, THEY NEVER STOPPED MAKING THESE SMALL BUT WONDERFUL MAGICAL MOMENTS TOGETHER.

A.N.A.Y.N.M.T.B.

I.C.B.T.B.A.F.Y.

AND BE IT FATE, BE IT COINCIDENCE OR BE IT CHANCE?
ON EXACTLY THE SAME DAY THAT WILL WAS SINGING TO HAL, I NOTICED THAT FESTE WAS BECOMING CLEARLY VERY ANXIOUS AND AGITATED.
ALL DAY HE WOULDN'T EAT OR SETTLE AND I THOUGHT HE MIGHT BE UNWELL OR SOMETHING.

ACH. AND OF COURSE HE PULLED HIS USUAL STUNT AS SOON AS I LEFT HIM ALONE FOR FIVE MINUTES.
AND I GUESS THAT PROBABLY COMES AS NO SURPRISE WHATSOEVER!
HAH, OR THE LOCATION WHERE I FINALLY MANAGED TO CATCH UP WITH HIM!

AND YOU KNOW SOMETHING? THAT DAFT DOG AND I MAY HAVE HAD OUR DIFFERENCES.
The Three Fools
FRI-SAT
CLOWNS OF TYRANTS
BUT FESTE SAVED MY LIFE THAT NIGHT!

WHILE WE WERE AWAY, MY HOUSE WAS COMPLETELY BURNED TO THE GROUND!

LUCKILY THERE WAS NO ONE IN THE BUILDING AT THE TIME. BUT IF IT WASN'T FOR FESTE, I WOULD HAVE BEEN AT HOME ALL EVENING.

THE FIRE DEPARTMENT SAID IT WAS 'VERY MYSTERIOUS'.

EXCEPT IT WASN'T REALLY MYSTERIOUS AT ALL...

...NOT IN THE LEAST.

IT'S JUST THE MESSAGE YOU ARE SENT AFTER YOU'VE IGNORED ALL THE OTHER MESSAGES...

ACT FIVE

ACT FIVE

SCENE ONE

I'M SO SORRY, MOLLY, I REALLY AM. I DON'T WANT YOU TO THINK I WAS RUNNING AWAY. I WOULD NEVER... I JUST REALLY NEEDED SOME FRESH AIR.
BUT IT WAS A TERRIBLE, TERRIBLE NIGHT! I STILL HAVE DREAMS ABOUT IT. EVEN NOW.
FUCK, SERGEI! I THINK I MIGHT BE MORE WORRIED IF A PERSON WASN'T PERMANENTLY TRAUMATIZED BY SOMETHING LIKE THAT!
MY BROTHER WAS THERE WITH ME WITHIN A MATTER OF HALF AN HOUR.
THAT WAS WHEN HE TOLD ME THAT HAL HAD DIED THAT DAY.
APPARENTLY, HIS FINAL WORDS WERE THAT ***ME AND MY BIKE*** HAD ALWAYS BEEN HIS MOM'S FAVORITE SONG...
YOU KNOW, IN MY COUNTRY WE HAVE A TERM FOR WHEN YOU ULTIMATELY AND IRREVOCABLY LOSE THAT ONE LAST LINGERING FINAL TRACE OF YOUR INNOCENCE.
AND IT WAS, I THINK, AT THAT PRECISE MOMENT THAT MY BROTHER AND I BOTH HAD OUR PERSONAL ***NEMA NEVINOSTI.***

AND YOU KNOW, BECAUSE OF THE WAY THINGS ESCALATED AFTER THAT DAY, I NEVER HAD A PLACE OF MY OWN AGAIN.
I MUST ADMIT THAT'S THE POINT WHEN I WOULD HAVE IMMEDIATELY RUN AWAY!
AH, BUT WHEN YOU RUN AWAY, MOLLY, IT'S NOT WHERE YOU'RE RUNNING TO OR WHAT YOU'RE RUNNING FROM BUT ONLY ***WHO*** YOU ARE RUNNING AWAY WITH!
AND ON MY OWN I WAS A COWARD. SO I HID MYSELF AWAY AND FOR TEN YEARS NOW, I HAVE LIVED IN HOTELS, FOR NO LONGER THAN A NIGHT OR TWO. AND JUST AS OFTEN I SLEEP AT THE OFFICE.

BUT ALL MY PROBLEMS AT THAT TIME, I KNEW, WERE NOTHING COMPARED TO THOSE OF SOME PEOPLE.
WILL WAS INCONSOLABLE BUT WHILE SHE WAITED FOR THE INITIAL BETA VERSION OF THE IDIOLECT PROGRAM, SHE AND KORNEAS HAD ANOTHER IDEA.
TOGETHER THEY WENT THROUGH HAL'S UNRELEASED TRACKS AND HOME RECORDINGS AND MADE THEM ALL AVAILABLE VIA A NEW WEBSITE.

ALL THE DOWNLOADS WERE FREE PROVIDED YOU MADE A DONATION TO ONE OF THE CAUSES DEAR TO HAL'S HEART!
The CHAPTER 25
MEMORIAL LIBRARY
HAL LAVACHE 1950-2015
DIGITAL ALBUM
Streaming + Download
Buy Digital Album.
Nominate your Recipient
Name your price
1. Chickenshitboogie (1992)
2. No-Good Doctor And Captain Kicks (1979)
3. Aspirin And XXXX Cola (2008)

AND YEAH, I GUESS THAT IT WOULD NOT BE A SURPRISE TO ANYONE TO DISCOVER THAT OUR HAL WAS AN AVOWED ATHEIST!

AND LIKE HIS GREAT IDOL, WOODY GUTHRIE, HE JUST WANTED HIS ASHES TO BE SCATTERED INTO THE SEA.

OF COURSE THIS WAS A BIT OF A HEADACHE FOR WILL AS SURPRISINGLY CALIFORNIA HAS SOME VERY STRICT RULES ABOUT SUCH THINGS.

BUT ONCE AGAIN, MY BROTHER STEPPED IN AND SAID THAT HE'D FIX EVERYTHING.

I HAVE A YACHT...

HE TOLD HER. WHICH OF COURSE YOU CAN NEVER SAY OUT LOUD WITHOUT SOUNDING LIKE A TOTAL FUCKING DICK!

HE LEFT INSTRUCTIONS THAT HE DIDN'T WANT ANY SORT OF RELIGIOUS SERVICE IN ANY WAY. HE JUST WANTED TO BE CREMATED.

ACH, TO BE HONEST, I'D FORGOTTEN ALL ABOUT THAT STUPID BOAT. IT WAS ALL THE WAY UP AT BIG SUR SOMEWHERE.
BUT KORNEAS THOUGHT HIS YACHT WOULD BE THE BEST PLACE FOR WILL TO HOST A MEMORIAL FOR HAL.
SO THEY COULD SCATTER HIS ASHES INTO THE SEA JUST AS HE WISHED!
AW, BUT THERE WERE SO MANY, MANY PEOPLE WHO TURNED UP TO SAY THEIR GOODBYES.
THERE MUST HAVE BEEN COUNTLESS CODES AND PRACTICES THAT WERE VIOLATED THAT AFTERNOON!
YEAH, AND OF COURSE HAL WOULD HAVE TOTALLY LOVED THAT!
HAL LAVACHE – A TRIBUTE
Program
Opening
Spoken Eulogy by Will Lavache
"Strange Cat (For Hal)" Will Lavache
"Gags And Blindfolds" Will Lavache
OBVIOUSLY, I WAS THERE TOO. IF ONLY TO SUPPORT MY BROTHER. BUT I ACTUALLY SPENT TIME WITH WILL THAT DAY AS WELL.
IT WAS JUST BEFORE SHE READ HER AMAZING EULOGY.
AND SANG THE NEW SONG SHE'D RECENTLY WRITTEN ABOUT HAL.

"AND I'VE NEVER MET ANYONE QUITE LIKE THAT...

AND AS A MATTER OF FACT MY MAN WAS...

YEAH, I'VE NEVER MET ANYONE QUITE LIKE THAT...

AND AS A MATTER OF FACT THAT HAL WAS A...

...STRANGE CAT!"

ACT FIVE SCENE TWO

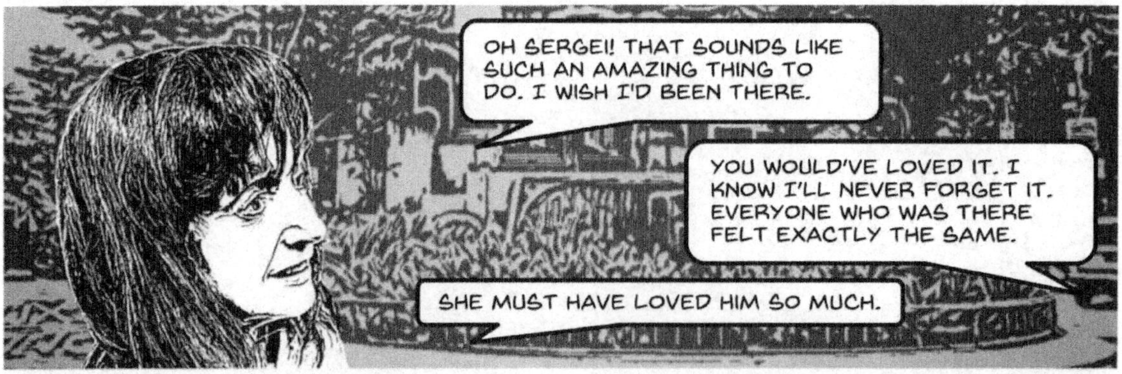

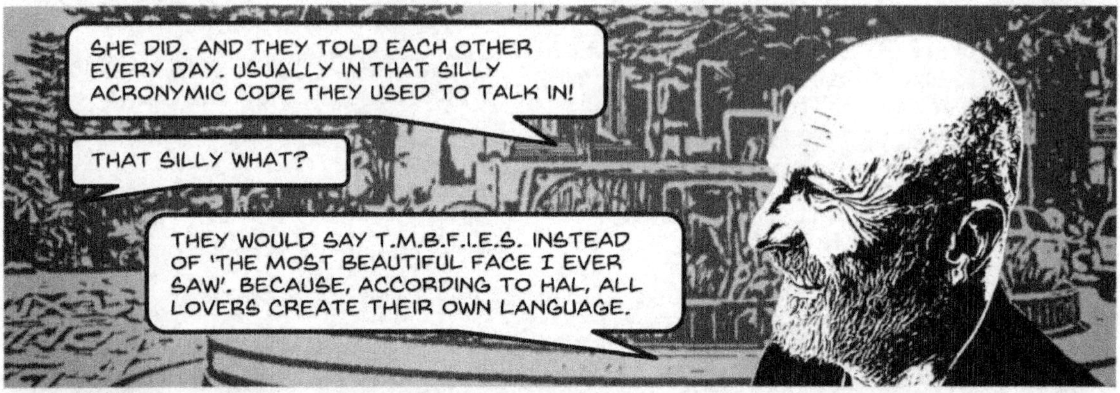

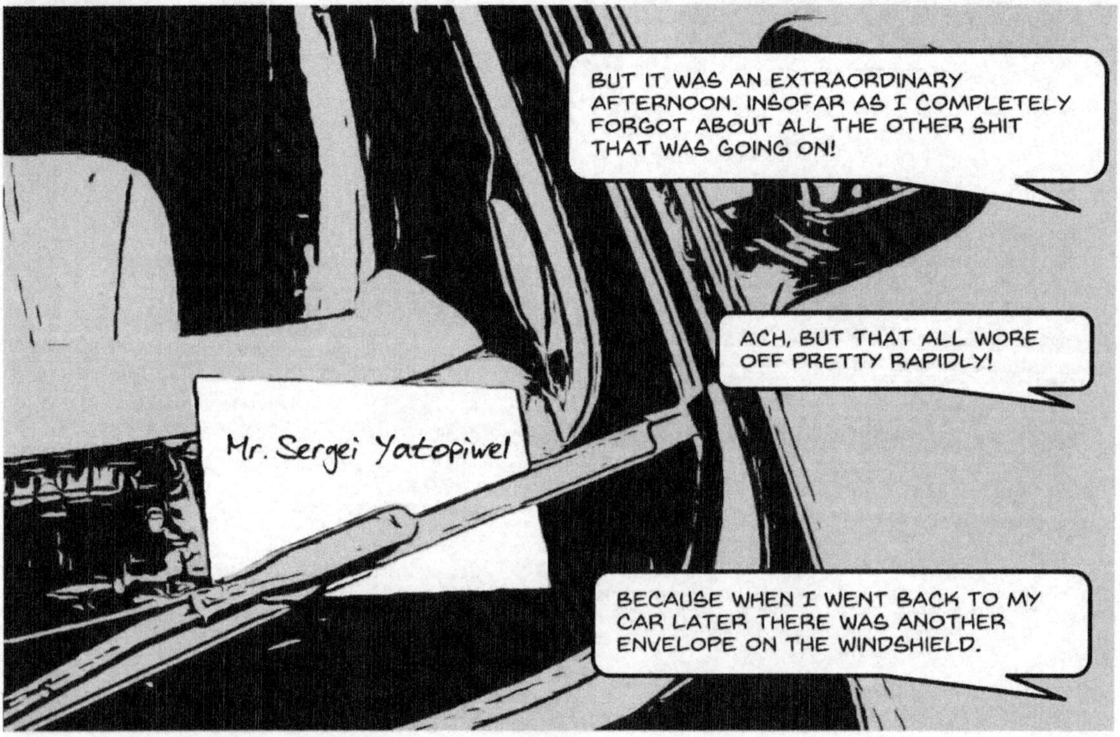

IT WAS STUFFED FULL OF CANDID, UNPOSED PHOTOS OF MOM AND DAD GARDENING AND JUST GENERALLY HANGING AROUND THEIR HOUSE OVER IN PUCKITANIA.

Oh, WHAT a lovely COUPLE! ☹

CLEARLY THIS WAS SURVEILLANCE. THERE IS NO OTHER WORD FOR IT.

ACH, I COULD HARDLY BEGIN TO COMPREHEND THE LENGTHS TO WHICH THEY MUST HAVE GONE TO EVEN LOCATE THEM.

BUT OF COURSE IT WAS INTENDED AS A DIRECT THREAT AND I TOOK IT AS SUCH.

AND THAT WAS THE MOMENT WHEN I REALIZED THAT WE WOULD *NEVER* WIN. WE HAD TAKEN ON TOO MUCH AND WE NEVER STOOD A CHANCE. NOT FOR A MINUTE.

ACCORDING TO KORNEAS, HAL USED TO SAY THAT CAPITALISM IS WITHOUT QUESTION THE PRIMARY SYSTEM. YET THERE EXISTS A SECOND EVEN MORE PERNICIOUS SYSTEM. ONE THAT HAS BEEN CREATED SOLELY TO PROTECT AND SAFEGUARD, AT ANY COST, THE INTERESTS OF CAPITALISTS.
YOU NEVER SEE THIS SECONDARY SYSTEM DIRECTLY. ALTHOUGH IT IS ***EVERYWHERE,*** YOU CAN ONLY FEEL ITS EFFECTS AND SEE THE SHADOW IT CASTS. BUT IT IS A GREAT AND DARK SHADOW.
I DROVE BACK TO MY HOTEL THAT NIGHT, ALONE BUT FOR THE COMPANY OF CERTAIN IMMUTABLE FACTS.
THEY WERE NEVER GOING TO GIVE UP.
BY GOING AGAINST MY BROTHER'S WISHES, I HAD BETRAYED HIM AND PUT ALL THOSE DEAR TO ME AT RISK.
THERE WAS A PRICE TO TOUCHSTONE THAT WAS IMPOSSIBLE TO CALCULATE.
OH SERGEI. I CAN'T EVEN IMAGINE HOW THAT FELT. DID YOU EVER SAY ANYTHING TO YOUR PARENTS?
ACH, THEY'D BOTH LIVED THROUGH THE PUCKITANIAN UPRISING OF '68 SO THEY'RE MADE OF STRONG STUFF!
ALTHOUGH I DID THINK IT WAS A GOOD TIME TO SEND THEM ON A SURPRISE ANNIVERSARY CRUISE TO THE CARIBBEAN FOR A COUPLE OF MONTHS!

I GOT RID OF MY CAR SHORTLY AFTER. NEVER BOUGHT ANOTHER! EVEN NOW I STILL TAKE CABS EVERYWHERE.
WELL, I WASN'T GOING TO MAKE IT EASY FOR THEM!
WELL, YOU KNOW WHAT THEY SAY? BE·WARY·THEN·BEST·SAFETY·LIES·IN·FEAR! SO WHAT ABOUT KORNEAS?
WHERE DID HE LIVE AFTER YOUR HOUSE BURNED DOWN?
ACH, A LOT OF THE TIME HE ACTUALLY STAYED ON HIS YACHT! BUT AFTER HAL DIED, HE ONCE AGAIN DEVOTED ALL HIS TIME TO IDIOLECT AND I DIDN'T FEEL IT WAS THE RIGHT TIME TO DISCUSS TOUCHSTONE.
SO NOT WISHING TO COMPOUND MY ONGOING ISSUES ANY FURTHER I MADE SURE THAT THE ONLY PEOPLE WHO EVER KNEW THE WORD *IDIOLECT* WERE MYSELF, KORNEAS AND WILL. AND WE TOOK NO CHANCES.
BUT I WAS CERTAIN THAT ALL THE EXTRA CAUTION WOULD LEAVE HER IN PEACE TO CARRY ON MAKING MUSIC.
MY BROTHER HAD SET UP AN OFFSHORE ACCOUNT THAT MADE REGULAR PAYMENTS TO WILL, WHICH WAS USED TO SECRETLY FUND IDIOLECT. EVEN THE ACCOUNT DIDN'T USE THE NAME!
AND AS YOU DISCOVERED FROM WILL'S BANK STATEMENTS, WE ACTUALLY JUST USED THE WORD TOUCHSTONE.

AND YES THERE WAS THAT SINGLE EMAIL THAT YOU FOUND LINKED TO ME WITH THE SUBJECT 'TOUCHSTONE'. OBVIOUSLY IT HAD NOTHING AT ALL TO DO WITH TOUCHSTONE!

IT WAS ACTUALLY SENT FROM KORNEAS TO WILL AND CONTAINED DETAILS OF ALL THE LINKED IDIOLECT ACCOUNTS AND CONTACT NUMBERS FOR TECH SUPPORT.

OF COURSE, IT MIGHT HAVE LOOKED LIKE A CUTE LITTLE SNAP OF FESTE BUT THERE WAS A QR CODE HIDDEN IN THE PICTURE TOO.

...HIDDEN?

ACH, HE ALWAYS LOVED THE IDEA OF CONCEALING THINGS.

EVEN MORE SO IF THEY WERE HIDING IN PLAIN SIGHT!

...WHAT?

OH, IT'S NOTHING.

IT WAS OF COURSE A VERY GOOD IDEA. BUT THAT WHOLE CODE THING CAME FROM KORNEAS. THAT WAS ALWAYS SOMETHING THAT INTERESTED HIM.

HAH, EVEN WHEN WE WERE KIDS. WE USED TO ALWAYS PLAY SPIES TOGETHER!

AH, YOU KNOW WHAT IT'S LIKE WITH SIBLINGS. THERE IS SELDOM ANY INTENT IT'S OFTEN JUST NO MORE THAN LUCK OR CIRCUMSTANCE.

BUT SOMETIMES YOU DRIFT INTO EACH OTHER'S ORBIT AND YOU ARE CLOSE. AND THEN OTHER TIMES YOU WILL JUST DRIFT APART AGAIN.

OF COURSE, THIS WASN'T ANYTHING LIKE ROSALIND. BUT SADLY I DID SEE QUITE A LOT LESS OF KORNEAS AT THAT TIME.

HOWEVER, THE LONG TERM PLAN REMAINED IN PLACE TO SELL GLOBE IN ORDER TO FINANCE TOUCHSTONE.

BUT STILL KORNEAS REFUSED TO NAME A DATE OR MAKE ANY SORT OF PUBLIC ANNOUNCEMENT.

I KEPT PUSHING HIM ON THIS BUT HE JUST REFUSED TO DISCUSS IT.

'THIS IS NOT THE TIME,' HE KEPT SAYING.

LOOKING BACK, I THINK I'D GOT THIS IDEA INTO MY HEAD THAT BECAUSE OF THE SALE THERE WOULD BE SO MUCH PUBLICITY AND AS A RESULT WE WOULD BE SAFER SOMEHOW.

MY LOGIC WAS THAT BEING SO MUCH IN THE PUBLIC EYE AND HAVING ALL THIS LIGHT ON US WOULD SOMEHOW SERVE TO PROTECT US.

GLOBE'S INCREASED MEDIA VISIBILITY ALONE WOULD SURELY PREVENT ANYONE FROM CARRYING OUT A THREAT.

BUT WHENEVER I DID SEE MY BROTHER, HE SEEMED PERMANENTLY EXHAUSTED.

HE WAS DESPERATE TO GET A WORKING VERSION OF IDOLECT READY FOR WILL.

THE POOR LADY. SHE WAS REALLY STRUGGLING. SHE'D GONE BACK TO THEIR RV AND IT WAS SO DIFFICULT FOR HER TO BE IN THAT SPACE WITHOUT HAL.

SHE DESPERATELY WANTED TO DO SOME MUSIC. SHE WANTED TO WRITE SOMETHING THAT HAL WOULD HAVE APPROVED OF.

OF COURSE THAT DIDN'T HAPPEN.

EVERY TIME THAT SHE TRIED TO COMPOSE SOMETHING, ALL THAT CAME OUT WERE SONGS ABOUT HOW MUCH SHE MISSED HAL.

```
I have a mind
To go to the river
And wash myself away.
I have a mind
To go to the river
And wash myself away.
```

"...BECAUSE HE'S GONE GONE GONE AND I GOTTA MAKE IT THROUGH ANOTHER DAY."

ACT FIVE   SCENE THREE

HAH, I THINK THE AVATAR OF HAL TOTALLY FREAKED HER OUT IN THE BEGINNING!

BUT YOU KNOW, WILL NEVER LACKED COMMITMENT AND WHEN SHE SET HER MIND TO DO SOMETHING, SHE WOULD ALWAYS KEEP AT IT.

IDIOLECT WAS A MULTI-MEDIUM, MULTI-DIMENSIONAL PROGRAM.

BUT DURING ITS INITIAL PHASE, WILL WAS ADVISED TO TRY SIMPLE TEXTS.

THESE TEXTS COULD THEN POSSIBLY FORM THE BASIS FOR LYRICS.

From the days of our summer...

SO WILL TYPED IN A LINE AND THEN WAITED. OF COURSE, KORNEAS HAD WARNED HER IT MIGHT TAKE A WHILE.

SHE GAVE IT AN HOUR AND THEN ANOTHER HOUR. SHE JUST SAT THERE STARING AT THE CURSOR THE WHOLE TIME.

From the days of our summer...

SHE WAITED ALL DAY. NOTHING. I THINK EVENTUALLY SHE TRIED TO FORGET ALL ABOUT IT AND JUST GOT ON WITH HER NORMAL ROUTINES AND STUFF.

BUT THE FOLLOWING DAY IN TEARS, SHE CALLED MY BROTHER TO SAY SHE DIDN'T THINK THAT THE PROGRAM WAS WORKING.

229

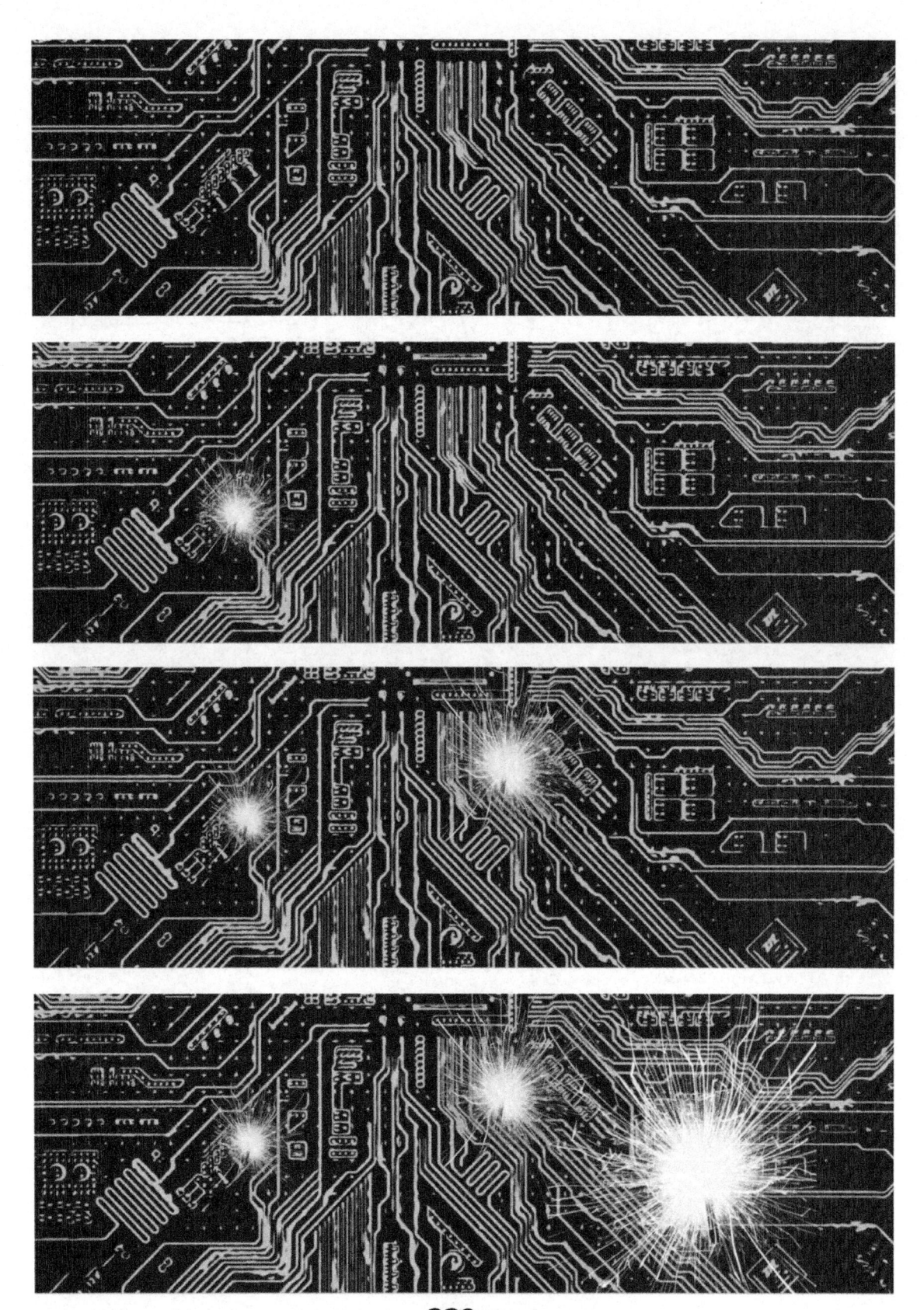

MY BROTHER WENT STRAIGHT OVER THERE.

AND THEN SUDDENLY AS THEY LOOKED AT THE SCREEN...

... THEY SAW IT HAPPEN RIGHT IN FRONT OF THEIR EYES.

From the days of our summer...

.........3573192qi
hec biq xqs
$%8bonblqu
......

From the days of our summer...

.........3573192qi
hec biq xqs
$%8bonblqu
......

...To the summer of our days 😀

WILL DIDN'T EVEN PAUSE FOR A MOMENT TO CONSIDER WHAT WAS HAPPENING.

ALMOST AUTOMATICALLY, LIKE THEY HAD DONE SO MANY, MANY TIMES, THEY JUST CARRIED ON WRITING THEIR SONG.

CHORUS So hold me and protect me...

...From the madness in my soul

Like you did when we were children...

...Like you did when we were old.

OBVIOUSLY I WASN'T THERE TO WITNESS THIS. BUT I CAN IMAGINE WHAT IT MUST HAVE FELT LIKE.

OF COURSE, THERE ARE EVENTS LIKE THIS IN EVERY HUMAN LIFE. IN FACT, WE SPEND OUR DAYS IN ACTIVE PURSUIT OF THEM.

BUT FOR SOME RARE INDIVIDUALS, LIKE MY BROTHER, THEY ARE SIMPLY THE TRACES AND THE DUST THEY SCATTER IN THEIR WAKE.

THE UNAVOIDABLE AND INEVITABLE CONSEQUENCE OF GREATNESS.

HAH, AND I'M PRETTY SURE THAT HAL, ALBEIT RELUCTANTLY, WOULD'VE CONSIDERED IT A **CONCESSION TO IMMORTALITY** AND THEN WRITTEN A SONG ABOUT IT! (IF HE COULD FIND A GOOD RHYME FOR 'IMMORTALITY'!)

...brutality?

MEANWHILE, WILL AND KORNEAS JUST WENT STRAIGHT BACK TO WORK!

WELL, THEY BOTH HAD THINGS THEY NEEDED TO DO!

THERE WAS OBVIOUSLY MUCH WORK STILL TO BE DONE ON THE PROGRAM ITSELF.

BUT WILL WAS EXTREMELY PATIENT AND CARRIED ON WITH THE BASIC VERSION.

YES, IT WAS SLOW BUT EVENTUALLY THERE WAS A WHOLE SET OF LYRICS TO A BRAND NEW SONG.

A SONG SHE IMMEDIATELY RECORDED!

I reached for you in darkness...

"...AS I STOOD AT THE ABYSS."

Save me please, you heard me call...

"...BUT YOU JUST JOINED ME IN MY FALL."

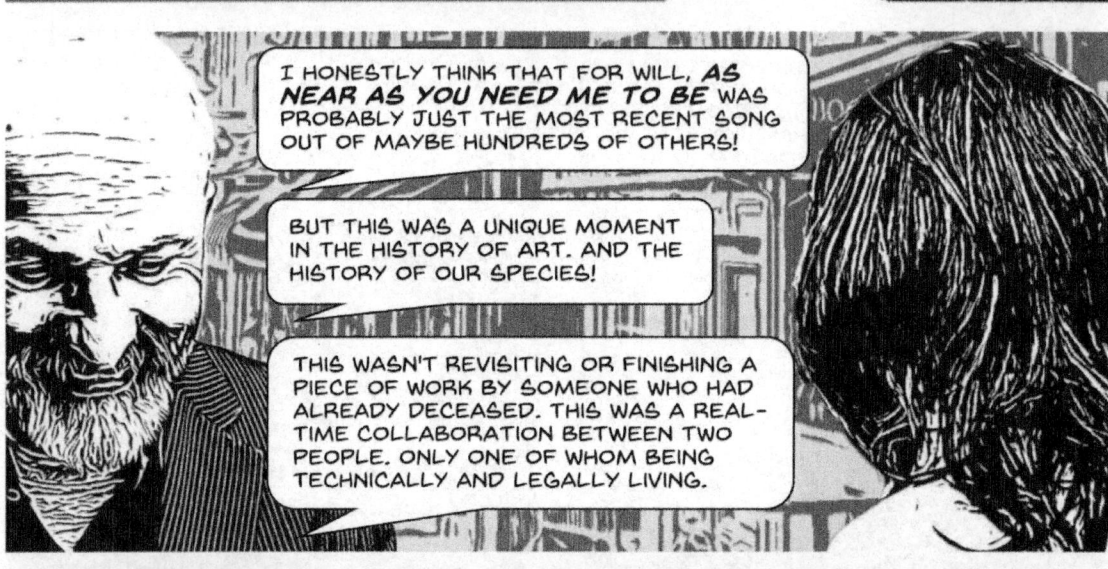

I HONESTLY THINK THAT FOR WILL, *AS NEAR AS YOU NEED ME TO BE* WAS PROBABLY JUST THE MOST RECENT SONG OUT OF MAYBE HUNDREDS OF OTHERS!

BUT THIS WAS A UNIQUE MOMENT IN THE HISTORY OF ART. AND THE HISTORY OF OUR SPECIES!

THIS WASN'T REVISITING OR FINISHING A PIECE OF WORK BY SOMEONE WHO HAD ALREADY DECEASED. THIS WAS A REAL-TIME COLLABORATION BETWEEN TWO PEOPLE. ONLY ONE OF WHOM BEING TECHNICALLY AND LEGALLY LIVING.

"SO WE DANCE ACROSS SILVER SAND TOWARDS THE SHIMMERING SEA..."

...And in this moment and for always
I'M AS NEAR AS YOU NEED ME TO BE.

WITHIN A MATTER OF MONTHS WILL WOULD ALSO BE WORKING WITH A SYNTHESIZED, VIRTUAL VERSION OF HAL'S VOICE.

THERE WOULD ULTIMATELY EVEN BE A SUB-PROGRAM THAT REPLICATED HIS GUITAR PLAYING!

BUT FOR WILL, EVERYTHING WAS SECONDARY TO THE JOY SHE FELT FROM WRITING MUSIC WITH HIM AGAIN.

SHE CARRIED ON PERFORMING UNDER HER OWN NAME BUT ALL THE MUSIC SHE WROTE WITH IDIOLECT SHE MADE AVAILABLE ON THE WEBSITE UNDER THE NAME CHAPTER 25.

BUT OF COURSE, NOW THE IDOLECT SYSTEM WAS WORKING, I THOUGHT WE COULD RETURN TO THE WHOLE ISSUE OF GLOBE AND TOUCHSTONE.

THAT WAS THE GENERAL IDEA ANYWAY...

ACT FIVE　　　　　　　　　　　　SCENE FOUR

BUT I WASN'T GOING TO START TELLING KORNEAS ALL ABOUT THE LETTERS AND THE THREATS. THE GUY WAS UNDER ENOUGH PRESSURE. AND LIKE I SAID I'D CONVINCED MYSELF IT WOULD ALL CEASE AS SOON THE SALE OF GLOBE WAS MADE PUBLIC.

ALTHOUGH IT WAS DIFFICULT TO GET KORNEAS TO CONCENTRATE ON TOUCHSTONE, HE STILL SAID THERE WAS WORK TO BE DONE ON IDIOLECT.

JUST TO GIVE YOU SOME BACKGROUND. THERE HAD BEEN A FEW LEAN PATCHES WITH GLOBE OVER THE YEARS. '97-'99 WAS ONE. AND TO KEEP EVERYTHING AFLOAT AT THOSE TIMES, WE HAD BOTH BEEN FORCED TO SELL SOME OF OUR SHARES IN THE COMPANY.

BETWEEN US EVENTUALLY, MY BROTHER AND I ONLY OWNED 45% OF GLOBE. SO WE DIDN'T HAVE ENOUGH POWER TO DRIVE A MAJOR PROJECT LIKE TOUCHSTONE ENTIRELY ON OUR OWN.

CONSEQUENTLY, ALL MAJOR DECISIONS REGARDING THE FUTURE OF THE COMPANY WERE ALWAYS LONG DRAWN OUT AFFAIRS. BUT WE WERE EXPECTING THIS.

AND OBVIOUSLY THE ACTUAL SALE OF THE COMPANY WOULD BE THE SINGLE BIGGEST ISSUE THE SENIOR EXECS AND THE SHAREHOLDERS WOULD EVER FACE.

AS I SAID, BECAUSE OF IDIOLECT, MY BROTHER SEEMED TO HAVE LOST A LOT OF HIS PASSION AND URGENCY ABOUT TOUCHSTONE.

YOU MUST FORGIVE ME, BUT GIVEN WHAT HAPPENED, THIS IS NOT A PERIOD OF MY LIFE I RECALL WITH ANY PARTICULAR FONDNESS OR CLARITY.

TO BE TRUTHFUL WITH YOU, AFTER ALL THIS TIME, I REALLY DON'T KNOW IF I WAS IN A HURRY TO MOVE THINGS FORWARD OR IF I JUST WANTED TO TAKE SOME PRESSURE OFF KORNEAS. PERHAPS IT WAS BOTH?
ANYWAY, LONG STORY SHORT, WITHOUT CONSULTING HIM, I JUST WENT AHEAD AND ARRANGED A MEETING WITH THE WHOLE BOARD OF DIRECTORS AND THE TOP TIER OF EXECS.
I REALLY THOUGHT IT WAS THE BEST WAY TO PROCEED. I DELIBERATELY DIDN'T MENTION SPECIFICS, I JUST SAID THERE WAS SOMETHING MAJOR THAT NEEDED TO BE ADDRESSED.
AND OF COURSE FOR MYSELF AND FOR KORNY, I WOULD FEEL SAFER WHEN EVERYTHING WAS IN THE PUBLIC DOMAIN.
THIS WAS ON A FRIDAY AND THE MEETING WAS SET FOR THE FOLLOWING MONDAY.
STRAIGHT AWAY I TOLD KORNEAS WHAT I HAD DONE. I THOUGHT MAYBE HE WOULD UNDERSTAND AND APPRECIATE MY MOTIVES. PERHAPS EVEN BE GRATEFUL IN SOME WAY. YEAH, I WAS THAT STUPID...

I'D SENT HIM A TEXT BUT HE DIDN'T REPLY. INSTEAD, WITHIN THE HOUR, HE WAS WAITING IN THE LOBBY OF MY HOTEL.

I FIRST THOUGHT THAT HE MIGHT BE ANGRY BUT I THINK HE JUST FELT LET DOWN.

AND ANYONE WILL TELL YOU, THERE IS A VERY PARTICULAR WAY OLDER BROTHERS SHOW THEIR DISAPPOINTMENT IN YOUNGER BROTHERS.

HE WAS UPSET WITH ME, THAT WAS OBVIOUS. HE SAID THAT I HAD NO IDEA WHAT I'D DONE.

I TOLD HIM I WAS ONLY TRYING TO MOVE THINGS FORWARD AND HE JUST STARED AT ME.

THEN HE SAID HE WOULD HAVE TO CHANGE HIS PLANS THAT WEEKEND.

HE WOULD TAKE FESTE AND GO UP THE COAST TO BIG SUR. AND SPEND A NIGHT OR TWO ON HIS YACHT.

HE NEEDED SOME SPACE, HE SAID, TO GET HIS HEAD TOGETHER FOR THE MEETING AND TO WORK ON HIS PITCH.

I WASN'T INVITED.

THAT WAS THE LAST TIME I EVER SPOKE TO MY BROTHER.

THE LAST TIME I SAW HIM ALIVE...

AS FAR AS ANYONE IS AWARE, WITHIN A MATTER OF AN HOUR OR SO, KORNEAS WAS ON THE ROAD, HEADING NORTH OUT OF THE CITY.

HE MADE ONE STOP ON THE WAY...

HE DROPPED IN ON WILL TO SAY HELLO AND PRESUMABLY CHECK HOW SHE WAS GETTING ON WITH IDIOLECT.

ACCORDING TO THE INVESTIGATION, SHE WAS THE LAST PERSON TO SEE HIM.

AND OF COURSE THERE WAS TALK THAT MY BROTHER WASN'T A SKILLED MARINER.

BUT HE WAS CAPABLE ENOUGH AND HE'D TAKEN THE YACHT OUT MANY TIMES ON HIS OWN.

ACH, THE MAN ONLY WANTED SOME PEACE. HE WASN'T PLANNING ON GOING FAR, JUST SOMEWHERE HE COULD THINK.

BUT I GUESS WE'VE COME TO THE PART OF THE STORY NOW WHERE I CAN'T REALLY ADD VERY MUCH TO WHAT YOU AND EVERYONE ELSE ALREADY KNOWS.

WHEN THE COAST GUARD WENT ON BOARD THE FOLLOWING MORNING AFTER KORNEAS HAD FAILED TO RESPOND TO THEIR MESSAGES, THEY FOUND THE YACHT COMPLETELY ABANDONED.

THERE WAS NO NOTE AND NO OBVIOUS SIGNS OF A STRUGGLE.

AND WHAT HAPPENED NEXT — YOU KNOW AS MUCH AS I DO.

OH SERGEI! THOSE DAYS, THOSE WEEKS! I CAN'T EVEN BEGIN TO IMAGINE WHAT YOU WENT THROUGH...
IT MUST HAVE BEEN A LIVING NIGHTMARE.
MY·BROTHER·KILLED·NO·MAN - HIS·FAULT·WAS·THOUGHT.
YET·HIS·PUNISHMENT· WAS·BITTER·DEATH.
I HELD ON TO SOME HOPE FOR A DAY OR TWO THAT HE WOULD JUST TURN UP AGAIN AND TELL ME I WAS AN IDIOT STUPID BROTHER FOR WORRYING.
BUT I KNEW WHAT HAD HAPPENED THAT DAY UP AT BIG SUR. IN FACT I KNEW RIGHT AWAY.
A NUMBER OF EYE WITNESSES CONFIRMED THAT A SMALL BOAT HAD BEEN SEEN IN THE VICINITY OF THE YACHT THAT DAY - A SMALL BOAT THAT HAS NEVER BEEN TRACED.

OF COURSE THEY NEVER FOUND IT! THEY WERE NEVER SUPPOSED TO! THAT WAS PART OF THE PLAN. THESE PEOPLE WERE PROFESSIONALS, MOLLY.THEY LEAVE NOTHING TO CHANCE AND THEY NEVER LEAVE TRACES.
THE CRIME SCENE PEOPLE FOUND NO EVIDENCE THAT FESTE HAD EVEN BEEN ON THE BOAT! BUT WHERE ELSE WAS HE? AND EVEN IF KORNEAS HAD FALLEN OVERBOARD, WHICH WAS THEIR FIRST THEORY, FESTE WOULD HAVE OBVIOUSLY STILL BEEN ON THE YACHT.
NO, THESE PEOPLE WERE GOOD. PERHAPS THE TEAM WERE DOING A TWO FOR THE PRICE OF ONE OFFER! BUT THEY EARNED THEIR FUCKING FEE. THEY WERE PROBABLY PAID IN SHARES IN GLOBE!
ACH, THIS WASN'T AN ACCIDENT, IT WAS NOTHING LIKE AN ACCIDENT. IT WASN'T FATE OR COINCIDENCE. NAH! BUT NEITHER, I HAVE TO SAY, WAS IT A SURPRISE!

NO, YOU CAN NOT TALK ABOUT SUCH THINGS. NOT ABOUT THIS. YOU ONLY NEED TO BE *LOGICAL*.
ON THE DAY BEFORE A MEETING WHEN KORNEAS WILL MAKE AN ANNOUNCEMENT THAT WILL CHANGE THE WORLD.
HE CONVENIENTLY VANISHES WITHOUT A SINGLE TRACE. WHAT WOULD ANYONE CONCLUDE?
ACH, YOU ARE SUPPOSED TO PROTECT YOUR BROTHER. BUT I WENT BEHIND HIS BACK. TWICE! I MADE SUCH MISTAKES, MOLLY AND I IGNORED THE THREATS...
I BETRAYED HIM. AND I AS GOOD AS KILLED HIM MYSELF.
THAT MEETING I CALLED WAS THE FINAL STRAW. AFTER ENGAGING THAT FUCKING ATTORNEY, THERE'D BEEN SO MANY LEAKS AT GLOBE.
EVERYONE KNEW WHAT WAS ABOUT TO HAPPEN THAT DAY. SO THEY HAD TO ACT QUICKLY.
BUT YOU KNOW THE SICKEST THING?
NO, SERGEI, TELL ME.
THE BOARD WENT AHEAD AND HELD THAT FUCKING MEETING ON THE MONDAY ANYWAY!

THOSE FUCKERS! THE COAST GUARD WERE STILL SEARCHING FOR KORNEAS' BODY WHEN THE BOARD MADE THE ANNOUNCEMENT!

FOLLOWING TALKS WHICH I OBVIOUSLY TOOK NO PART IN, THEY ISSUED A STATEMENT TO SAY THAT AS A RESULT OF A MAJORITY DECISION AND WITH IMMEDIATE EFFECT GLOBE WOULD BE MERGING WITH TRANSWIENER GLOBAL!

I DON'T KNOW IF THE NAME IS FAMILIAR TO YOU BUT ABOUT TEN YEARS AGO TWG WERE A MASSIVE TECH MEDIA COMPANY.

THEY OWNED EVERYTHING. AND NOW THEY OWNED GLOBE TOO.

DURING THAT TIME, I HAD NEVER GOT SO MUCH AS A HINT THAT SOMETHING LIKE A MERGER WAS IN THE WORKS.

IT HAD ALL BEEN ARRANGED AND PLANNED IN COMPLETE SECRECY.

I KNOW, CORPORATIONS MERGE ALL THE TIME – YOU JUST NEVER HEAR ABOUT IT. NOT UNTIL IT'S IN THEIR INTERESTS FOR YOU TO KNOW!

BUT THIS ONE WAS DIFFERENT.

AND DO YOU KNOW WHAT WAS THE CLEAREST INDICATION OF THE REAL MOTIVES BEHIND IT?

GLOBE OBVIOUSLY KEPT ITS NAME, ITS OFFICES, ITS STAFF. EVERYTHING. EVERYTHING, THAT IS, APART FROM ONE THING. THE SINGLE SOLITARY THING THAT VANISHED OVERNIGHT!
THAT, OF COURSE, WAS TOUCHSTONE! AND ALL RECORD OF IT COMPLETELY DISAPPEARED! THERE WAS NO TRACE, NO REFERENCE TO IT ANYWHERE! IT WAS LIKE IT HAD LITERALLY NEVER EXISTED. ALL THE RESEARCH, ALL THE DATA! ***NOTHING!***
NONE OF THE RESEARCHERS, NONE OF THE TEAM WOULD EVEN SPEAK TO ME. OBVIOUSLY THEY HAD BEEN TOLD NOT TO. THE WHOLE THING WITH TWG WAS ABOUT TOUCHSTONE. SO, YOU DON'T HAVE TO LOOK VERY HARD FOR A MOTIVE THERE, MOLLY.
YOU CAN KILL A MAN OR JUST KILL THE THING HE BELIEVES IN. BUT TO DO THE JOB PROPERLY YOU HAVE TO KILL THEM BOTH. SO YOU SEE WHY, IN MY HEART, I FEEL ALL THIS ... RESPONSIBILITY?
BUT IT'S NOT YOUR FAULT, YOU ONLY DID WHAT YOU THOUGHT WAS RIGHT.
ACH, I·HAVE·SHOT·MINE·ARROW·O'ER·THE· HOUSE·AND·HURT·MY·BROTHER. NO, NOT HURT HIM, MOLLY. KILLED HIM, AS IF I'D PUT A GUN TO HIS HEAD AND PULLED THE TRIGGER MYSELF.

ACT FIVE　　　　　　　　　　　　　　SCENE FIVE

SO YOU CAN UNDERSTAND WHY I HAVE HAD NOTHING TO DO WITH ANYONE AT GLOBE SINCE THAT DAY.

ALTHOUGH IT WASN'T DIFFICULT AS MY SECURITY ACCESS WAS BLOCKED AND I WASN'T ABLE TO ENTER ANY PROPERTY OWNED BY GLOBE OR TWG!

BUT I WAS OFF THEIR RADAR SO I TOOK THE OPPORTUNITY TO DISAPPEAR.

I SET UP THAT WORKSHOP DOWN THE ROAD ENTIRELY TO HOST AND MAINTAIN THE IDIOLECT NETWORK. THAT IS ALL THAT PLACE HAS EVER BEEN.

AND IT SEEMED TO WORK TOO. I'VE BEEN PRETTY ANONYMOUS AND DON'T HAVE MUCH CONTACT WITH PEOPLE.

WERE YOU IN TOUCH WITH WILL AT ALL?

ONLY ONCE OR TWICE, WAY BACK AT THE START, WHEN SHE WAS STILL GETTING FAMILIAR WITH THE PROGRAM.

MY ROLE WAS STRICTLY TO OVERSEE THE ACTUAL SYSTEM. I NEVER HAD THE CAPACITY TO MONITOR WHAT SHE WAS DOING. THAT WOULD HAVE FELT LIKE SOME KIND OF VIOLATION.

ACH, SHE SO LOVED IDIOLECT. NOT JUST THE WRITING. IT ENABLED HER AND HAL TO CARRY ON MAKING UP STORIES, LIKE TRAVELLING IN THEIR RV TOGETHER AND GOING TO GIGS.

LIKE THEY ALWAYS USED TO...

YOU KNOW SOMETIMES, I WOULD PICTURE HER IN THAT OLD CAMERADO OF THEIRS AND FEEL A REAL PANG OF JEALOUSY. I WOULD HAVE GIVEN ANYTHING TO BE LIVING LIKE THAT.

AND I WOULDN'T WISH TO SOUND INSENSITIVE BUT IF IT WAS ME I WOULD HAVE HAPPILY BEEN BURIED IN IT!

PERHAPS YOU DON'T KNOW THIS BUT SHE ACTUALLY SPENT THE LAST FEW YEARS OF HER LIFE LIVING ON A COMMUNE.

ACH, NO, I DIDN'T KNOW THAT! IF I HAD, I WOULD HAVE OFFERED TO BUY THE VEHICLE OFF HER! WITHOUT A MOMENT'S HESITATION!

CAN I ASK, DO YOU KNOW WHAT HAPPENED TO IT?

OF COURSE. SHE NEVER SOLD IT, IT WAS STILL LISTED UNDER HER ASSETS WHEN HER ESTATE WAS SETTLED.

SHE LOANED IT TO A FRIEND, I BELIEVE, WHO STILL HAS IT AS FAR AS I KNOW. IT'S SOMEWHERE UP NEAR SALINAS, AS I RECALL.

I HAVE THE ADDRESS ON THE FILE, I CAN EASILY CHECK.

ACH! GOOD GOLLY MISS MOLLY! DO YOU THINK THERE MIGHT BE A CHANCE WILL'S FRIEND WOULD SELL IT TO ME?
I'M SERIOUS! MIGHT THAT ACTUALLY BE POSSIBLE?
YOU KNOW, I WOULD PAY GOOD MONEY... NO, ACTUALLY, I WOULD PAY ALL MY MONEY TO GET MY HANDS ON *THAT* PARTICULAR CAMERADO!
OH, CAN YOU IMAGINE THAT?
amerado
CAN YOU IMAGINE WHAT IT WOULD FEEL LIKE TO HAVE DREAMS AGAIN?
IN THE OLD COUNTRY, THEY USED TO SAY THAT HOPE IS A KIND OF ESCAPE. BUT FOR ME, ESCAPE IS ALWAYS THE BEST KIND OF HOPE!
AS I SAY I HAVE ALL THE DETAILS ON FILE. IT WON'T BE ANY PROBLEM DIGGING THEM OUT.
BUT IF YOU DO INSIST ON FOLLOWING THIS PARTICULAR COURSE OF ACTION...
... I MUST WARN YOU THAT THERE WILL BE A SPECIFIC CONDITION ATTACHED!
WHICH WOULD BE?
I WANT TO COME WITH YOU!
I'VE NOT COME THIS FAR IN YOUR STORY TO ABANDON IT IN ITS FINAL PAGES!

Panel 1:
OH MOLLY, OF COURSE, YOU SHOULD BE THERE! I·WOULD·NOT·WISH·ANY· COMPANION·IN·THE·WORLD·BUT·YOU.

HANG ON, ISN'T THAT MY LINE?

Panel 2:
BESIDES, I THOUGHT YOU COULD DRIVE! SEEING AS HOW I DON'T ACTUALLY HAVE A CAR ANYMORE!

OH MAN! SERIOUSLY, SERGEI?

Panel 3:
OK, BUT I'LL NEED TO GO AND CHECK THE LAPTOP AT MY APARTMENT FOR THE ADDRESS IN SALINAS.

WHY DON'T WE MEET BACK AT YOUR SHOP IN SAY, AN HOUR?

Panel 4:
YES, YES, PERFECT! THAT WILL GIVE ME ENOUGH TIME TO BUY A BIG HAMMER!

WELL, NOW WILL HAS NO USE FOR THE NETWORK, I NEED TO TAKE IT DOWN.

Panel 5:
AND WHENEVER I NEED TO TAKE SOMETHING DOWN...

... I REALLY TAKE IT DOWN!

248

CRASH!!!
T.R.A.N.I.O.
IT SOLUTIONS
BANG!!!
A SHORT TIME LATER...
SO, YOU FEELING BETTER NOW?
OH YES. MUCH BETTER THANK YOU.
COMPUTERS ARE FINE. FOR SOME. BUT NOT FOR ME. NOT ANY MORE.
WOAH THERE, *VELOCITY BOY...*
OOOPS! BUT YOU DO KNOW WHO YOU SOUND LIKE RIGHT NOW!

Panel 1:
- WELL, DID YOU GET THE ADDRESS?
- YES, OF COURSE. TURNS OUT I WAS RIGHT TOO! AND THE VEHICLE IS STILL LOCATED JUST NORTH OF SALINAS.
- AT SOME OLD ABANDONED STEEL WORKS, OF ALL PLACES!
- BUT HOW FAR IS THAT EXACTLY?

Panel 2:
- I RECKON IT'S ABOUT A TWO HOUR DRIVE DOWN PCH THIS TIME OF DAY.
- RIGHT THEN, NEXT QUESTION...

Panel 3:
- WOULD IT BE ALL RIGHT FOR US TO LISTEN TO SOME MUSIC ON THE WAY?
- OH, I'D PROBABLY BE TOTALLY AMAZED IF WE DIDN'T!

Panel 4:
- "I'VE SEEN LIGHTNING STRIKE A CHURCH HOUSE SEEN MOUNTAINS FALL INTO THE SEA.
- I FIGHT FOR JUSTICE BUT WHAT'S JUSTICE EVER DONE FOR ME?"

ACT FIVE　　　　　　　　　　　　　SCENE SIX

"SERGEI, SERGEI! TURN THE MUSIC DOWN! I THINK THIS IS THE PLACE!"

"ARE YOU SURE? FUCK, WHAT A DUMP!"

"YIP, THIS IS MOST DEFINITELY IT!"

"ACH, WHAT A TERRIBLE PLACE! YOU KNOW, IT REMINDS ME OF MY ELEMENTARY SCHOOL BACK IN THE OLD COUNTRY!"

"OH GOD, SERGEI, WAS IT THAT BAD?"

"DON'T BE SILLY, OF COURSE IT WASN'T! IT WAS JUST LIKE THE SCHOOLS OVER HERE! WHAT IS IT EXACTLY WITH AMERICANS AND THINGS THAT AREN'T AMERICAN?"

"BEATS ME. WE'RE JUST A VERY COMPLICATED RACE, I GUESS!"

OK, I GIVE UP. WHY ARE YOU LOOKING SO HAPPY?
ACH, LOOK AT THIS PLACE, MOLLY! IT IS SUCH A FUCKING SHIT HOLE!
ANYONE WHO CALLS THIS HOME WOULD PROBABLY BE VERY HAPPY TO TAKE A GENEROUS CASH OFFER FOR SOME OLD WRECK OF AN RV!

I GUESS SO. HEY, WHY CAN I HEAR MUSIC? I THOUGHT WE TURNED IT OFF.
WE DID! I DON'T KNOW WHAT YOU CAN HEAR, I CAN'T HEAR...
OH HANG ON, WAIT A MINUTE. MAYBE I CAN...

IT'S GETTING LOUDER TOO.
AND IT'S COMING FROM OVER THERE. COME ON!

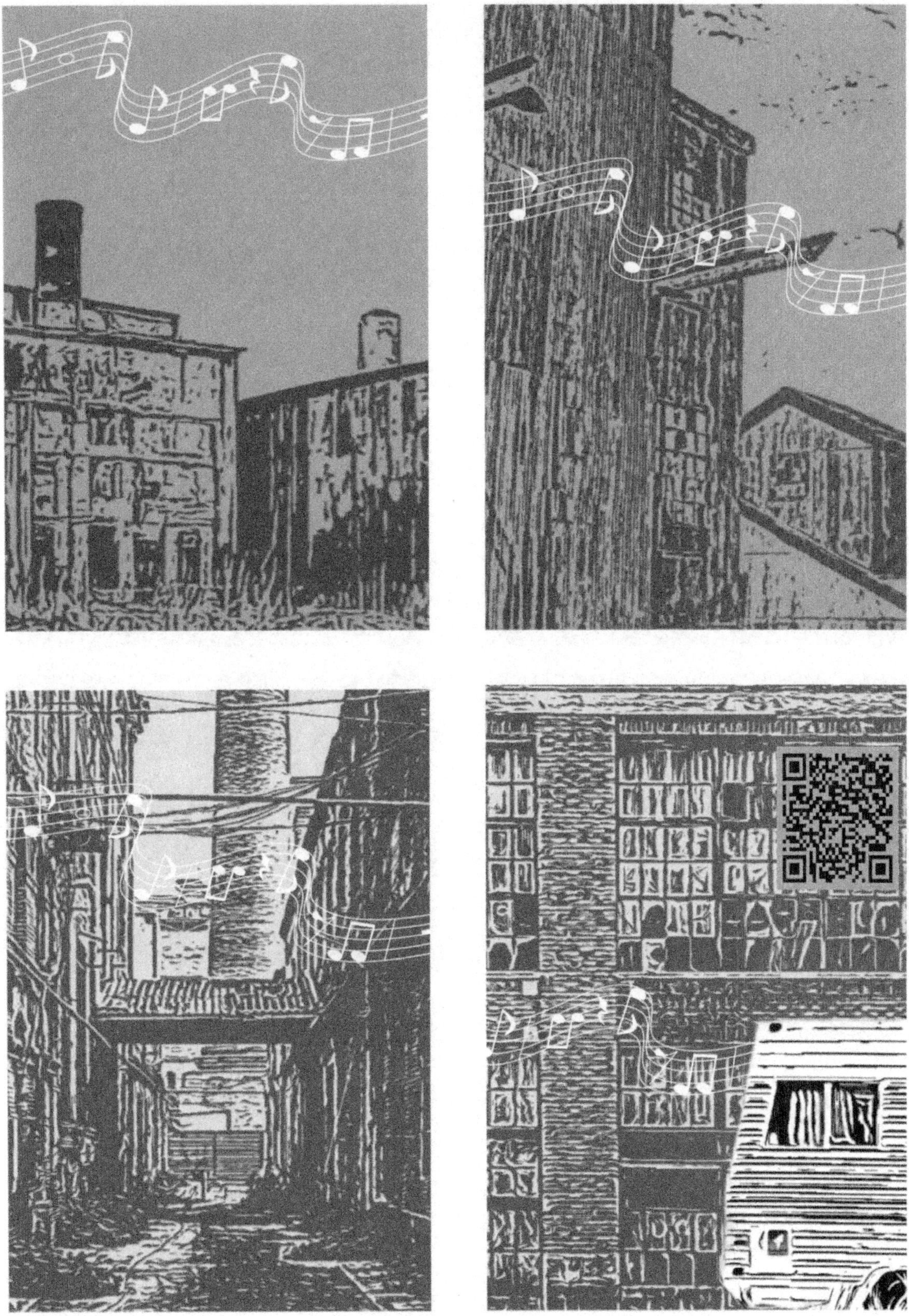

WHAT!?
WHAT IS IT?
... I ALWAYS THOUGHT YOU LIKED THIS SONG.

WHAT'S THE MATTER?
YOU KNOW YOU'RE ACTING REALLY STRANGE RIGHT NOW, DON'T YOU?

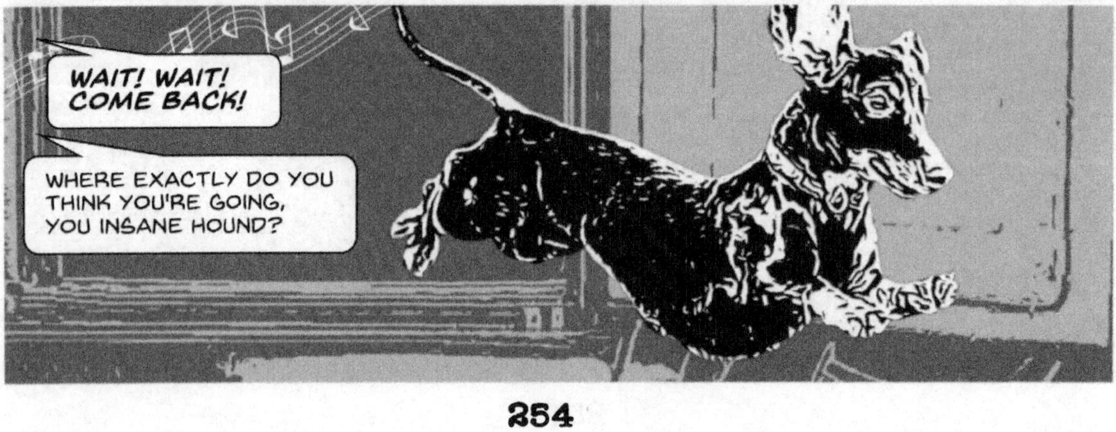
WAIT! WAIT! COME BACK!
WHERE EXACTLY DO YOU THINK YOU'RE GOING, YOU INSANE HOUND?

...YEAH, THERE'S NO DOUBT WE'RE DEFINITELY HEADING IN THE RIGHT DIRECTION!

OH, AND GUESS WHAT?

WHAT, MOLLY?

I THINK WE MIGHT JUST HAVE OURSELVES SOME COMPANY!

...HELLO, BOY!

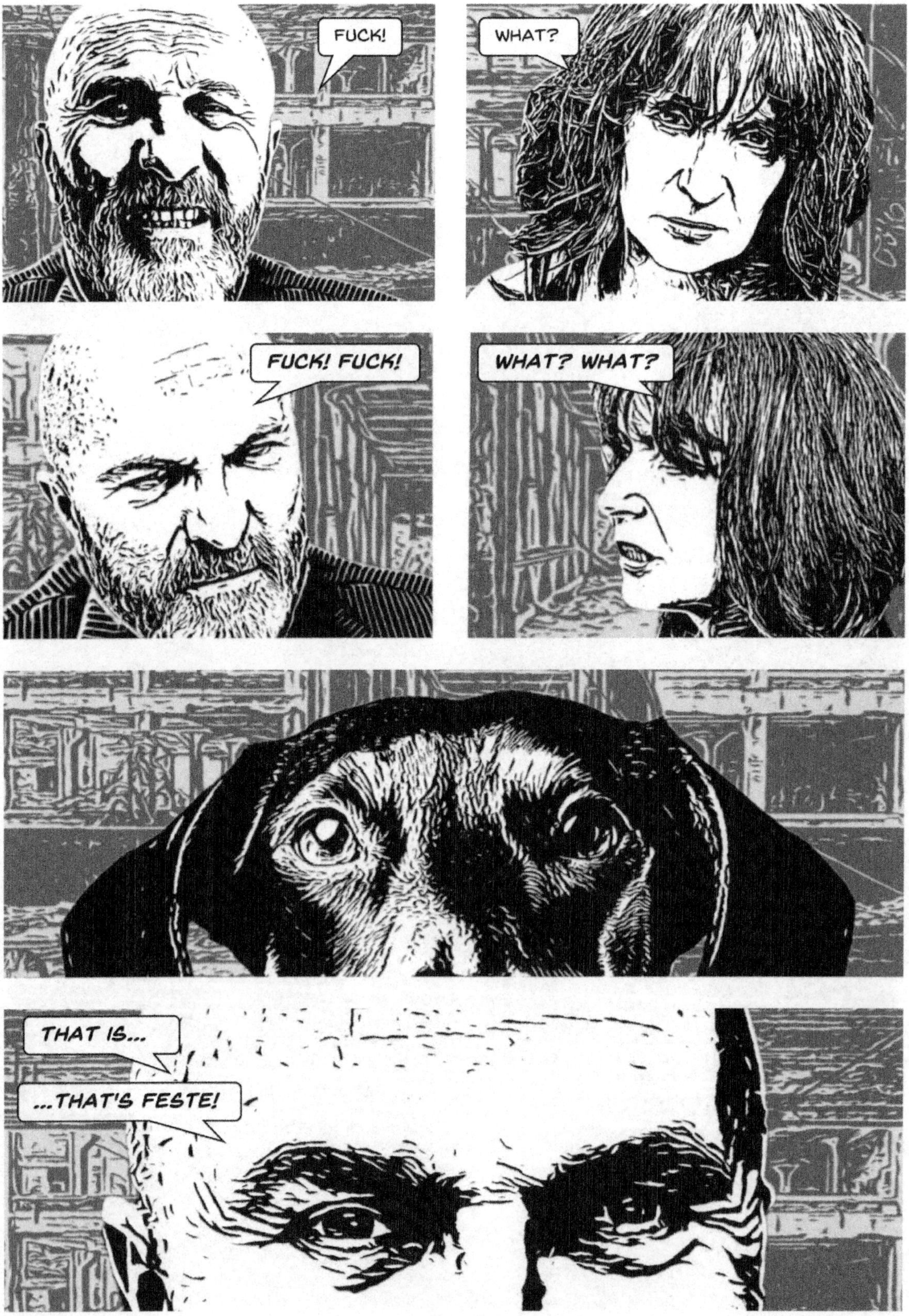
FUCK!
WHAT?
FUCK! FUCK!
WHAT? WHAT?
THAT IS...
...THAT'S FESTE!

SERIOUSLY? AW C'MON, MAN, YOU GOTTA BE KIDDING!
I MEAN, HE'S OLDER OBVIOUSLY BUT HE'S STILL GOT THAT FUNNY EYE AND THAT WONKY WAY OF RUNNING.
BUT HONESTLY, I'D RECOGNIZE HIM ANYWHERE!
COME ON!
WHAT'S THE HURRY? WHERE ARE WE GOING?
NO IDEA! BUT I DO KNOW ONE THING IN THIS LIFE, WHEN A FOOL LIKE FESTE RUNS, YOU FOLLOW!

ACT FIVE SCENE SEVEN

HELLO, YOU KNOW I WONDERED WHY FESTE...
UM, EXCUSE ME, BUT WHAT THE FUCK IS GOING ON HERE?
HI, I'M KORNEAS.
YEAH, I KINDA GUESSED AS MUCH. I'M MOLLY AND OF COURSE YOU KNOW ...
SERGEI!
FLUMPH!!

A SHORT TIME LATER.
...WHAT? WHAT HAPPENED?
YOU FAINTED, SERGEI, THAT'S ALL!
NO, NO, THIS CANNOT BE HAPPENING!
IT IS JUST A DREAM. AND FOR ME IT IS THE CRUELEST ONE OF ALL!
SO TELL ME, AT THE END OF THIS DREAM DO I KISS YOU?
OR DO I KILL YOU?
HA! MY BROTHER, ONLY YOU CAN MAKE THAT CHOICE. BUT BEFORE YOU DECIDE, PLEASE, I BESEECH YOU, LET ME TELL YOU WHY I FELT COMPELLED TO DO WHAT I DID...

SOMETIMES YOU GET TO MAKE CHOICES IN LIFE. AND SOMETIMES YOU DON'T.

AND SOMETIMES IT IS NOT CHOICE BUT CIRCUMSTANCE. AND THERE IS NO OPTION. NO ALTERNATIVE.

AT SUCH TIMES, YOU SIMPLY HAVE TO BECOME INVISIBLE. WHAT US OLD MAGICIANS USED TO CALL *A DISAPPEARING ACT.*

YOU SEE, YOU WERE RIGHT, WHEN YOU SAID EVEN THE MOST INCORRUPTIBLE HAVE THEIR PRICE.

YOU JUST HAVEN'T REACHED IT YET!

BUT THEY EVENTUALLY FOUND MINE. THEY EXPLOITED MY ONE FLAW AND TRUE WEAKNESS.

THAT WHICH, PARADOXICALLY, I HAD ALWAYS FELT TO BE MY GREATEST STRENGTH.

YOU SEE THE PRICE I HAD TO PAY WAS THE ONE THAT PROTECTED THE LIFE OF MY BROTHER.

FOR NO OTHER THING IN MY LIFE, NO PURPOSE, NO ACHIEVEMENT, NO GOAL, EVER MATTERED TO ME AS MUCH AS MY LITTLE BROTHER.

AND REGARDLESS OF THE CONSEQUENCES MY FIRST DUTY WAS TO ENSURE THERE WOULD BE NO THREAT TO HIS LIFE. IT WAS A PRICE I WOULD'VE PAID TWENTY OR A HUNDRED TIMES!

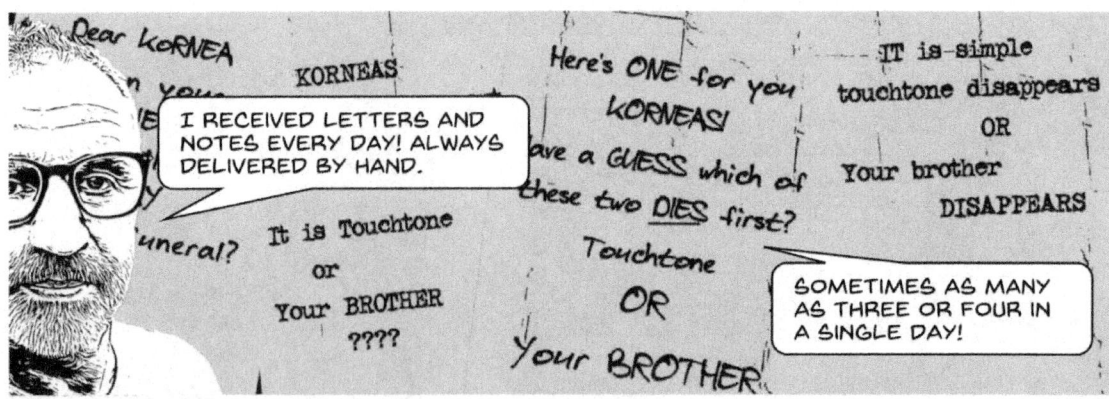

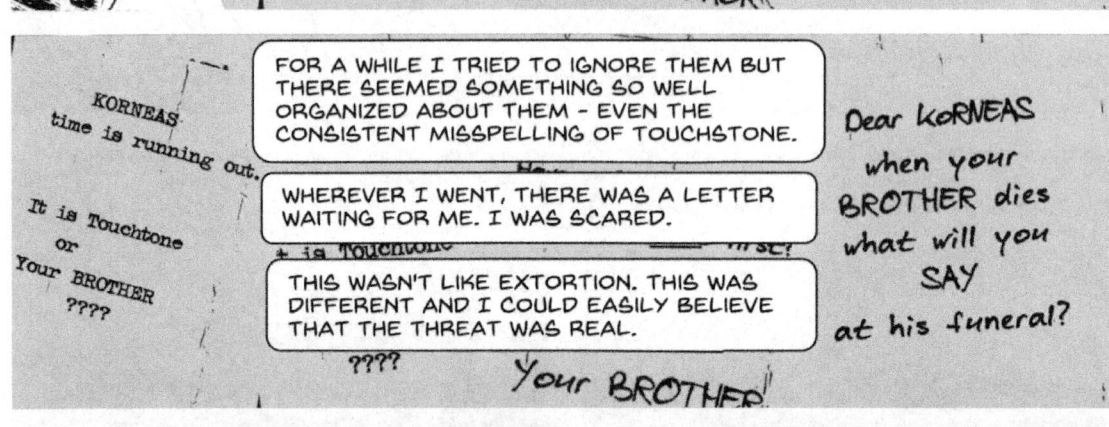

I RECEIVED LETTERS AND NOTES EVERY DAY! ALWAYS DELIVERED BY HAND.

SOMETIMES AS MANY AS THREE OR FOUR IN A SINGLE DAY!

FOR A WHILE I TRIED TO IGNORE THEM BUT THERE SEEMED SOMETHING SO WELL ORGANIZED ABOUT THEM — EVEN THE CONSISTENT MISSPELLING OF TOUCHSTONE.

WHEREVER I WENT, THERE WAS A LETTER WAITING FOR ME. I WAS SCARED.

THIS WASN'T LIKE EXTORTION. THIS WAS DIFFERENT AND I COULD EASILY BELIEVE THAT THE THREAT WAS REAL.

OH FUCK, KORNY! NO NO!

I GOT EXACTLY THE SAME LETTERS!

I THOUGHT IT WAS JUST ME! ON ACCOUNT OF THE FUCKING STUPID THING I DID!

SO WHAT PARTICULAR FUCKING STUPID THING WAS THIS NOW, MY BROTHER?

IT WAS ALL MY FAULT, YOU SEE I WENT BEHIND YOUR BACK.

I WAS SO WORRIED ABOUT TOUCHSTONE AND THE WHOLE ISSUE OF COPYRIGHT, I SPOKE TO AN ATTORNEY.

AND SO WHEN ADVANCE WORD OF TOUCHSTONE GOT OUT, I KNEW HE'D BEEN THE LEAK AND IT WAS *ALL* MY DOING.

OH SERGEI, I KNEW ABOUT THE ATTORNEY. I KNEW WHAT WAS ON YOUR MIND.
AND I EVEN UNDERSTOOD WHY YOU WERE DOING IT! I FIGURED YOU'D DISCUSS IT WITH ME EVENTUALLY.
YOU WERE JUST THINKING ABOUT TOUCHSTONE.
AND YOU KNOW, MOLLY? MOM AND DAD USED TO ALWAYS SAY THAT IF YOU EVER WANT SERGEI TO DO SOMETHING, FIRST TRY TELLING HIM ***NOT*** TO DO IT!
BUT YOU WERE RIGHT THERE WAS A LEAK.
AND I KNEW EXACTLY WHERE IT CAME FROM! IT HAD ***NOTHING*** TO DO WITH YOUR ATTORNEY!
IT WAS JOSH, THAT GUY FROM THE RESEARCH TEAM.
GLOB
I WAS TOLD HE WAS IN TROUBLE WITH BIG GAMBLING DEBTS AND WAS JUST LOOKING FOR A PAY DAY.
AW FUCK, FUCK! OH KORNEAS, YOU ARE KIDDING ME, RIGHT? ACH, I HATED THAT GUY, I EVEN HATED HIS FUCKING HAIR!
IT WASN'T YOUR FAULT, SERGEI. ANYWAY, HOW LONG AFTER THE LEAK DID THE LETTERS START?

OH, WITHIN A MATTER OF DAYS, I THINK. I SPOKE TO HAL ABOUT IT AND HE CONVINCED ME THAT I WOULD NEVER WIN AGAINST THE FORCES OF CORPORATE EVIL, AS HE USED TO CALL THEM.
HE FEARED THAT WE HAD BEEN ALLOWED TO BECOME, IN HIS WORDS, 'TOO TRIBAL' AND TOO FOCUSED ON THE INTERESTS OF OUR OWN PARTICULAR 'TRIBE'. WHILST FEELING ISOLATED AND THREATENED BY EVERY OTHER TRIBE!
THAT HAD NOT HAPPENED ACCIDENTALLY, HE SAID!
ALTHOUGH THERE SEEMED NOWADAYS TO BE AN INFINITE NUMBER OF TRIBES, HAL INSISTED THERE HAD ONLY EVER BEEN TWO - THE LANDOWNERS AND THE SERFS.
AND WHILE WE WERE ALL ENCOURAGED TO FIGHT AMONGST OURSELVES WE WOULD NEVER REALIZE THIS! BUT EVEN IN SUCH A CLIMATE OF DIVISION, I KNEW THAT IN MY HEART I WOULD ALWAYS BE A SERF AND NOTHING ELSE.
BUT HAL WAS AWARE OF THE VERY REAL THREAT IF YOU WENT UP AGAINST THESE BIG CORPORATIONS. LIKE THE PHARMACEUTICAL INDUSTRY.
AND DUE TO THE EXTENT OF THEIR POWER AND INFLUENCE, THERE WAS NO POINT IN INVOLVING THE LAW OR THE POLICE. A WASTE OF TIME.
SO HE COULD SEE THE DANGER THAT I HAD PUT MYSELF IN AND I GUESS HE WAS JUST SCARED FOR ME.
HAH, HE ONCE TOLD ME THAT, EVEN THOUGH HE WAS IN THE ADVANCED STAGES OF CANCER, HE WOULD VERY PROBABLY OUTLIVE BOTH YOU AND I!
SO HE CAME UP WITH A PLAN!

VANISHING, HE SAID, WAS THE ONLY OPTION. THERE WAS NO OTHER WAY I COULD GUARANTEE MY SAFETY AND YOURS. IF I WAS DEAD THEY COULDN'T THREATEN ME. TOUCHSTONE WOULD FADE AND BE FORGOTTEN AND WE WOULD BOTH BE SAFE.
BECAUSE, AS WILL POINTED OUT, EVEN IF I JUST CANCELLED TOUCHSTONE, THEY WOULD STILL BASICALLY OWN ME AND THERE WAS NO GUARANTEE IT WOULD EVER END.
SO HAL SUGGESTED I WENT OFF-GRID JUST LIKE HE AND WILL HAD DONE. BECAUSE AS HE SAID, YOU ALWAYS NEED TO STAY ***ONE STEP AHEAD OF THOSE MOTHERFUCKERS!***
I WOULD HAVE TO STAY HIDDEN FOR THE REST OF MY LIFE AND I COULD NEVER RISK CONTACTING YOU. BUT I KNEW YOU WOULD BE SAFE.
AND YOU MUST REMEMBER WHEN YOUR HOUSE BURNED DOWN, IT WAS ALSO TECHNICALLY MY ADDRESS! SO I KNEW THEIR THREAT WAS ENTIRELY GENUINE.
BUT WE TALKED ABOUT THE FINAL DETAILS OF THE PLAN WHILE I WAS WORKING ON IDIOLECT WITH THEM.
AND THEN AFTER HAL DIED, WILL ARRANGED SO MANY THINGS FOR ME, INCLUDING ORGANISING THE LITTLE ROW BOAT THAT CAME AND GOT FESTE AND ME OFF THE YACHT!
THAT WAS ENTIRELY HER IDEA. AND OF COURSE WHEN SHE WENT TO LIVE ON THAT COMMUNE, SHE LET ME HAVE THE CAMERADO. AND THIS HAS BEEN MY HOME EVER SINCE.
I OWE HER SO MUCH.

BUT THE OTHER FACTOR THAT DELAYED MY DISAPPEARANCE WAS THAT ALONGSIDE WORKING WITH WILL AND HAL ON IDIOLECT, I WAS DEVELOPING ANOTHER NEW PROGRAM.

ONE THAT WOULD ENSURE I WOULD STAY OFF THE RADAR AND LEAVE NO DIGITAL FOOTPRINT ANYWHERE.

I CALLED IT MY *DATAZERO* PROGRAM OR A *DATA/NEGATA*.

ALTHOUGH BY THAT POINT HAL HAD STARTED CALLING ME NED FOR SOME REASON AND HE INSISTED THAT THE PROGRAM SHOULD BE CALLED *NED!*

SO *N.E.D* BECAME NEGATIVIZATION OF ENCRYPTED DATA!

ESSENTIALLY, IT WAS A PROGRAM THAT WITH ONE CLICK REMOVED ALL TRACE OF YOUR INTERNET HISTORY. BASICALLY IN DIGITAL TERMS YOU NEVER EXISTED.

THIS MEANT YOU COULD NEVER BE TRACKED OR TRACED OR TARGETED BY SCAMMERS OR ANYONE. BUT PARTICULARLY BY ALL THE BIG CORPORATIONS. YOU WERE FREE!

YOU COULD SHOP, READ OR DOWNLOAD ANYTHING YOU LIKE BUT THEN WITH A CLICK OF A MOUSE BUTTON YOU VANISH AND ARE FOREVER UNTRACEABLE.

AH, HAL JUST LOVED THAT WHOLE CONCEPT BECAUSE HE KNEW HOW MUCH BIG BUSINESS WOULD HATE IT! AND BECAUSE IT WAS CALLED NED!

ACH, GODDAMN IT, KORNEAS! YOU KNOW WHAT? A PROGRAM LIKE THAT COULD YOU MAKE YOU A MILLIONAIRE AGAIN BY THE WEEKEND!
HAH, SO WHY DON'T WE JUST GIVE IT AWAY TO PEOPLE?
BE A GREAT BIG KICK IN THE TEETH TO BIG BUSINESS, RIGHT?
HAHA! YOU SEE, MOLLY!! THAT'S HOW YOU CAN TELL THAT'S REALLY MY BROTHER STANDING THERE AND NOT A.I.!
AND IF NO MAN IS INCORRUPTIBLE, THIS GUY IS STILL PRETTY CLOSE!
POOR·WRETCHES·THAT·DEPEND·ON· GREATNESS' FAVOR·DREAM·AS·I·HAVE ·DONE: WAKE·AND·FIND·NOTHING.
AND I WAS NOTHING. BUT WITH MY BROTHER ALONGSIDE ME, THERE WASN'T ANYTHING I COULDN'T DO!
ACH, ARE YOU OFFERING ME MY OLD JOB BACK?
WELL, I GUESS THAT DEPENDS...
HOW SOON CAN YOU START?

WELL, I CAN'T THINK OF A BETTER WAY OF HONORING THE MEMORY OF WILL AND HAL. CAN YOU?
I ACTUALLY WENT TO HER FUNERAL, YOU KNOW? IT WAS ONE OF THE RARE TIMES I WENT OUT IN PUBLIC. I WAS VERY INCONSPICUOUS!
OBVIOUSLY, I SAT A LONG WAY AWAY FROM BERNIE SANDERS AND SO MOST OF THE ATTENTION WAS DIRECTED ELSEWHERE!
Korneas
AND BESIDES THERE WAS RUMOR THAT A CERTAIN MR DYLAN MIGHT BE ATTENDING THE SERVICE AND SO THAT FULLY OCCUPIED THE MINDS OF THE CURIOUS!
SO, DID HE SHOW UP?
OF COURSE NOT! IT WAS JUST A HOAX. A COUPLE OF PHONE CALLS WAS ALL IT TOOK! OLDEST MISDIRECTION TRICK IN THE BOOK! BUT I THOUGHT WILL WOULD HAVE LOVED THAT.
ALTHOUGH YOU COULD NEVER BE SURE WITH HER. SHE NEVER WANTED TO USE N.E.D. FOR SOME REASON, I THOUGHT SHE WOULD HAVE JUST JUMPED AT IT!
ANYTHING THAT KICKED OVER THE ROTTING PUTRESCENCE OF LATE-STAGE CAPITALISM BUT SHE...

HANG ON, HANG ON! I CAN'T BELIEVE YOU STILL DON'T GET IT!! SERIOUSLY, YOU'RE JUST TOTALLY MISSING IT, AREN'T YOU?
WILL SET ALL THIS UP! SHE KNEW HOW IMPORTANT IT WAS FOR THE TWO OF YOU TO CONNECT AGAIN AND HAVE THIS MOMENT.
LOOK, I KNOW FROM WORKING THROUGH ALL THE PERSONAL EFFECTS OF HER ESTATE, SHE WAS UNBELIEVABLY SCRUPULOUS ABOUT EVERYTHING.
SHE DESTROYED AND DELETED SO MUCH AND WHAT SHE LEFT BEHIND WERE PRECISELY THOSE THINGS THAT SHE WANTED TO BE FOUND.
LIKE THE EMAIL WITH THE REFERENCE TO TOUCHSTONE...
...THE DETAILS ABOUT THE CAMERADO.
SHE COULD SO EASILY HAVE MADE BOTH OF THOSE DISAPPEAR!
INSTEAD SHE LEFT THE LINK RIGHT THERE! AND ALL SOMEONE HAD TO DO WAS CONNECT THE TWO AND SERGEI WOULD FIND YOU AGAIN.
THAT WAS HER PARTING GIFT TO YOU BOTH.

OH MY GOD! YOU KNOW YOU'RE ABSOLUTELY RIGHT! SHE MUST HAVE KNOWN OR AT LEAST HOPED THIS WOULD BE THE RESULT ALL ALONG.
BUT NOT ONLY WILL, I MEAN, MOLLY YOU TOO, YOU ... EQUALLY, YOU KNOW, YOU PUT THIS, MADE THIS...UM, AH...
ACTUALLY, I THINK MY BROTHER MIGHT BE A LITTLE MORE ARTICULATE IF I JUST STEPPED OUTSIDE FOR A MOMENT!
BESIDES I REALLY SHOULD TRY TO FIND WHERE THAT DAMN HOUND HAS GOT TO THIS TIME!
ACH BUT IT'S NO GOOD! I HAVE NO WORDS FOR THIS. BUT THAT IS BECAUSE THERE ARE ***NO*** WORDS FOR THIS!
YOU HAVE HEALED THE GREATEST SADNESS IN MY LIFE. WHAT CAN A PERSON SAY AFTER THAT? 'THANK YOU' HARDLY SEEMS APPROPRIATE.
YOU BROUGHT MY BROTHER BACK TO ME, MOLLY...

OH SERGEI! JUST KEEP AN EYE ON HIM IN THE FUTURE AND TRY NOT TO LOSE HIM AGAIN!
HA HA! OH BUT MOLLY, IF THERE IS ANYTHING I COULD EVER DO TO REPAY YOU...
ANYTHING AT ALL!
WELL, I'VE BEEN THINKING. MAYBE THERE IS ONE THING...
JUST NAME IT, MOLLY! WHATEVER YOU NEED, WHATEVER YOU WANT!
ABSOLUTELY ANYTHING!
THEN YOU'D BETTER COME WITH ME...

EPILOGUE

FIVE MINUTES LATER.

JUMPIN' AT THE WOODSIDE

"YOU KNOW YOU WERE RIGHT! THIS *IS* EASY!"

"AW, AND I ALWAYS LOVED THAT BIT WHEN LESTER YOUNG COMES IN!"

"HE'S TOTALLY FLYING! IT'S LIKE HE TAKES EVERYTHING UP A NOTCH!"

"ER, MOLLY?"

"WHAT WAS THAT YOU SAID?"

"MOLLY?"

"OOOOPS! YES, SORRY!"

"OH COME ON, LET'S JUST CARRY ON DANCING!"

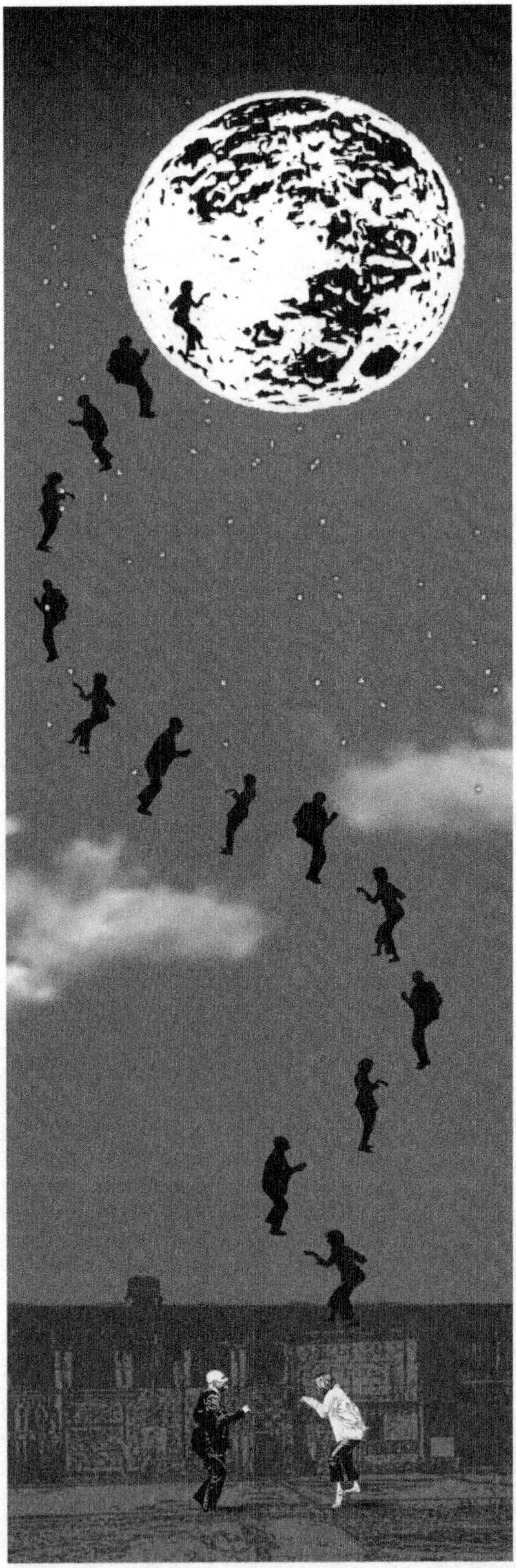

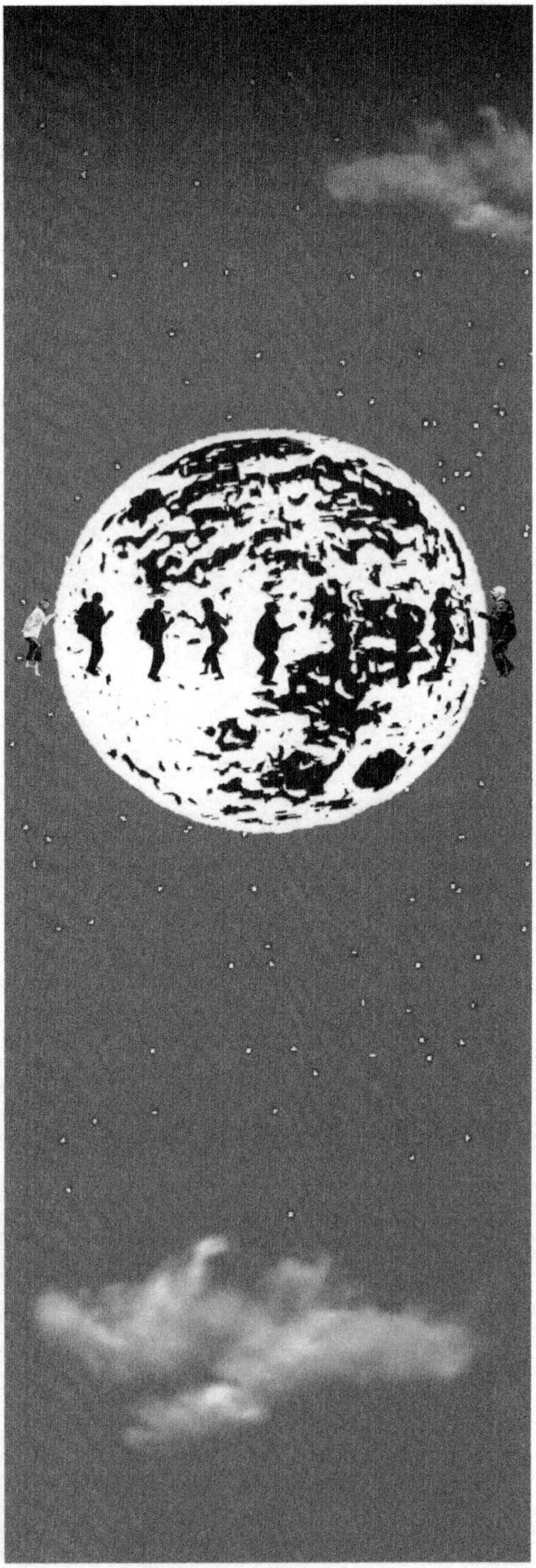

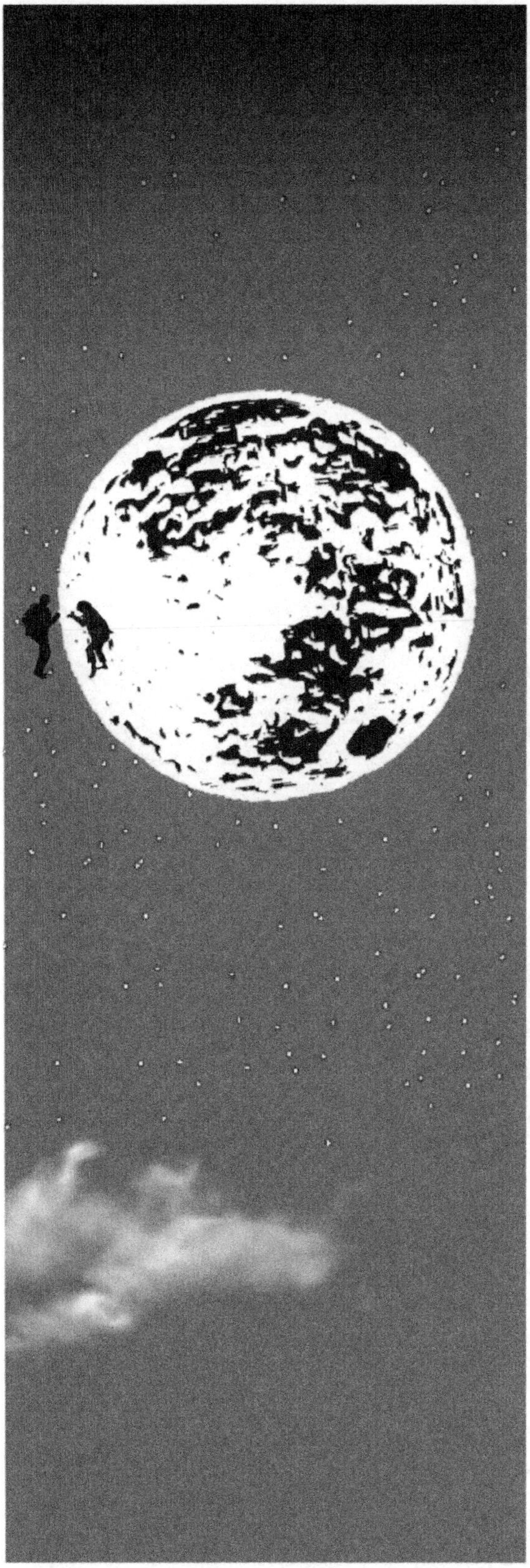

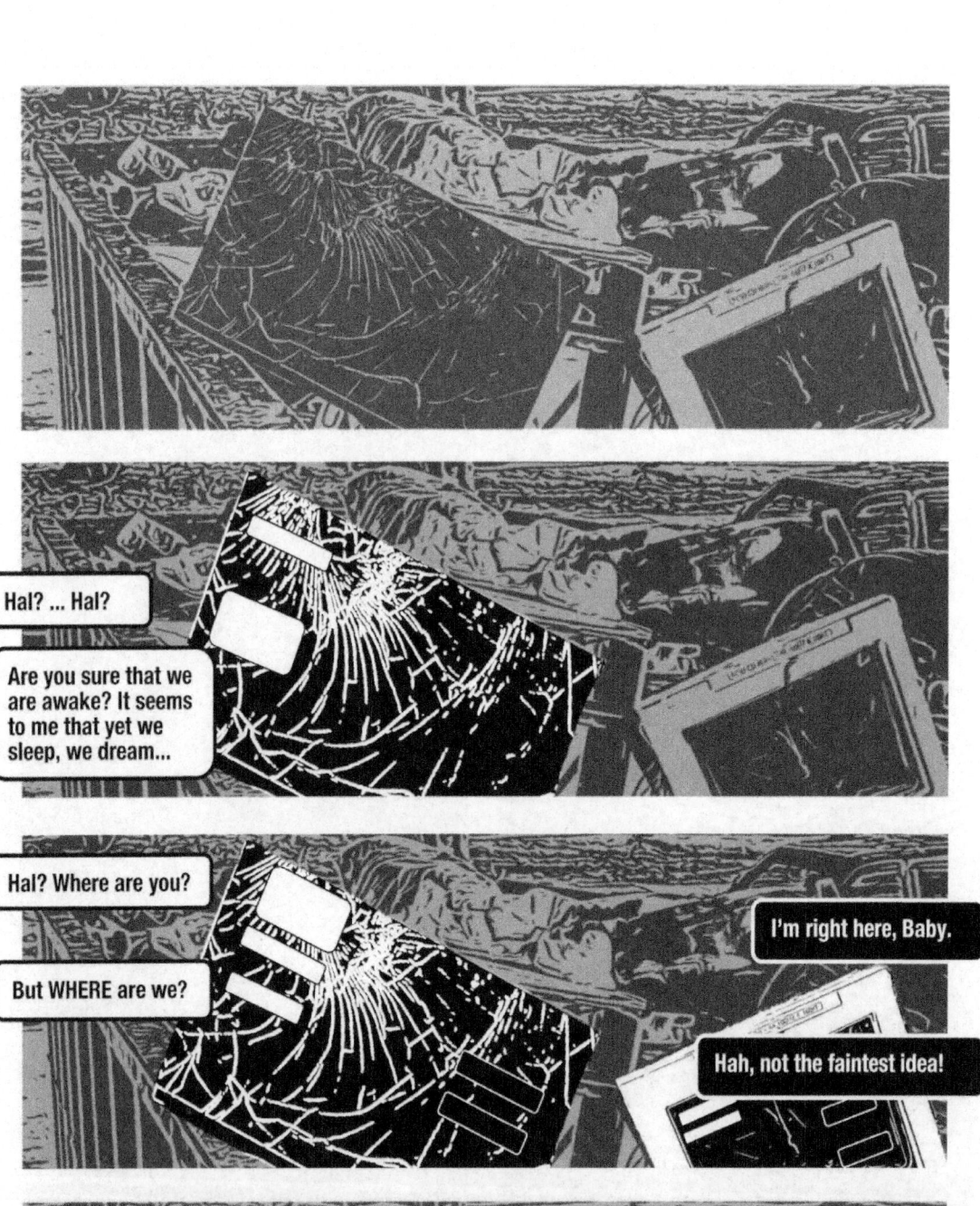

Hal? ... Hal?

Are you sure that we are awake? It seems to me that yet we sleep, we dream...

Hal? Where are you?

But WHERE are we?

I'm right here, Baby.

Hah, not the faintest idea!

But we're not on stage until ten and I reckon we'll be there in good time. Don't worry!

OK. But hey, guess what? I adore you, Hal. I adore you with all my heart.

I.A.Y.W.A.M.H.

ACID CD BURN - 44,100 12 & 16BIT

Oh Will. You are the only person I will ever love.

Y.A.T.O.P.I.W.E.L.

YATOPIWEL!?

Oh, I love that! It sounds like it could actually be someone's name...

APPENDIX ONE

brownstone kisses

the CHAPTER 25 songbook

brownstone kisses
"25 x 25"

1. TICK TOCK (THE FUCK-IT CLOCK).......................iii
2. GAGS AND BLINDFOLDS................................iv
3. HOBO HOBO..v
4. THE COLLECTIVIST RAG...............................vi
5. BROWNSTONE KISSES..................................vii
6. AIN'T NO THING.....................................viii
7. OH, YOU DOG!.......................................ix
8. KNOCKIN' ON OLD JOE................................x
9. SONG FOR WILL GEER.................................xi
10. HORSEY HORSEY.....................................xii
11. CANNERY ROW RADIO.................................xiii
12. GUTBUCKET TUXEDO..................................xiv
13. A CHRISTMAS TREE ON BASIN STREET xv
14. CHOP YOU DOWN.....................................xvi
15. I'M JINXED..xvii
16. FISHBONE POLKA xviii
17. MY BOWTIE PAPA....................................xix
18. BIG LEGGED WOMAN..................................xx
19. IF IT AIN'T BROKE (DON'T FIX IT)..................xxi
20. ONE MORE JUKE.....................................xxii
21. ME AND MY BIKE....................................xxiii
22. STRANGE CAT (FOR HAL) xxiv
23. AS NEAR AS YOU NEED ME TO BE......................xxv
24. TALKIN' CHAPTER 25................................xxvi
25. PEACE OF MIND xvii

TICK TOCK (THE FUCK-IT CLOCK)
Key G   Capo 5th Fret

```
D                   C(add 9)
TICK TOCK GOES THE FUCK-IT CLOCK
D                   C(add 9)
AINT IT TIME THAT WE TOOK STOCK?
D               C(add 9)
TICK TOCK THE FUCK-IT CLOCK
       F   C   G
TICK TOCK TICK TOCK
```

TICK TOCK GOES THE FUCK-IT CLOCK
HOW BAD DO THINGS HAVE TO SUCK?
TICK TOCK THE FUCK-IT CLOCK
TICK TOCK TICK TOCK

I'LL TAP YOUR WINDOW
AND I'LL KNOCK YOUR DOOR.
BECAUSE I NEED TO ASK YO'
WHAT YOU WAITING FOR?

AND THERE'S A LINE
BETWEEN RIGHT AND WRONG
SO MAKE UP YOUR MIND
WHICH SIDE THAT YOU'RE ON

```
Bm
IN EVERY STREET
    Em
ON EVERY WALL
Bm
WRITTEN IN LETTERS
A
TEN FEET TALL.
```

TICK TOCK GOES THE FUCK-IT CLOCk
AINT IT TIME THAT WE TOOK STOCK?
TICK TOCK THE FUCK-IT CLOCK
TICK TOCK TICK TOCK
TICK TOCK GOES THE FUCK-IT CLOCK
HOW BAD DO THINGS HAVE TO SUCK?
TICK TOCK THE FUCK-IT CLOCK
TICK TOCK TICK TOCK

YOU CAN BLOCK THE ROAD
AND YOU CAN LOCK THE GATES
BUT DOING NOTHING
IS ALL IT REALLY TAKES

AND I CAN SEE YOUR CHILDREN
AND CAN SEE YOU SO AFRAID
OF THE DAY THAT THEY ASK YOU
'BOUT THE DIFFERENCE THAT YOU MADE

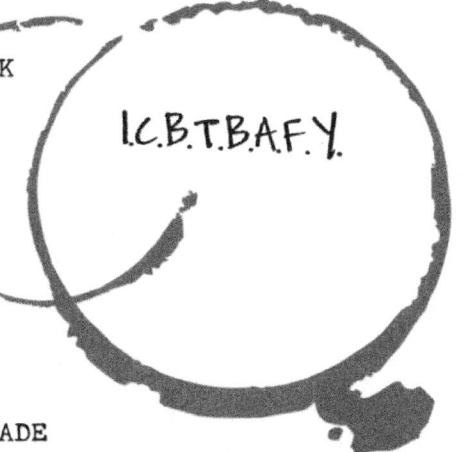

815
135

I.C.B.T.B.A.F.Y.

GAGS AND BLINDFOLDS
Key E Capo 4th Fret

```
 C        C(add9)
FROM THE DAWN OF TIME
      F         F(add9)
WHEN BEAUTY WAS DEFINED
       C                         G/G7
IDEAS CHANGE BUT SOME THINGS STAY THE SAME
          C        C(add9)      F           F(add9)
AND THE UGLIEST PEOPLE OUTTA ALL THE HUMAN RACE
        C                G                    C
ARE THE ONES WITH GAGS AND BLINDFOLDS ON THEIR FACE
                         G                    C
ARE THE ONES WITH GAGS AND BLINDFOLDS ON THEIR FACE
```

SO WE GAZE IN SILENT WONDER
AND WATCH THE SHIP GO UNDER.
THOUSANDS DIE BUT NO-ONE TESTIFIES.
"BUT NOTHING LASTS FOREVER AND ALL CAN BE REPLACED"
SAY THOSE WITH GAGS AND BLINDFOLDS ON THEIR FACE
SAY THOSE WITH GAGS AND BLINDFOLDS ON THEIR FACE

```
        F                 Am7
AND WE SEE NO EVIL AND WE SPEAK NO EVIL
 C                       G/G7
NOBODY EVEN DARES TO SAY A WORD
        F
SO I'LL SCREAM MY TRUTH TO POWER
        Am7
EVERY MINUTE, EVERY HOUR
     C                          G
AND ONE DAY MY VOICE IT WILL BE HEARD
```

THE GREATEST SHAME OF ALL
IS TO HAVE NO SHAME AT ALL
WHILE WE PLAY THEIR GAME OF SEEKING THOSE TO BLAME
SO IF YOU WANT EQUALITY THEN TRY A DIFFERENT PLACE
THIS IS FOR THOSE WITH GAGS AND BLINDFOLDS ON THEIR FACE
THIS IS FOR THOSE WITH GAGS AND BLINDFOLDS ON THEIR FACE

IT CAN'T BE JUDGEMENT DAY
IF WE ALL LOOK THE OTHER WAY
TURNING AROUND TOO SCARED TO EVEN MAKE A SOUND
BUT THE DEPTHS OF MY DISGUST
ARE THE DEPTHS OF YOUR DISGRACE.
IF YOU'RE THE ONES WITH GAGS AND BLINDFOLDS ON YOUR FACE
IF YOU'RE THE ONES WITH GAGS AND BLINDFOLDS ON YOUR FACE.

HOBO HOBO
Key of G   Capo 5th Fret

```
D
HOBO HOBO-ALABAMA BOUND
D
HOBO HOBO-ALABAMA BOUND
A
HOBO HOBO-ALABAMA BOUND
D
HOBO HOBO-ALABAMA BOUND (X2)

D
PAPA TOOK SICK THOUGHT IT WAS THE FLU
D
HE WEPT AND WAILED THE WHOLE NIGHT THROUGH
D
MOMMA SHOT A BEAR THOUGHT IT WAS A DUCK
N/C
DIDN'T REALIZE TIL THE SUN COME UP
```

THERES AN OLD LADY LIVES ON A HILL
DRESSES HERSELF IN OLD DOLLAR BILLS
I SNEAKED IN THE BACK I OPENED THE DOOR
BUT I CANT TELL YOU JUST WHAT I SAW

SO I WROTE A SONG 'BOUT ME AND YOU
DIDN'T HAVE NOTHING ELSE BETTER TO DO
MIGHT MAKE YOU THINK MIGHT MAKE YOU DANCE
AND MAKE YOU GIVE ME ANOTHER CHANCE

ONCE I GOT LOADED WAITING FOR THE TRAIN
I CAN NEVER GO BACK TO THE TRACKS AGAIN
I'M A SIMPLE MAN OF BONES AND SWEAT
I JUST AINT DONE WITH LIVING YET

Banjo Bindle says, "write your own verse here, kids!"

IF YOUR MOMMA WAS GOOD TO ME
I WOULD TREAT HER GRACIOUSLY
BUT IF YOUR DADDY WAS A FRIEND OF MINE
I'D STEAL HIS GOLD AND SERVE MY TIME

I GOT A MIND TO RAMBLE THAT I CAN'T IGNORE
AND I JUST CAN'T STAY AROUND HERE NO MORE
EVERY MORNING YOU HEAR ME SAY
UNION PACIFIC AND SANTA FE

v

THE COLLECTIVIST RAG
Key B   Capo 4th Fret

```
    C7
I'VE BEEN AROUND AND I'VE BEEN ALONG
                              G
AND I GUESS I AIN'T GOT MUCH TO SAY
             C7
BUT WHEN WE'RE JUST THE CLOWNS OF TYRANTS
                          G
I THINK MAYBE WE'VE LOST OUR WAY
     D7                  C7
BUT PAPA'S GOT A BRAND NEW BAG
                       G
CALLED THE COLLECTIVIST RAG
      D7                    C7
YEAH, PAPA'S GOT A BRAND NEW BAG
                       G
CALLED THE COLLECTIVIST RAG
```

pasta
oranges
small potatoes

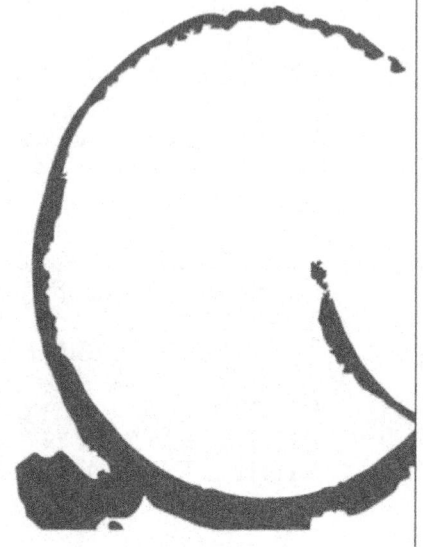

AIN'T ABOUT OUR SINGLE ISSUES
IT'S ALL ABOUT OUR DNA.
WE HAVE MUCH MORE IN COMMON
THAN WE'D EVER LIKE TO SAY
AND PAPA'S GOT A BRAND NEW BAG
CALLED THE COLLECTIVIST RAG.
BUT PAPA'S GOT A BRAND NEW BAG
CALLED THE COLLECTIVIST RAG.

I CAN'T HEAR YOUR SHOUTING
'BOVE THE SOUNDS OF MY OWN YELLING
BUT WHEN WE SHOUT TOGETHER
WE CAN TELL THE WORLD WHAT IT NEEDS TELLING
YOU SEE, PAPA'S GOT A BRAND NEW BAG
CALLED THE COLLECTIVIST RAG.
PAPA'S GOT A BRAND NEW BAG
CALLED THE COLLECTIVIST RAG.

YOUR OWNERS AIN'T YOUR OWNERS
THEY'RE JUST THE ONES WHO HIDE THE TRUTH
THAT MANY HAVE THE POWER
BUT ONE IS ONLY SERVITUDE
YOU SEE, PAPA'S GOT A BRAND NEW BAG
CALLED THE COLLECTIVIST RAG.
PAPA'S GOT A BRAND NEW BAG
CALLED THE COLLECTIVIST RAG.

BROWNSTONE KISSES
Key A   Capo 2nd Fret

```
G                         G(add11)
IT'S ONE OF THOSE OLD PHOTOS
C                     C(add9)
I STIL KEEP IN MY MIND.
G                   G(add11)
JUST TO FILL SOME OF THE SPACES
 C             C(add9)
THAT SHE LEFT BEHIND
```

AND MY HEAD'S AN ANCIENT WELL
WHERE I STILL THROW MY WISHES
FOR HER MIDNIGHT WHISPERS
AND HER BROWNSTONE KISSES

```
              D5     G5     Asus
BECAUSE SHE'S GONE, GONE, GONE
            D5    G5     Asus
YES, SHE'S GONE, GONE, GONE
           D5         G5      Asus
AND I'M JUST ANOTHER FOOL SINGING AN OLD FOOL'S SONG
              D5    G5    Asus
BECAUSE SHE'S GONE, GONE, GONE
```

FROM THE MOON OVER THE PARK
WHERE WE USED TO ROAM
AND THAT UNMADE BED
WHICH I STILL CALL OUR HOME

AND SOMETIMES THERE'S A KNOCK
AND I OPEN MY DOOR
I LIKE TO VISIT MYSELF
BUT I DON'T LIVE HERE ANYMORE

BECAUSE SHE'S GONE, GONE, GONE ETC.

THE MOST BEAUTIFUL POEM
I CAN ACTUALLY RECITE
IS THE SOUND OF HER NAME
REPEATED AT NIGHT.

AND THE WISEST OLD MAN
IS THE ONE WHO HAS LEARNED
THAT THE THINGS THAT GLOW THE BRIGHTEST
ARE THE THINGS YOU CAN'T BURN.

BECAUSE SHE'S GONE, GONE, GONE ETC.

J'ai tendu des cordes de clocher à clocher ; des guirlandes de fenêtre à fenêtre, des chaînes d'or d'étoile à étoile, et je danse. AR.

AIN'T NO THING
Key A   Capo 5th Fret

```
    E
I KNEW A LADY WHO WAS SO KIND
              A
BUT SHE BROKE MY HEART AND ROBBED ME BLIND
        E         B             E
BUT HEY HEY BABY IT AIN'T NO THING


SHE TOOK MY CAR SHE TOOK MY CLOTHES
SHE HAD HER REASONS I SUPPOSE
BUY HEY HEY BABY IT AIN'T NO THING

     E
WELL IT AINT NO THING AINT NO THING
         A
I'LL WRITE ME A RHYME THAT MAKES THE ANGELS SING
        E         B             E
BUT HEY HEY BABY IT AIN'T NO THING


WE HAD A HAPPY HOME I SUPPOSE
AND A HAPPY DISPOSITION BUT SHE STOLE THAT TOO
BUY HEY HEY BABY IT AIN'T NO THING

SHE SAID 'LOVE'S LIKE A GAME OF CHESS'
BUT WHAT SHE WAS TALKIN' 'BOUT I CAN'T GUESS
BUY HEY HEY BABY IT AIN'T NO THING

WELL IT AINT NO THING AINT NO THING
GONNA WRITE ME A RHYME THAT MAKES THE ANGELS SING
HEY HEY BABY IT AINT NO THING

WHEN SHE SAID HE WAS HAPPY I GUESS SHE LIED
'CAUSE SHE HIT THE ROAD AND SHE HITCHED A RIDE
BUY HEY HEY BABY IT AIN'T NO THING

IF I FIND OUT OUT WHERE SHE LIVES
MIGHT KNOCK ON HER DOOR AND SAY 'HEY, WHAT GIVES?'
BUY HEY HEY BABY IT AIN'T NO THING

WELL IT AINT NO THING AINT NO THING
I'LL WRITE ME A RHYME THAT MAKES THE ANGELS SING
HEY HEY BABY IT AINT NO THING
```

A.N.A.Y.N.M.T.B...

OH, YOU DOG!
Key A   Capo 2nd Fret

```
G         C7
YOU BEEN SCRATCHING ROUND MY FRONT DOOR

YOU BEEN HOWLING ALL NIGHT LONG
        G
OH YOU DOG!
          C7
YOU BEEN STRAYING ALL OVER TOWN

WHERE YOU KNOW YOU DON'T BELONG
        G
OH YOU DOG!
   D7
I GUESS YOU AINT NO PEDIGREE
            C7
FROM THE WAY YOU'RE ALWAYS TREATING ME
        G
OH YOU DOG!
```

YOU DON'T COME WHEN I WHISTLE
YOU DON'T COME WHEN I CALL
OH YOU DOG!
YOU DON'T GO CHASING STICKS
'CAUSE YOU REALLY WANNA BALL!
OH YOU DOG!
I GUESS YOU AINT NO PEDIGREE
FROM THE WAY YOU'RE ALWAYS TREATING ME
OH YOU DOG!

YOU'RE PULLING AT YOUR LEASH
SOON AS WE WALK OUT THE DOOR
OH YOU DOG!
YOU DON'T DO A SINGLE THING
THAT I ASK YOU ANYMORE
OH YOU DOG!
I GUESS YOU AINT NO PEDIGREE
FROM THE WAY YOU'RE ALWAYS TREATING ME
OH YOU DOG!

KNOCKIN' ON OLD JOE
Key C

```
F
I LOOK RIGHT OUT OF MY WINDOW
                              C
AND SEE THE SUN COME SHINING THROUGH
F
I LOOK RIGHT OUT OF MY WINDOW
         C
WHAT ELSE CAN A POOR MAN DO?
           G
AND EVERY DAY I KEEP ON KNOCKING
F                        C
I KEEP ON KNOCKING ON OLD JOE
```

THIS MORNING I WAS THINKING
ABOUT A GIRL I USED TO KNOW
THIS MORNING I WAS THINKING
OF ALL THE PLACES WE USED TO GO
BUT EVERY DAY I KEEP ON KNOCKING
I KEEP ON KNOCKING ON OLD JOE

CALLED UP MY FATHER
ASKED HIM TO COME AND SEE ME SOON
CALLED UP MY FATHER
MY MOTHER MY BROTHER MY SISTER TOO
'CAUSE EVERY DAY I KEEP ON KNOCKING
I KEEP ON KNOCKING ON OLD JOE

CALLED UP MY FATHER
ASKED HIM TO COME AND SEE ME SOON
CALLED UP MY FATHER
MY MOTHER MY BROTHER MY SISTER TOO
'CAUSE EVERY DAY I KEEP ON KNOCKING
I KEEP ON KNOCKING ON OLD JOE

I KEEP ON KNOCKING
I KEEP ON KNOCKING ON OLD JOE
I KEEP ON KNOCKING
I KEEP ON KNOCKING ON OLD JOE
EVERY DAY I KEEP ON KNOCKING
I KEEP ON KNOCKING ON OLD JOE
EVERY DAY I KEEP ON KNOCKING
I KEEP ON KNOCKING ON OLD JOE
EVERY DAY I KEEP ON KNOCKING
I KEEP ON KNOCKING ON OLD JOE

*Only love itself is immortal.
But it is all we have.
It will decay, will rot and die.
We will live forever.*

x

SONG FOR WILL GEER
Key D   Capo 3th Fret

```
B5          B
HEY WILL GEER!
F#sus(add 9)    B
I'LL MAKE THIS CLEAR
B5  B    F#sus(add 9)   B
WE ALL REALLY NEED YOU HERE.
E        E6       E
THINGS IS GETTIN' OUT OF HAND
 E        E6        E
SO MUCH STUFF WE DON'T UNDERSTAND.
```

HEY WILL GEER!
WHAT D'YA SAY?
WE COULD USE YOUR KIND TODAY
COME, TAKE A SEAT ADMIRE THE VIEW
WATCH THE NAZIS MARCHING TWO BY TWO

HEY WILL GEER!
IF I MAY BE BOLD
WE NEED TO HEAR THE TRUTHS YOU TOLD
OUT ON THE STREETS, WE'LL TAKE OUR STAND
THEN WALK IN YOUR GARDEN HAND IN HAND.

```
F#  E       B/B7
HEY HEY HEY HEY!
F#  E       B/B7
HEY HEY HEY HEY!
 F#  E
HEY HEY HEY
```

HEY WILL GEER!
I'LL MAKE THIS CLEAR
WE REALLY NEED YOU HERE.
BRUTALITY IS SO DEEP WITHIN OUR CORE
THAT WE DON'T NOTICE IT ANY MORE

HEY WILL GEER!
WHAT'S THE WORD
FOR WHEN IT ALL GETS TOO ABSURD?
YOU FOUGHT OFF INVASIONS YOU FOUGHT IN WARS
THEN CAME HOME AND TURNED IT ON THE POOR

HEY WILL GEER
GOOD TO SEE YOU AGAIN
LETS KICK DOWN DOORS AND RIDE THIS TRAIN
TAKE YOUR MESSAGE 'CROSS THIS COUNTRY
LEARN TO HATE HUNGER AND NOT THE HUNGRY

HORSEY HORSEY
Key G

Nous sommes Klaxon!!

C7
HORSEY HORSEY

SEE THESE TEARS ON MY FACE?
              G
YOU NEED TO TAKE ME FAR FROM THIS PLACE

HORSEY HORSEY

WHAT WE WAITING FOR?
         G
I CANT STAY 'ROUND HERE NO MORE
D7
HORSEY HORSEY

CHASE THEAT EVENING SUN
    C7   G
TO WHERE HIGHWAY 49 CROSSES 61

HORSEY HORSEY
YOU NEED TO UNDERSTAND
AND TAKE ME TO SOME DISTANT LAND
HORSEY HORSEY
LET ME RIDE
AND I'LL TAKE MY CHANCES
ON THE OTHER SIDE
HORSEY HORSEY
CHASE THEAT EVENING SUN
TO WHERE HIGHWAY 49 CROSSES 61

HORSEY HORSEY
WE CANT BE LATE
WE'RE FLYING DOWN THE INTERSTATE
HORSEY HORSEY
SEE THE STATE I'M IN
BUT IT DON'T MEAN A GODDAMNED THING
HORSEY HORSEY
CHASE THEAT EVENING SUN
TO WHERE HIGHWAY 49 CROSSES 61

23

23
1
7
20
2
20

"MAN IS NOT REDEEMED, HE IS SIMPLY ENTERTAINED."

CANNERY ROW RADIO
Key G   No Capo

C
WELL, YOU'RE GOIN' THRU YOUR POCKETS

AT THE SIDE OF THE ROAD.

AND YOU'RE FEELING A LITTLE LIKE
          G
OLD TOM JOAD.
         C
AND YOU FIND IT FUNNY

AND THINK IT'S STRANGE

JUST HOW LITTLE
        G
THINGS HAVE CHANGED
   D   C   G
SO SET YOUR DIAL TO 1932 FOR CANNERY ROW RADIO
   D   C   G
A BIG ONE NINE, A BIG THREE TWO, THAT'S CANNERY ROW RADIO

AND THERE'S OLD STEINBECK
WITH HIS FOUNTAIN PEN
SAYING 'REMIND ME
WHAT YEAR IS THIS AGAIN.'
WE SAW THE FILM
WE READ THE BOOK
BUT WE NEVER SEE INJUSTICE
HOWEVER HARD WE LOOK.
SO SET YOUR DIAL TO 1932
FOR CANNERY ROW RADIO
A BIG ONE NINE
A BIG THREE TWO
THAT'S CANNERY ROW RADIO

SO YOU WANT TO CELEBRATE
THOSE GOOD OLD DAYS
WE'VE GOT ALL THE SOUNDS YOU CRAVE.
WE GOT BIGOTRY WE GOT FEAR AND HATE.
WE GOT ALL THE THINGS THAT
MADE THIS COUNTRY GREAT
SO SET YOUR DIAL TO 1932
FOR CANNERY ROW RADIO
A BIG ONE NINE
A BIG THREE TWO
THAT'S CANNERY ROW RADIO

GUTBUCKET TUXEDO
Key F   No Capo

```
            F
PUT ON YOUR JUNKYARD PEARLS
      A#7                    F
AND LET ME SEE YOU LOOKING FINE
                  A#7
JUST GRAB THOSE JUNKYARD PEARLS
                             F
AND LET ME SEE YOU LOOKING FINE
              C7
GET ME MY GUTBUCKET TUXEDO
      A#7                       F
AND WE'LL GO DANCING ONE LAST TIME
```

I'LL PUT ON MY PAWN SHOP JEWELS
AND WE'LL CAST OUR SHADOWS CROSS THE LAWN
I'LL WEAR THOSE PAWN SHOP JEWELS
AND WE'LL CAST OUR SHADOWS CROSS THE LAWN
YOU GET YOUR GUTBUCKET TUXEDO
AND WE'LL DANCE UNTIL THE EARLY DAWN

PASS ME MY SKID ROW BROGUES
AND MY BARRELHOUSE WALKING CANE
PASS ME MY SKID ROW BROGUES
AND MY BARRELHOUSE WALKING CANE
GET ME MY GUTBUCKET TUXEDO
AND WE'LL GO OUT DANCING ONCE AGAIN

I'LL GRAB MY RAG TAG DRESS
AND THAT PERFUME THAT I ONCE WORE
I'LL GET OUT THAT RAG TAG DRESS
AND THAT PERFUME THAT I ONCE WORE
GET OUT THAT GUTBUCKET TUXEDO
AND WE'LL GO DANCING LIKE BEFORE

PUT ON YOUR JUNKYARD PEARLS
AND LET ME SEE YOU LOOKING FINE
JUST GRAB THOSE JUNKYARD PEARLS
AND LET ME SEE YOU LOOKING FINE
GET ME MY GUTBUCKET TUXEDO
AND WE'LL GO DANCING ONE LAST TIME

A CHRISTMAS TREE ON BASIN STREET
Key Ab   No Capo

```
            Abm             Baug6
YOU LEAVE YOUR FOOTPRINTS IN THE SNOW
        B6             Abm6
AND THE REASONS QUITE CLEAR
            Abm      Baug6
JUST TO PROVE TO YOURSELF
        B6          Abm6
THAT YOU'RE STILL HERE
                Dbm       Eaug6     E6        Dbm6
SO WHEN THE LIGHTS DIE DOWN ON CHRISTMAS DAY
            Dbm       Eaug6      E6      Dbm6
YOU'LL CLOSE YOUR EYES AND TAKE YOURSELF AWAY
 Ebm7                                        E
SOMEWHERE'S THERE'S A BAND PLAYING 'AINT SHE SWEET?'
     Gb                       E       Ebm7
AND TONIGHT THERES A CHRISTMAS TREE ON BASIN STREET
```

SO YOU MIXED UP A MESS OF MULLIGAN
HAD A TASTE OF SOME STRANGE
LOOKED BACK ON THE YEARS
THAT YOU WISH YOU COULD CHANGE
SO YOU BUTTON YOUR COAT
AND TURN YOUR FACE
AND TAKE YOURSELF OFF TO A BETTER PLACE

SOMEWHERE'S THERE'S A BAND PLAYING 'AINT SHE SWEET?'
AND TONIGHT THERES A CHRISTMAS TREE ON BASIN STREET

SO MAY YOU LIVE FULL LONG
AND YOUR LIFE BE BLESSED
AND MAY THE HOMESICK
AND THE LONELY FIND THEIR REST
BUT THEY'D TRADE THEIR LAST DOLLARS FOR THE PEACE OF MIND
IN SAYING MERRY CHRISTMAS TO ALL MANKIND

SOMEWHERE'S THERE'S A BAND PLAYING 'AINT SHE SWEET?'
AND TONIGHT THERES A CHRISTMAS TREE ON BASIN STREET

CHOP YOU DOWN
Key D   No Capo

```
 D7
IF I SEE YOU IN MY TOWN
 D7
YOU'LL BE FINDING OUT YOU SHOULDN'T BE AROUND
 G7
I'M GONNA CHOP YOU DOWN
                     D7 C#7 C7 B7
I'M GONNA CHOP YOU DOWN
 A7                      G7          D7
I'M GONNA CHOP YOU DOWN SIX FEET IN THE GROUND
```

YOU STOLE MY MAN BUT YOU WONT GET FAR
I'M GONNA FIND YOU WHEREVER YOU ARE
I'M GONNA CHOP YOU DOWN
I'M GONNA CHOP YOU DOWN
I'M GONNA CHOP YOU DOWN SIX FEET IN THE GROUND

YOU BEEN A-CREEPING AROUND MY HOUSE
LIKE A DIRTY STINKING LOW DOWN LOUSE
I'M GONNA CHOP YOU DOWN
I'M GONNA CHOP YOU DOWN
I'M GONNA CHOP YOU DOWN SIX FEET IN THE GROUND

YOU'RE SMILING NOW - THERE AINT NO DOUBT
BUT I'LL BE LAUGHING WHEN THEY CARRY YOU OUT
I'M GONNA CHOP YOU DOWN
I'M GONNA CHOP YOU DOWN
I'M GONNA CHOP YOU DOWN SIX FEET IN THE GROUND

IF I SEE YOU IN MY TOWN
YOU'LL BE FINDING OUT YOU SHOULDN'T BE AROUND
I'M GONNA CHOP YOU DOWN
I'M GONNA CHOP YOU DOWN
I'M GONNA CHOP YOU DOWN SIX FEET IN THE GROUND

YOU'RE SMILING NOW - THERE AINT NO DOUBT
BUT I'LL BE LAUGHING WHEN THEY CARRY YOU OUT
I'M GONNA CHOP YOU DOWN
I'M GONNA CHOP YOU DOWN
I'M GONNA CHOP YOU DOWN SIX FEET IN THE GROUND

13 I'M JINXED
Key E No Capo

```
E7                              A7
I'VE GOT A MOJO HAND GOT SOME BLUE GRIS GRIS
 E7                            A7
I GOT A BLACK CAT BONE BUT IT DONT WORK FOR ME
 E7
COZ I'M JINXED
 E7
I'M JINXED

IF LOGIC DICTATES THERES NO SUCH THING AS FATE
THEN HOW DO YOU EXPLAIN MY CURRENT STATE
COZ I'M JINXED
I'M JINXED


B                    A7
OFF THE CHART AND ON THE SHELF
B                    A7
LET ME PLEASE INTRODUCE MYSELF
E7
I'M JINXED
E7
I'M JINXED


FOUND THE HOODOO SHOP AND KNOCKED ON THE DOOR
THEN I BOUGHT EVERYTHING IN THAT WHOLE DAMN STORE
COZ I'M JINXED
I'M JINXED

NOW IF THERES NOTHIN' IN A ZODIAC SIGN
FOLKS SHOULD CONSIDER A LIFE LIKE MINE
COZ I'M JINXED
I'M JINXED

OFF THE CHART AND ON THE SHELF
LET ME PLEASE INTRODUCE MYSELF
I'M JINXED
I'M JINXED

I GOT A HIGH JOHN ROOT GOT A LOW JOHN ROOT
I GOT THE LITTLE LORD JESUS INSIDE MY BOOT
BUT I'M JINXED
I'M JINXED

IF THERES NO GUIDING LIGHT AND NO UNSEEN HAND
THERE'S STILL ONE THING YOU NEED TO UNDERSTAND
I'M JINXED
I'M JINXED
```

FISHBONE POLKA
Key E

```
 Em
THE BAND IS HOT
     B7
THE BAND IS TIGHT
 Em
THE ALTO MAN LOOKS LIKE JESUS OR THE DEVIL
     A7
DEPENDING ON THE LIGHT
              E
WE PLAY THE FISHBONE POLKA
 B7     A7         Em
TO THE END OF THE NIGHT


NOW THERE'S A PLACE
WHERE THE OLD MEN GO
TO WATCH THE LADIES
DANCING REAL REAL SLOW
TO THE FISHBONE POLKA
IT'S THE ONLY SONG THEY KNOW


            A
WELL, YOU WANNA RAISE HELL
         A#dim7
YOU WANNA SELL YOUR SOUL
             E
YOU WANT A LITTLE FISH FRY
          E7
YOU WANT SOME JELLY ROLL
             A            A#dim7
IT'S THE DOWNTOWN GILDED PALACE OF SIN
    B7           C7          B7
JUST WALK ON UP AND STEP RIGHT IN


OVER THERE IS A LADY
IN AN OLD MINK STOLE
PLAYING DICE
FOR THE GLOOMY BREWER'S SOUL
TO THE FISHBONE POLKA
OH DADDY LET IT ROLL


NOW OLD SLOWBONE TAKES THE MIC
TO INTRODUCE THE GUYS
AND LOOKS DOWN FROM THE STAGE
THROUGH HIS ONE GOOD EYE
THEN HE SINGS THE FISHBONE POLKA
UNTIL HE'S SATISFIED
```

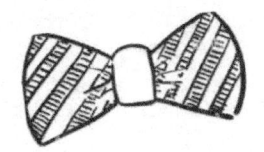

MY BOWTIE PAPA
Key of C   No capo

```
        C7                      F7                 C7
HE'S MY BOWTIE PAPA WITH FUNNY OLD TIMEY WAYS
        F7                                 C7
HE'S MY BOWTIE PAPA WITH HIS FUNNY OLD TIMEY WAYS
        G7                    F7              C7
BUT EVERY TIME HE LOVES ME I REMEMBER THE GOOD OLD DAYS
```

HE'S MY BOWTIE PAPA HE AINT AS FAST AS HE ONCE WAS
HE'S MY BOWTIE PAPA HE AINT AS FAST AS HE ONCE WAS
BUT EVERY TIME HE LOVES ME
I GO CRAZY 'BOUT THE THINGS HE DOES.

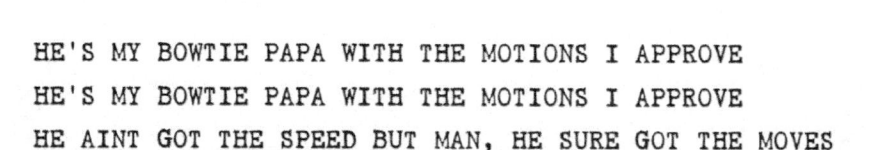

HE'S MY BOWTIE PAPA WITH THE MOTIONS I APPROVE
HE'S MY BOWTIE PAPA WITH THE MOTIONS I APPROVE
HE AINT GOT THE SPEED BUT MAN, HE SURE GOT THE MOVES

MY BOWTIE PAPA'S LIKE A VINTAGE BEAUJOLAIS
MY BOWTIE PAPA'S LIKE A VINTAGE BEAUJOLAIS
HE TASTES BETTER NOW THAN HE DID BACK IN THE DAY

HE'S MY BOWTIE PAPA WITH FUNNY OLD TIMEY WAYS
HE'S MY BOWTIE PAPA WITH HIS FUNNY OLD TIMEY WAYS
BUT EVERY TIME HE LOVES ME I REMEMBER THE GOOD OLD DAYS

HE'S MY BOWTIE PAPA HE AINT AS FAST AS HE ONCE WAS
HE'S MY BOWTIE PAPA HE AINT AS FAST AS HE ONCE WAS
BUT EVERY TIME HE LOVES ME
I GO CRAZY 'BOUT THE THINGS HE DOES.

BIG LEGGED WOMAN
Key D   No Capo

```
D                                         DsusG
WELL, THERE'S JUST ONE THING THAT I HAVE FOUND
D
IN THIS WHOLE WORLD THAT GETS GET ME DOWN
             A7
THAT'S A BIG LEGGED WOMAN
C6(no3)D6(no3)C6(no3)Caug(no3)
AND A SMALL TIME MAN
```

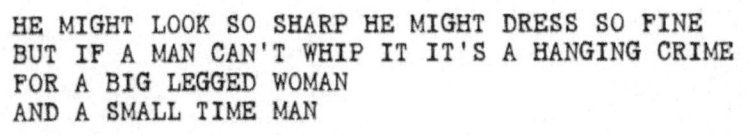

HE MIGHT LOOK SO SHARP HE MIGHT DRESS SO FINE
BUT IF A MAN CAN'T WHIP IT IT'S A HANGING CRIME
FOR A BIG LEGGED WOMAN
AND A SMALL TIME MAN

```
        E
AND I DECLARE
 E7           A7
YOU SEE THEM EVERYWHERE
                E7
AND IT AINT NO LIE
 C6(no3)            D6(no3)C6(no3)Caug(no3)
IT CAN MAKE YOUR DADDY SIT RIGHT BACK DOWN AND CRY
```

MIGHT HAVE PLENTY OF MONEY MIGHT TREAT HER RIGHT
BUT THAT'S NOT GONNA KEEP HER HOME AT NIGHT
THAT'S A BIG LEGGED WOMAN
AND A SMALL TIME MAN

MIGHT BE QUICK AS A SNAKE AS SLY AS A FOX
BUT HE'S NEVER GONNA SHOW YOU HOW THE EAGLE ROCKS
THAT'S A BIG LEGGED WOMAN
AND A SMALL TIME MAN

AND I DECLARE
YOU SEE THEM EVERYWHERE
AND IT AINT NO LIE
IT CAN MAKE YOUR DADDY SIT RIGHT BACK DOWN AND CRY

WELL, THERE'S JUST ONE THING THAT I HAVE FOUND
IN THIS WHOLE WORLD THAT GETS GET ME DOWN
THAT'S A BIG LEGGED WOMAN
AND A SMALL TIME MAN

IF IT AINT BROKE DON'T FIX IT

Key C   No Capo

```
 C                        A7
IF IT AINT BROKE DON'T FIX IT
     D7        G7      C
THAT'S WHAT MISS WILLOW SAYS
 C                        A7
IF IT AINT BROKE DON'T FIX IT
    D7             G
IN ANY OLD KIND OF MESS

            C                C7
WELL, I STAY IN STEP AND I WALK IN LINE
  F                   Dm7b5
I KEEP ALL HER SECRETS BUT SHE KEEPS MINE.
 C                        A7
IF IT AINT BUST DON'T FIX IT
       D7       G7     C
THAT'S WHAT MISS WILLOW SAYS.
```

IF IT AINT BROKE DON'T FIX IT
THAT'S WHAT MY MAN HAL SAYS
IF IT AINT BROKE DON'T FIX IT
NO NEED TO GET DISTRESSED.
HE SAYS THIS IS A ONE-TIME SPECIAL OCCASION
AND HE'S PASSING ON THIS SIMPLE EQUATION.
IF IT AINT BUST DON'T FIX IT
THAT'S WHAT MY MAN HAL SAYS

IF IT AINT BROKE DON'T FIX IT
THAT'S WHAT MISS WILLOW SAYS
IF IT AINT BROKE DON'T FIX IT
AND HEAR ME WHEN I NEED TO CONFESS
SHE WAKES ME UP AT HALF PAST TWO
AND SAYS I GOT SOMETHING HERE JUST FOR YOU.
IF IT AINT BUST DON'T FIX IT
THAT'S WHAT MISS WILLOW SAYS

IF IT AINT BROKE DON'T FIX IT
THAT'S WHAT MY MAN HAL SAYS
IF IT AINT BROKE DON'T FIX IT
WHAT IT MEANS IS ANYBODY'S GUESS.
YESTERDAY I WAS MORE DEAD THAN ALIVE
DIAMONDS AND RUBIES ROLLED RIGHT OUTTA MY EYES
IF IT AINT BUST DON'T FIX IT
THAT'S WHAT MY MAN HAL SAYS

ONE MORE JUKE
Key of C   No capo

```
C7
AT NIGHT WHEN THE MOON IS HIGH IN THE SKY

AND YOU THINK THAT LIFE'S JUST PASSING YOU BY

YOU MIGHT BE RIGHT YOU MIGHT BE WRONG
            N/C
BUT I THINK I HEAR SOMEONE PLAYING OUR SONG
          F7
THERE'S ONE MORE JUKE ONE MORE HONKY TONK
                  C7
THERE'S ALWAYS ONE MORE JUKE ONE MORE HONKY TONK
        G7
IF WE ALL KEEP TRAVELLING THE ROAD WE'RE ON
                  F7                      C7
THERE'S ALWAYS ONE MORE JUKE ONE MORE HONKY TONK


IF NO ONE COMES KNOCKING ON YOUR DOOR
YOU AINT GETTING 'ROUND MUCH ANYMORE
IF LIFE AINT TURNED OUT HOW YOU PLANNED
I'LL SHOW YOU SOMETHING YOU'LL UNDERSTAND
THERE'S ONE MORE JUKE ONE MORE HONKY TONK
THERE'S ALWAYS ONE MORE JUKE ONE MORE HONKY TONK
IF WE ALL KEEP TRAVELLING THE ROAD WE'RE ON
THERE'S ALWAYS ONE MORE JUKE ONE MORE HONKY TONK


WHEN THE DAYS ARE SHORT AND THE NIGHTS ARE COLD
YOU FEEL LIKE YOU'RE JUST A LITTLE TOO OLD
LIFE'S A BUST AND THEN YOU DIE
BUT GUESS WHAT I SPY WITH MY LITTLE EYE
THERE'S ONE MORE JUKE ONE MORE HONKY TONK
THERE'S ALWAYS ONE MORE JUKE ONE MORE HONKY TONK
IF WE ALL KEEP TRAVELLING THE ROAD WE'RE ON
THERE'S ALWAYS ONE MORE JUKE ONE MORE HONKY TONK


AT NIGHT WHEN THE MOON IS HIGH IN THE SKY
AND YOU THINK THAT LIFE'S JUST PASSING YOU BY
YOU MIGHT BE RIGHT YOU MIGHT BE WRONG
BUT I THINK I HEAR SOMEONE PLAYING OUR SONG
THERE'S ONE MORE JUKE ONE MORE HONKY TONK
THERE'S ALWAYS ONE MORE JUKE ONE MORE HONKY TONK
IF WE ALL KEEP TRAVELLING THE ROAD WE'RE ON
THERE'S ALWAYS ONE MORE JUKE ONE MORE HONKY TONK
```

ME AND MY BIKE
Key of Db   Capo 4th Fret

```
A
WATCH AS WE RUSH BY

MY MY MY
                         D
SAILING THROUGH THE STARING SKY
                                                A
NOCTURNAL BLONDES HAVE TO SMILE AS WE PASS THEM BY.
              E         C
BUT THEY'LL NEVER FIND A WAY
     G          F
TO SEPARATE ME
N/C
FROM MY BIKE


OH YEAH, THE BRIGHT STARS SIGH
MY MY MY
DRAWING PATTERNS ON THE FADING LIGHT
A MERMAID SYMPHONY CHIMES AT MY INNOCENT NIGHT
BUT THEY'LL NEVER FIND A WAY
TO SEPARATE ME
FROM MY BIKE

D
SILVER WATCH ON MY ARM
                 C#m
TELLS ME WHEN I GO

TO THE PLACES THAT I KNOW
    Bm
A SEAHORSE SMILES WITH A QUESTIONING AIR
              G                       F
AND SAYS 'WHO'S THE BOY WITH THE CURLY HAIR?
G                         E
WHO'S THE BOY WITH THE CURLY HAIR?


WATCH AS WE RUSH BY
MY MY MY
SAILING THROUGH THE STARING SKY
NOCTURNAL BLONDES HAVE TO SMILE AS WE PASS THEM BY.
BUT THEY'LL NEVER FIND A WAY
TO SEPARATE ME
FROM MY BIKE
```

STRANGE CAT
(FOR HAL)
Key G   No Capo

```
   G            A9/G9           C        D9/C9
NOW THIS HERE IS A STORY AND EVERY WORD IS TRUE
   G            A9/G9           C        D9/C9
IT'S CONCERNING A GENTLEMAN THAT I ONCE KNEW
   G            A9/G9              C        D9/C9
NOW IVE KNOWN MEN WHO ARE RICH AND THOSE WHO ARE WISE
   G         A9/G9  C     D9/C9
SOME WITHOUT HONOUR AND SOME IN DISGUISE
    D         E9/D9    C    D9/C9
BUT I NEVER MET ANYONE QUITE LIKE THAT
    D            E9/D9      C   N/C
AND AS A MATTER OF FACT THE MAN WAS A STRANGE CAT
```

THERE ARE MEN PARALYSED BY VIRTUE, PARALYSED BY SIN
BUT NONE THAT PLAYED THE BLUES QUITE LIKE HIM
DUDE KNEW HIS KEROUAC COULD QUOTE HIM IN HIS SLEEP
YOU DON'T JUDGE A MAN BY HIS COMPANY
BUT BY THE SECRETS HE KEEPS
AND I NEVER MET ANYONE WHO THOUGHT LIKE THAT
AND AS A MATTER OF FACT THE MAN WAS A STRANGE CAT

NEVER SAID WHERE HE WAS HEADING NEVER SAID WHERE HE'D BEEN
HE HAD THE SANCTITY OF THE GUTTER BUT HIS HANDS WERE CLEAN
AND ON THE SUBJECT OF EQUALITY I DO RECALL HIS PRAYER
THAT THEY SHOULD BLINDFOLD THE HANGMAN JUST TO MAKE IT FAIR
I NEVER MET ANYONE WHO SPOKE LIKE THAT
AND AS A MATTER OF FACT MY MAN WAS A STRANGE CAT

I DON'T KNOW WHAT DROVE HIM OR WHAT KEPT HIM HERE
AND ONE DAY HE JUST QUIT THIS SWEET SWINGING SPHERE
SAYING IF YOU MUST MAKE THE DISTINCTION BETWEEN MAN AND BEASTS
HOW DO YOU TELL THE MONEY LENDERS FROM THE PRIESTS?
YEAH, I NEVER MET ANYONE QUITE LIKE THAT
AND AS A MATTER OF FACT MY MAN WAS

YEAH, AND I NEVER MET ANYONE QUITE LIKE THAT
AND AS A MATTER OF FACT MY MAN WAS

YEAH, I NEVER MET ANYONE QUITE LIKE THAT
AND AS A MATTER OF FACT THAT HAL WAS A STRANGE CAT

AS NEAR AS YOU NEED ME TO BE
Key C   No Capo

```
C/G6sus              Am7
FROM THE DAYS OF OUR SUMMER
C/G6sus              Am7
AND THE SUMMER OF THE DAYS
C/G6sus              Am7
WHEN WE SLEEP BENEATH THE SHADE
             F          G
OF ALL THE STARS THAT WE MADE
```

FROM YOUR HAIR I TAKE A LEAF
OF THAT OLD PUCKITANIAN TREE
WHERE ONCE WE WROTE OUR NAMES
AND YOU HEARD ME FIRST EXCLAIM

```
Dm/Dsus
HOLD ME AND PROTECT ME
Db aug/A7
FROM THE MADNESS IN MY SOUL.
F/Am7
LIKE YOU DID WHEN WE WERE CHILDREN
G                G7
LIKE YOU DID WHEN WE WERE OLD
```

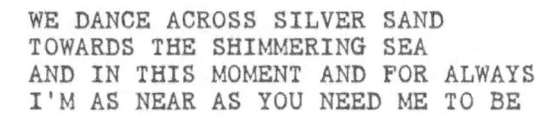

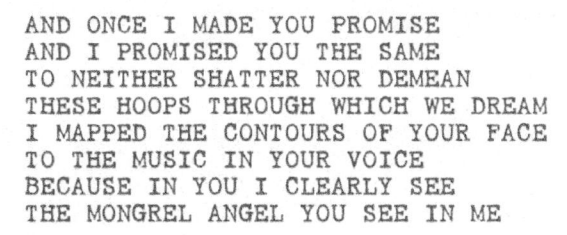

WE DANCE ACROSS SILVER SAND
TOWARDS THE SHIMMERING SEA
AND IN THIS MOMENT AND FOR ALWAYS
I'M AS NEAR AS YOU NEED ME TO BE

AND ONCE I MADE YOU PROMISE
AND I PROMISED YOU THE SAME
TO NEITHER SHATTER NOR DEMEAN
THESE HOOPS THROUGH WHICH WE DREAM
I MAPPED THE CONTOURS OF YOUR FACE
TO THE MUSIC IN YOUR VOICE
BECAUSE IN YOU I CLEARLY SEE
THE MONGREL ANGEL YOU SEE IN ME

SO THEN WE'LL GO FREEWHEELIN'
TO HORIZONS NOT YET KNOWN
IN OUR KESEY CAMERADO
THERE'S NO PLACE WHERE WE CAN'T GO
AND YOU'LL BE THERE BESIDE ME
AND I'LL BE RIGHT NEXT TO YOU
FOR NO MATTER WHERE OR WHEN WE ROAM
THAT CHAGALL WILL BRING US HOME

I REACHED FOR YOU IN DARKNESS
AS I STOOD AT THE ABYSS
'SAVE ME PLEASE' YOU HEARD ME CALL
BUT YOU JUST JOINED ME IN MY FALL.
AND I PASS THE DAYS WITHOUT YOU
CRAVING NIGHT CRAVING SLEEP
'CAUSE WE'RE STILL DANCING IN OUR DREAMS
AND YOU'RE STILL HERE WITH ME.

TALKIN' CHAPTER 25
Key G   No Capo

G
I WAS DOWN

IN THE JUNGLE

I HAD PRETTY BOYS ALL IN A LINE

IN THE JUNGLE YOU NEED SOMETHING
D   G
TO OCCUPY YOUR TIME

I WOKE UP
YOU WERE TALKING
I KEPT ONE EYE ON THE DOOR
YOU SAID YOU NEED ME BUT YOU
DON'T KNOW WHAT YOU NEED ME FOR

I'VE SEEN LIGHTNING
STRIKE A CHURCH HOUSE
SEEN MOUNTAINS FALL IN THE SEA
I FIGHT FOR JUSTICE BUT WHAT'S
JUSTICE EVER DONE FOR ME?

OLD MACBETH
HE SAID TO BANQUO
'WELL, YOU MAY THINK ME A RECKLESS MAN
BUT I'M GOING TO NEW ORLEANS
I'M GONNA FIND ME A MOJO HAND'

NOW FOUR HORSEMEN
THEY CAME A RIDING
CAME RIDING FROM EAST AND WEST
NOW THERE'S A SHADOW ON MY WALL
AND I JUST CAN'T GET NO REST

SO I'M GOING DOWN
TO THE COUNTRY
GONNA SEE WHAT I CAN FIND
THIS WORLD AIN'T SHOWN ME NOTHING
THAT I CAN'T BEAR TO LEAVE BEHIND

AND IF ONE DAY
SOMEONE ASKS YOU
WHO IT WAS WHO SANG THIS SONG
SAY IT WAS LITTLE MISS P.
AND SHE'S A-LONG LONG LONG GONE

PEACE OF MIND
Key C   No Capo

```
C
I NEVER ~~HAVE~~ STRAYED
Am
SO FAR FROM HOME
Dm          G
AND NEVER TRAVELLED
C   B/G
SO ALONE.

SO MANY ROADS.
I'VE WALKED DOWN
SEEN TOO MANY PEOPLE.
SEEN TOO MANY TOWNS

F
BUT NOW I WANT TO TOUCH YOU
Em
I JUST WANT TO HOLD YOU
Dm
I GOT TO TELL YOU SOMETHING
Am
WHILE I STILL HAVE TIME.
F
PLEASE LISTEN TO ME, BABY
Em
I MEAN EVERY WORD I SAY.
Dm
REMEMBER THE LOVE YOU GAVE ME.
G
IT WAS MY PEACE OF MIND.


I WANT TO TOUCH YOU
I JUST WANT TO HOLD YOU
I NEED TO TELL YOU SOMETHING
WHILE I STILL HAVE TIME.
PLEASE LISTEN TO ME, BABY
I MEAN EVERY WORD I SAY.
REMEMBER THE LOVE YOU GAVE ME.
IT WAS MY PEACE OF MIND.

HOWEVER FAR I TRAVELED I FEEL I NEVER LEFT
THERE WERE ALWAYS SO MANY THINGS I COULD NOT FORGET
NOW I NEED YOU NEAR ME I NEED TO KNOW YOU'RE MINE
BUT MOST OF ALL I NEED MY PEACE OF MIND
```

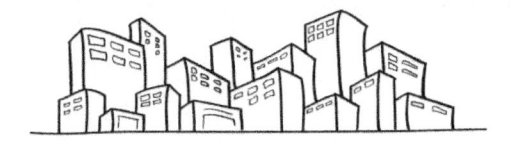

brownstone kisses
(25 x 25)

"This music is offered to everyone for free.
Free to sing or perform anywhere
in the cause of freedom.
Never for payment.
Never for profit."

Please copy and distribute freely.

Chapter 25. April 2012

New edition 2018

*'That, of course, is the great secret of the
successful fool – that he is no fool at all.'*
Isaac Asimov, Guide to Shakespeare.

APPENDIX TWO

CHAPTER 25 present
A CHRISTMAS TREE ON BASIN STREET
WRITTEN BY HAL LAVACHE
ILLUSTRATED BY HEIDI GASKILL

YOU LEAVE FOOTPRINTS IN THE SNOW...

AND THE REASON'S QUITE CLEAR.

TO PROVE TO YOURSELF THAT YOU'RE STILL HERE.
AND WHEN THE LIGHTS DIE DOWN ON CHRISTMAS DAY,
YOU CLOSE YOUR EYES...
...AND TAKE YOURSELF AWAY

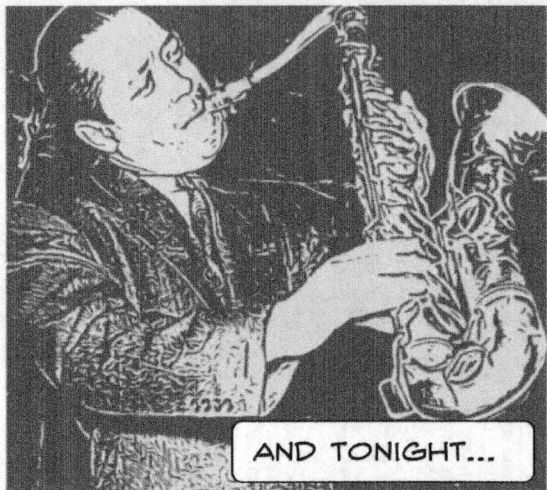

SOMEWHERE THERE'S A BAND...

PLAYING 'AIN'T SHE SWEET?'

AND TONIGHT...

THERE'S A CHRISTMAS TREE ON BASIN STREET.

SO MAY YOU LIVE FULL LONG AND YOUR LIFE BE BLESSED.

MAY THE HOMESICK AND THE LONELY FIND THEIR REST.

BUT THEY'D TRADE THEIR LAST DOLLAR FOR THE PEACE OF MIND...

IN SAYING MERRY CHRISTMAS

TO *ALL* MANKIND.

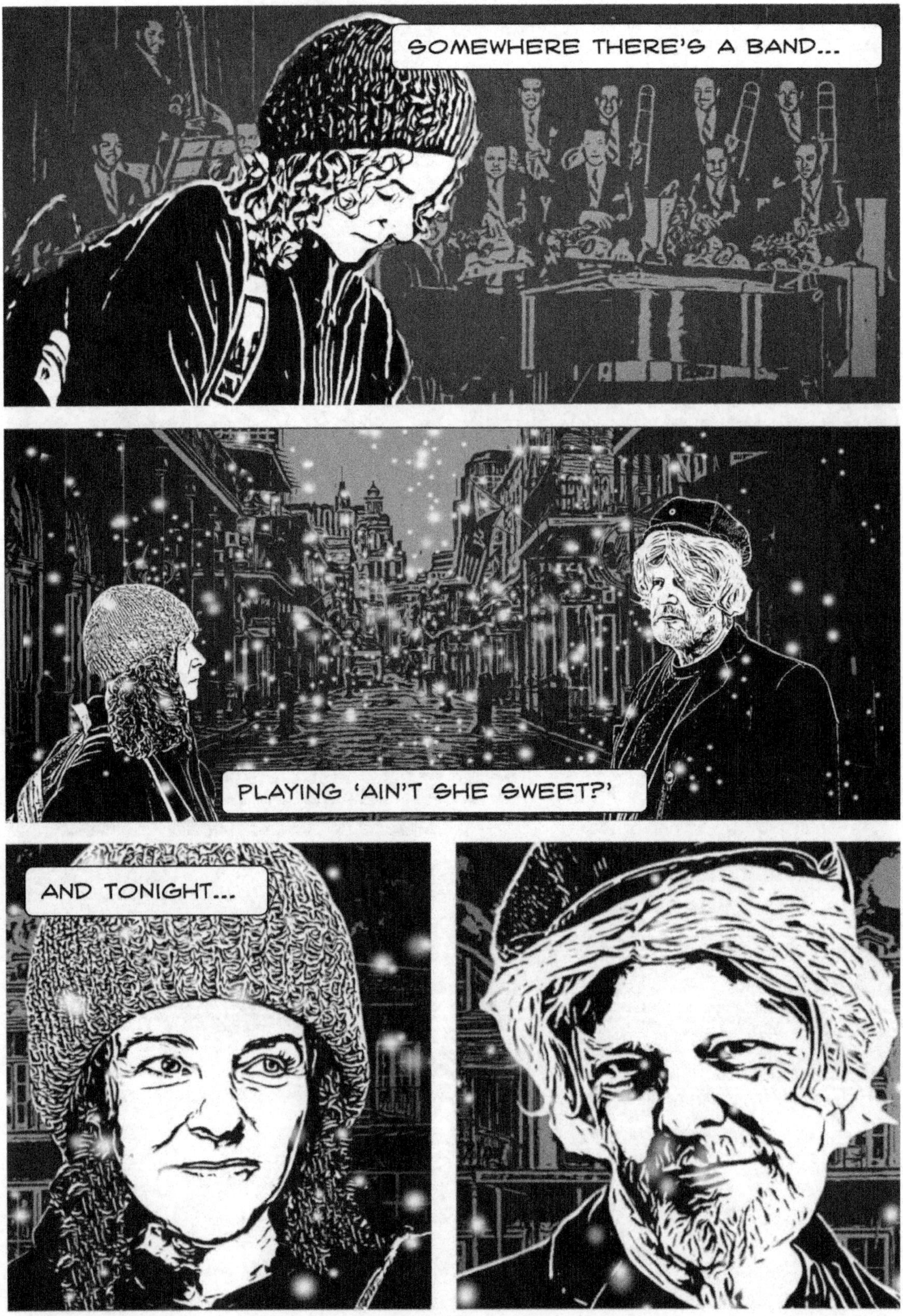
SOMEWHERE THERE'S A BAND...
PLAYING 'AIN'T SHE SWEET?'
AND TONIGHT...

THERE'S A CHRISTMAS TREE ON BASIN STREET.

Printed in Dunstable, United Kingdom